Liam. She'd know him anywhere.

Same dirty-blond hair, square jaw and broad shoulders. Though the tough-looking boy had morphed into a drop-dead sexy man. As their gazes met, she felt an instant jolt of attraction, eerily reminiscent of her sixteen-year-old self every time she'd been anywhere near him. Judging by how his eyes darkened, she affected him the same way.

The light changed and she started across, checking both ways to make sure traffic had stopped. Halfway there, she heard a loud pop, too loud to be a car backfiring. Gunshot? A woman a few paces behind her screamed and immediately everyone on the crosswalk panicked and started running. Since Ellie had instinctively crouched low, the mad rush of people trying to get away nearly ran her over, shoving her sideways into the cross street. Struggling to get to her feet, she'd just turned herself around and got upright when Liam sprinted out and grabbed her, yanking her away from traffic.

Somehow, they made it to the sidewalk. Heart pounding, blood pumping, Ellie struggled to catch her breath.

"Are you all right?" Liam asked, still holding on to her arm.

Dear Reader,

I love the Coltons! I know you do, too. I always get excited when I start working on one of these. *Colton's Body of Proof* was even more exciting, because it's set in one of the most magical cities ever—New York. Even better, the hero, Liam Colton, is a reformed bad boy, now doing his part to help keep troubled teens from making the same mistakes he did.

And the heroine, Ellie Mathers, is a crime scene investigator. Brilliant and beautiful. What fun! She and Liam were high school sweethearts, though they lost touch over the years. When they reconnect, sparks fly.

Add in the huge Colton family, the hustle and bustle of NYC and the unmistakable fact that someone is out to get Ellie—ever since she recognized her former best friend, who's been missing for sixteen years, in a crowded subway station. When Liam offers to help keep Ellie safe, she can't pass up his offer. And as the attraction between them deepens, she wonders if she'll be able to protect her heart.

Come along with me for another wild Colton ride! I hope you enjoy the journey as much as I did.

Karen Whiddon

COLTON'S BODY OF PROOF

Karen Whiddon

HARLEQUIN
ROMANTIC SUSPENSE

Special thanks and acknowledgment are given to
Karen Whiddon for her contribution to
The Coltons of New York miniseries.

Recycling programs
for this product may
not exist in your area.

ISBN-13: 978-1-335-73830-1

Colton's Body of Proof

Copyright © 2023 by Harlequin Enterprises ULC

For questions and comments about the quality of this book, please contact us at CustomerService@Harlequin.com.

Harlequin Enterprises ULC
22 Adelaide St. West, 41st Floor
Toronto, Ontario M5H 4E3, Canada
www.Harlequin.com

Printed in U.S.A.

Karen Whiddon started weaving fanciful tales for her younger brothers at the age of eleven. Amid the gorgeous Catskill Mountains, then the majestic Rocky Mountains, she fueled her imagination with the natural beauty surrounding her. Karen now lives in north Texas, writes full-time and volunteers for a boxer dog rescue. She shares her life with her hero of a husband and four to five dogs, depending on if she is fostering. You can email Karen at kwhiddon1@aol.com. Fans can also check out her website, karenwhiddon.com.

Books by Karen Whiddon

Harlequin Romantic Suspense

The Coltons of New York

Colton's Body of Proof

Visit the Author Profile page at Harlequin.com for more titles.

To my daughter, Stephanie Waters, and all the other educators out there. I'm so proud of you for making such a huge difference in the world.

Chapter 1

Sometimes Ellie Mathers wished she had the kind of nine-to-five job she could leave at work. Instead, she tended to take her cases home with her, reviewing the evidence, looking for that one thing that would finally provide the answer NYPD needed her to provide. She loved her job and was good at it, even though the constant need to stay *on* could be exhausting and counterproductive. She'd tried yoga and meditation, learned she didn't have the patience for either, and settled on hitting the gym three to four times a week for grueling workouts with weights and machines. She'd found a good morning workout prior to going into the precinct helped get her blood pumping, which tended to clarify her thought process. Which served her well, since her job as a crime scene investigator required her to be sharp and focused.

Which was why today, leaving her gym and heading for the subway to begin her forty-minute trip to Brooklyn, she couldn't help constantly scanning her surroundings as she hurried to catch the train at 42nd Street. As she jogged down the steps, mentally urging the slow-moving people in front of her to go faster, she eyed the crowded platform and quietly groaned. She needed to make a quick decision where she wanted to wait for quick access off, which meant she needed to get on last. Whether she got a seat or not, she never cared, but she had to be as close to the exit as possible. Some of the awful things she saw at her job had taught her to always keep her back toward the wall whenever possible and have an escape route mapped out.

As she reached the bottom step, she once again scanned the crowd. Most people barely even noticed her, but as a woman with short, dark hair looked up and met her gaze, Ellie froze. Their gazes locked before the woman looked away.

It couldn't be. Aliana Martin. Ellie wanted to rub her eyes. Instead, she battled her way through the crowd on the platform, determined to reach the woman's side.

Just then, the train arrived, coming to a stop with the familiar screeching sound. The doors opened, the crowd moved and somehow the dark-haired woman melted into the throng and disappeared. Heart pounding, Ellie followed.

Inside the car, Ellie grabbed the pole closest to the door, ignoring the swirl of people moving around her. Holding tight, she continued searching for Aliana. If indeed, that was who she'd seen. After all, Aliana had vanished without a trace sixteen years ago. Despite the fact that this woman had dark hair and Aliana had been blond, Ellie would recognize her face anywhere. After all, they'd been best friends, as close as sisters, inseparable since kindergarten.

Finally, Ellie thought she'd found her, standing at the other end of the same packed car, gripping a pole close to the last set of doors. Taking a deep breath, Ellie began to make her way toward her. This earned her several glares from her fellow passengers, which she ignored.

But when she managed to reach the opposite end of the car, the dark-haired woman with Aliana's face was nowhere to be found.

Damn. "Maybe I'm just working too hard," Ellie muttered to herself. "Seeing things." Except she'd long ago learned to trust her gut feelings. And she knew without a doubt that she'd seen her long-missing best friend.

Which meant Aliana had to be here somewhere on this moving train car.

It would take about forty minutes to get from Midtown to Queens. Plenty of time to find her. Unless she got off at one of the earlier stops. Which hopefully Ellie would see.

Unless… Ellie glanced at the door between cars. Illegal unless an emergency, but people still did it. She thought she remembered reading that there had been eight deaths so far this year due to people trying to move from car to car while the train was in motion.

Since Aliana wasn't here, that had to be what she'd done. Eyeing the door, with the warning sign clearly posted above it, Ellie decided to wait until they reached their destination. If she could spot Aliana again, when they got out, she could catch up to her. Would catch up to her. Aliana had disappeared once. Ellie didn't intend to let her do so again.

The back of Ellie's neck crawled, alerting her that someone was watching her. Casually, she looked left, toward the next car. Sure enough, Aliana stood on the other side of the door, staring at her. As soon as Ellie met her gaze,, Aliana moved away. Soon, Ellie lost sight of her as she disappeared into the crowded car.

No matter. They were nearly at their destination. Aliana might try to move fast, but Ellie felt confident she'd be faster.

Finally, the announcement for Jamaica-179th Street came. Ellie moved as close as she could get to the exit door, ready to sprint the second it opened. She figured Aliana would try to get the jump on her since she clearly, for whatever reason, wanted to avoid Ellie. As the train shuddered to a screeching halt, a burly man stuffing a donut into his mouth elbowed his way in front of her just as the doors opened.

Somehow, Ellie managed to dart around him. Though she was one of the first to exit her car, the steady stream of people moving away from the train made it difficult for her to locate Aliana. But she tried. Weaving through the crowd, she searched for a tall woman with glossy brown hair wearing a pale blue sweater.

But after a good five solid minutes, she reluctantly had to admit defeat. Aliana had once again managed to disappear.

Walking to the lab, she began to question herself. Had she really seen Aliana, or just someone who resembled her? Every person had a doppelganger out there, or so she'd heard. Maybe this sighting was just a random, weird coincidence brought on by wishful thinking. After all, she'd just gone over the case for the umpteenth time. She always did as the anniversary of Aliana's disappearance came around.

But Ellie knew what Ellie knew. She felt certain she'd seen her missing former best friend. More than certain *positive*. Yes, life had been completely different back in high school. She and Aliana had been teenagers, joined at the hip, though when Ellie had started dating Liam Colton, Aliana had stepped back to give her some space.

Talk about a blast from the past. Liam Colton. He'd been cocky then, his bad boy persona and rakishly handsome looks drawing Ellie in like a magnet. Liam had been there for Ellie when her best friend had vanished, comforting her and even helping her search for clues as she tried to figure out what had happened.

Despite Ellie's attempts to reform him, however, Liam had drifted away, getting in more and more trouble. He ran around with what Ellie's mother had called a bad crowd and ultimately wound up in prison for helping steal a Lamborghini. When Ellie went to visit him in jail, he broke up with her. But that was a long time ago. Doing time had changed him. These days, he ran a scared straight program at high schools throughout the city, including the one where Ellie's mom worked as principal. Since she worked with Liam's older brother Sean, she'd heard about his transformation there too.

Liam. Despite his obvious failings as a teen, he'd become a steadfast, responsible adult. She almost couldn't picture that.

Shaking her head, she heaved a sigh. Odd how see-ing Aliana had brought to mind a man she'd managed to avoid thinking about too deeply for years.

Impulsively, she dug out her phone. Scrolling through her contacts, she stopped when she reached his name. How was it even still in here? And was it even current? He'd called her once, after he'd gotten out of prison. Though she hadn't picked up, she'd saved his infor-mation just in case she changed her mind. Since she'd eventually forgotten it, she hadn't.

Adrenaline still pumping, she stabbed the button to call him before she could reconsider. To her surprise, he picked up on the second ring.

The instant she heard his husky and still familiar voice, she started talking. Babbling, actually. "Hi, Liam. It's Ellie. I know it's been a long time, but I swear I saw Aliana today and you are the only person I could think of who might believe me."

Silence from his end. She filled that with an awk-ward laugh. "But then again, maybe I shouldn't have bothered you. In fact, I'm sorry I did. I'll let you go now…"

"Ellie, wait." He cleared his throat. "I have to admit, I'm surprised to hear from you."

Self-conscious now, she began to walk faster. "Yeah, when I saw Aliana…"

"This isn't a conversation for over the phone," he in-terrupted. "How about you meet me for coffee and we can discuss it?"

"When?" she asked, before she had time to think better of it.

"How about now?"

She checked her watch. "Where? I'm in Brooklyn right now. Greenpoint, to be specific."

"So am I," he said, sounding surprised. "I'm giving a talk at Midwood High School later this morning. I'm actually on my way over to Joe's. Do you want to grab a cup with me?"

"Midwood? You know my mom's the principal there?"

"I do." He laughed. "She sings your praises often. What do you think about having coffee?"

Joe's wasn't far from the NYPD Forensic Laboratory where she worked. "I can do that," she replied. "I should be there in five."

Ending the call, she continued at a good pace, though she still took time to appreciate the bright sunshine that promised a warmer afternoon. Since March mornings were still chilly, she kept her hands jammed in the pockets of her coat. Soon, bare branches would bud, then give way to lush green leaves. Since she took this route to work every morning, many of the shopkeepers recognized her and waved. She always smiled and waved back.

Though the building where she worked was only a few blocks away, she took a quick detour down Humboldt Street. Joe's Coffee Shop sat down the block, on the opposite side, almost at the end. She'd been there more than a few times since she loved their imported Jamaican coffee.

"Ellie!" someone shouted. There, on the other side of the street, a tall, muscular man with killer blue eyes grinned at her.

Her heart stopped, then started up again, rapid-fire.

Liam. She'd know him anywhere. Same dirty blond hair, square jaw and broad shoulders. Though the tough-looking boy had morphed into a drop-dead-sexy man. As their gazes met, she felt an instant jolt of attraction, eerily reminiscent of her sixteen-year-old self every time she'd been anywhere near him. Judging by the way his eyes darkened, she affected him the same way.

The light changed and she started across, checking both ways to make sure traffic had stopped. Halfway there, she heard a loud pop, too loud to be a car backfiring. Gunshot? A woman a few paces behind her screamed and immediately, everyone on the crosswalk panicked and started running. Since Ellie had instinctively crouched low, the mad rush of people trying to get away nearly ran her over, shoving her sideways into the cross street. Struggling to get to her feet, she'd just turned herself around and gotten upright when Liam sprinted out and grabbed her, yanking her away from traffic.

Somehow, they made it to the sidewalk. Heart pounding, blood pumping, Ellie struggled to catch her breath.

"Are you all right?" Liam asked, still holding on to her arm.

"I think so." She frowned, refusing to be embarrassed. "What the hell was that? It sounded like a gunshot."

"I agree." Letting go of her, Liam glanced around. "No one got hit if it was. It sounded as if it came from a car driving by, though I didn't see it. Like someone took a shot out of a car window."

Still stunned, Ellie took a deep breath. "What do you think they were shooting at?"

"You, Ellie," Liam replied. "I believe they were shooting at you."

Considering that, she stood stock-still. She had been ahead of everyone else in the crosswalk, by several feet. "If that's the case, they are a terrible shot. I made a perfect target."

The lack of emotion in her voice had him searching her face. "Are you okay?"

"I'm fine." She brushed off his concern. "Thank you for helping me back there. And while it might be tempting to go with supposition, there were a lot of other things someone could have been taking a shot at besides me."

"Maybe so. But I still think this needs to be reported."

She nodded. "You're right. I might as well head into the precinct and make a report on my way to my office."

"Would you mind if I escort you?"

Liking that he asked instead of insisting, she managed a smile. "Of course not. We still need to talk about my seeing Aliana. We can do that on the way there."

As they walked, side by side but not touching, she told him everything. "I'm absolutely positive it was her," she said, once she'd finished. "Without a doubt."

"Okay," he agreed, which she loved. Immediate acceptance. "Then we need to figure out what she's been doing the last sixteen years."

"And what happened to her." They'd reached her work building. She'd just started for the door to pull it open when Liam casily reached around her and did it instead. "After you," he said. His easy smile made her entire body buzz.

"Hey, Mathers." The woman manning the front desk motioned to her. "One of your friends stopped by and left you coffee and a bagel. She said it was your favorite."

Grateful, Ellie accepted the cardboard cup and paper bag she held out. "Did you get a name?"

"Sorry." She shrugged. "The phone started ringing and I barely had time to talk to her. Pretty brunette. That's all I've got."

Not too helpful since that described more than a few of her friends, but she smiled and thanked her. Two of her best friends often sent coffee or cookies and she reciprocated. "Come on, Liam. Let's go call your brother and make that report so I can get to work."

Following Ellie, Liam couldn't help but admire the sexy sway of her hips while at the same time marveling at her composure. Though neither of them could be positive that the shot had been meant for her, he considered it a very likely possibility. But then again, Ellie worked as a crime scene investigator, so likely she'd become inured to stuff like this. Either that, or she simply didn't believe him.

Spotting his brother Sean across the room, Liam grinned. "Looks like you won't need to make the call. Sean's here. He can take the report."

"Detectives from the various precincts stop by often. This time, I'm glad it's him." Ellie spun around and made a beeline for Sean. Liam simply went along after her.

"Hey, Ellie." After greeting her, Sean cocked his

head and eyed Liam. "And Liam. What brings you here today?"

"Ellie and I were meeting up for coffee at Joe's. When she started to cross the street, someone took a shot at her."

Immediately, Sean's broad smile turned into a frown. "Are you serious?"

"We don't know that for sure," Ellie interjected. "The shooter could have been aiming for someone else. There were other people there in the crosswalk with me."

Her words made Sean relax slightly. "Was anyone hit?" he asked. "I haven't heard about any 911 calls about an incident. But I can check."

"There were no injuries," Ellie replied. "I doubt anyone called. For all we know, it could have been someone firing a shot into the air or accidentally discharging their weapon." She shrugged. "Though I didn't look around for a bullet or anything. Maybe I should go back and do that."

"Not a good idea," Liam immediately said. "You don't need to be putting yourself at risk again."

Sean looked from one to the other. Liam could tell his brother wondered what exactly was going on. "Agreed," he finally said.

Ellie muttered something under her breath but didn't argue. "Fine. I'll just pretend it never happened."

"I still think you should file a report," Liam said. "Just to have it on record in case anything like this happens again."

She shrugged. "I'll write something up and email it to you, Sean. Will that work?"

"Definitely." Sean still watched Liam, his gaze narrowed.

"Good." Ellie smiled, her dark eyes warm as she looked from Sean to Liam. "Now what brings you to the forensic lab, Sean? Am I working on one of your cases?"

"Not you, but Radley is. He's not in yet, so I thought I'd hang around and wait for him."

"He should be here soon," she said. "Let me know if there's anything I can do to help." Then she turned her attention from Sean to Liam. "I'll see you around, hopefully. Maybe we can catch up another time. For now, I'm going to go eat my breakfast and drink my coffee before I get started with my day."

Clearly, she didn't want to discuss this in front of Sean. "See you around," he repeated.

"Great." With that, she walked off, releasing her long, dark hair from the ponytail so it cascaded down her back.

Damn. Liam didn't look away until she'd vanished.

"What's going on with you?" Sean asked, taking Liam's arm and steering him toward an empty desk. "I can't even remember the last time you talked to Ellie."

Since Sean knew all too well that Liam hadn't seen Ellie in years, Liam only smiled. He thought about telling Sean about Ellie believing she'd seen Aliana, but decided it wasn't his story to tell.

"Sit," Sean ordered, gesturing at one of the chairs across from the desk. Once Liam had gotten seated, Sean dropped into the other chair. "I see you at least once a week and you've never mentioned this."

"Mentioned what?" Liam asked, though he knew.

Sean gave an exaggerated sigh. "I didn't know you'd gotten reacquainted with Ellie. How'd that happen?"

"She called me," Liam replied. "It was kind of weird to hear from her after all these years, but I recognized her voice immediately."

"Interesting." Pleasantries out of the way, Sean checked his watch before he got down to business. "I'm surprised to see you here. Have you had any more thoughts about our conversation with Ciara Kelly?"

Liam had accompanied Sean and their other siblings, Eva and Cormac, on a visit to Ciara's apartment just about a week ago.

Ciara's husband, Humphrey, a well-respected psychiatrist who'd been like a second father to Sean and Eva, though he and Liam hadn't been as close, had been missing for two months. He hadn't been seen since he entered the criminal courthouse on Centre Street to testify in a trial. Not only had he never made it to the trial, but he'd missed two client appointments, hadn't checked in with Ciara at all and didn't show up at a dinner party he'd reportedly been looking forward to. He'd simply vanished without a trace. Although Liam had had his issues with Humphrey when he was younger, he was as worried as the rest of his siblings that they hadn't been able to locate the man in all this time.

"I was just as shocked as the rest of you when she admitted their marriage was a fake," Liam admitted. "While Ciara and Humphrey never acted really lovey-dovey, I always figured that was due to their need for privacy. But hearing Ciara say their marriage was one of convenience and that she and Humphrey didn't love each other? That felt like a punch in the gut."

"I know." Sean grimaced. "Did you believe her when she said she had nothing to do with his disappearance?"

After thinking for a moment, Liam finally nodded. "Yeah, I did. Clearly she cares about him."

"So she said." Ever the cynical cop, Sean didn't sound convinced. "This entire situation is just plain weird."

"I agree." Liam leaned forward in his chair, again thinking of the Aliana Martin disappearance. Like Humphrey, Aliana had seemingly vanished into thin air. The police had investigated, but hadn't been able to unearth anything, not even a single clue.

"Seeing you with Ellie sure brought back memories," Sean mused. "Even though you're both completely different people now."

That comment made Liam laugh. "We were teenagers back then," he said. "So yes, we grew up. Thirty-two is a far cry from sixteen."

"True," Sean conceded. "But you know what I meant. You were headed for a life of trouble back then."

Once, hearing his older brother say something like that would have made Liam bristle. But Sean was right. After losing both his mother and father so young, he'd been an angry teenager, especially after losing their father. Liam had been determined to do stupid stuff like steal fast cars. He'd loved the adrenalin rush and, in typical young, blockhead fashion, hadn't thought about the consequences.

"You always had a weakness for expensive luxury hot rods," Sean continued. "Even when you were a kid. Remember your Matchbox car collection?"

"I still have it somewhere," Liam admitted. "Why the trip down memory lane?"

Sean shrugged. "I don't know. Maybe seeing you with Ellie. You two sure were sweet on each other."

Uncomfortable for some reason, Liam cleared his throat.

"How bad is the coffee around here?" he asked, partly to change the subject.

Sean grimaced. "I don't know, but I'd guess it's about the same as it is at every other lab or precinct in the city. I doubt it's any better at the crime lab. That's why most of us get some on the way in to work."

"Which is exactly what I was about to do when Ellie called. Have you ever been to Joe's? They specialize in fresh-roasted, Jamaican coffee. It's really good." Just thinking about it made Liam's mouth water.

"How about we walk over there now?" Sean suggested. "It sounds like we could both use a cup of that coffee. Plus, it wouldn't hurt to take a look around, maybe see if we can find any bullets or anything."

Pushing to his feet, Liam waited for his brother to get up. "That's a great idea."

They started for the door. Halfway there, Liam stopped. "Where's Ellie's office? I want to see if she'd like us to bring her back a cup."

Sean studied him and finally shrugged. "Sure. Why not? It's this way."

A small metal sign on the door signaled Forensic Laboratory. "That's the actual lab," Sean pointed out. "They all use it. But each of the investigators has their own small office over here. Here's Ellie's."

Since the door was open, they didn't knock but simply walked inside. Ellie sat at her desk, her half-eaten breakfast in front of her. She looked up at them, her eyes wide, pupils dilated, her dusky skin clammy. And then, as she opened her mouth to speak, she doubled over, hands across her stomach.

Concerned, Liam rushed over. "Are you all right? You look—"

Before he could finish the sentence, she grabbed her trash can and vomited into it. Over and over she retched, the sound awful. Instead of moving away, Liam went closer and held her long, dark hair away from her face. He glanced back at Sean and his tough cop older brother looked slightly queasy, though he remained standing in the doorway.

Finally, after apparently emptying the contents of her stomach, Ellie sat up. Liam released her hair and took a step back, waiting while she grabbed a tissue from her desk and wiped her mouth.

"What the hell happened, Ellie?" Sean demanded.

Liam had already focused on the half-eaten bagel still on her desk. "Food poisoning doesn't act that quickly," he pointed out. When Ellie met his gaze, he could tell the same thought had occurred to her.

"Do you think?" she began, grimacing as she slurred her words.

"You were poisoned?" he finished. "Yes. I do."

"Why?" Sean wanted to know. "Why would anyone want to hurt you? It's not like you're working on some big, controversial case involving the mob or something."

Gaze still locked on Liam's, Ellie ignored him. "Good thing I vomited. If this was what I think it might be, it can cause renal failure." The slurring seemed slightly less pronounced. She grabbed a bottle of water from her desk and quickly drank nearly half of it.

"You really don't have any idea who might have delivered this bagel and coffee," he pointed out. "The woman working the front desk said she didn't get her name."

"True. What I do have are the resources to test the contents. If someone put some sort of poison in either the bagel or the coffee, I can find out what."

"Don't you think we should get you to the ER first?" Liam gently suggested. "Make sure you're okay?"

"I'm fine." She waved his suggestion away and got to her feet. When she stood, she swayed. "I'm a bit dizzy, but it will pass. I'm way more interested in testing your hypothesis." With that, she got up, grabbed the half-eaten bagel and the coffee cup, then the trash can liner. Balancing it all, she headed toward the lab, weaving only slightly.

Liam looked at Sean, who shrugged. "She's pretty damn headstrong," Sean commented. "I'd just assume that she's going to be all right and leave it at that. Do you still want to head to Joe's?"

"I'm not going anywhere until I find out the results of Ellie's tests," Liam said, crossing his arms. "In fact, I plan to wait right here in her office until she gets back."

"Suit yourself." Sean swung around as if to go. A second later, he turned back. "You know what? I'm going to wait too. I really need to get back to the precinct, but I want to find out what's going on here."

"I can't blame you," Liam said.

Though tempted to go into Ellie's lab, Liam decided not to bother her while she worked. Instead, he sent a quick text, letting her know he and Sean had decided to remain in her office.

A second later, she texted back. Come on into the lab.

Needing no second invitation, Liam showed Sean the text. After leaving her office, they pushed through the door marked Forensic Laboratory. Ellie looked up when they entered, then gestured for them to come closer.

"You've already seen me at my worst," she said without a trace of embarrassment. Though she spoke to both, she looked at Liam. "You might as well see me in my element."

The fact that she cared at all about how he saw her wasn't lost on him. He filed that information away to consider later. Right now, he approached her work surface, a large, stainless steel table lit by several overhead lights. Liam went around to the other side.

Ellie had already taken samples of the bagel, the cream cheese and the coffee and appeared to be in the process of testing them. "Ah-ha," she said. "I thought this coffee tasted sweet."

"What was in it?" Liam asked.

"Ethylene glycol. One of the main compounds in antifreeze." She shook her head. "Exactly what I suspected once I realized I'd been poisoned."

Sean swore. "Then someone really did try to poison you."

"Yes," Ellie replied. "I'm lucky I didn't drink more. This stuff can cause renal failure and…death."

Stunned, Liam stared. She could have died. "Do you guys have video cameras in your lobby?" he asked.

"Yes, of course." She met his gaze. "We'll definitely want to review the footage from this morning and see who dropped off my special breakfast."

"Maybe you should get checked out by a doctor?" Liam asked. "Just to make sure."

"If I have any other issues, I will," she promised. "Right now, I want to see the film."

They both looked at Sean. Mouth set in a grim line, he motioned to them to lead the way. "Let's find whoever is in charge of security. He'll know how we can see the tape."

Ellie picked up a phone on her desk and dialed a number. After speaking softly into it, she hung up and turned to them. "The security office is upstairs. They know we're coming and have promised to have the tape ready to view."

When they got off the elevator on the second floor, a uniformed officer met them. "This way," he said, marching them back to a small room with a medium-sized television mounted on the wall. "Wait here," he ordered. "I'll have it pulled up in a second and it will play on that screen."

A moment later, he returned. "Here we go."

They watched the black-and-white footage. A woman entered the precinct, wearing a baseball cap pulled low over her dark hair. Wearing a bulky sweater, she kept her face down, successfully avoiding a direct view of the camera.

"That's her," Ellie said. "Aliana Martin!"

Chapter 2

Aliana. The moment she saw the video, an awful certainty settled into Ellie's bones. That woman, despite her attempt to disguise her appearance, had to be Aliana. Ignoring her rising agitation, she forced herself to study the video. Her job had long ago taught her there was no benefit to allowing speculation. In any type of criminal activity, one could only go with the facts, especially in forensics.

"Are you absolutely certain?" Liam asked, his bright blue gaze locked with hers.

She loved that he'd never for one second doubted her. "Can you replay it?" she asked.

"Sure." Sean rewound and then hit Play.

As she watched the footage again, she spoke her thoughts out loud. "Because she takes care not to look at the camera, I can't be positive. And if it is her, she's wearing different clothing than when I saw her earlier. She added the baseball cap and that sweater is different. But that woman is about the right size and moves in a similar manner."

Which, as she knew better than anyone, wasn't enough to go on.

"Could she be one of your other friends?" Sean asked. "Or, considering that she tried to poison you, one of your enemies?"

Enemies. The word shouldn't have shocked her, but it did. "I don't really have any enemies," she said. "At least not that I know of."

Sean and Liam exchanged a glance.

"What?" she asked.

"With all the crimes you've investigated and helped solve, there's bound to be someone you've ticked off along the way," Sean said. "Believe me, as a detective, I see that all the time."

"Maybe so," she acknowledged. "But for now, I'm going to run with the supposition that Aliana Martin tried to poison me."

"And maybe tried to shoot you first," Liam interjected. "Since both of these things happened after your chance encounter on the subway this morning."

He had a point, though even she thought it might be a stretch. Right up until the day Aliana had disappeared, she and Ellie had been like sisters. "We were best friends," she mused. "Even if she hadn't wanted to be seen, why would she try to hurt me? New York is a big city. She wouldn't need to kill me when she can easily manage to avoid me for another sixteen years or longer."

"No idea." Liam studied her. "You still seem a bit shaky. Are you sure you don't want to stop by the hospital and let them check you out?"

"It just needs to work its way out of my system," she replied. The concern darkening his gaze made her feel warm all over. "I plan on chugging a bunch of water. But I promise you, if I have any more vomiting episodes or anything else that's even slightly concerning, I'll make sure to seek medical help."

Slowly, Liam nodded. "You're the scientist, but I still don't like it. I really think you need to make time to see a doctor." He sighed. "In the meantime, is there anything I can do to help?"

"No, but thank you for offering." Conscious of Sean watching them, she offered a sweet, impersonal smile. "I'll be in touch, if that's all right. We never did get a chance to catch up."

"I'll hold you to that," Liam said. "I live in Midtown Manhattan, but I'm in Brooklyn a lot since I do a bit of work for the 98th Precinct. In between giving talks at high schools all over the city."

Ellie nodded. "I've heard. My mom speaks very highly of you and your program."

The compliment made him grin. "That's good to hear. She's a very well-respected principal. I'm speaking there later today."

"Come on." Sean took Liam's arm and steered him toward the door. "Let's go grab that coffee before I head back to work."

Once they were gone, Ellie allowed herself to sink down onto a stool. Truth be told, she still felt a bit shaky. And dizzy. She could only be glad she hadn't chugged that coffee and that the bagel hadn't been laced with anything.

Poison. Directed at her. Since the food and coffee had been dropped off specifically for her, in that there couldn't be any doubt. Unlike the random gunshot, which might have been for any reason or directed at anyone.

None of this made sense. Assuming the woman she'd seen earlier had been Aliana—and Ellie knew in her heart she had been—why would Aliana want to hurt her? Yes, Aliana had vanished without a trace. Her parents had been devastated and Ellie had refused to accept she was gone. In fact, losing her best friend at age sixteen had been one of the reasons Ellie had chosen this career path. She'd never stopped investigating Aliana's disappearance. And she'd never, not once, allowed herself to believe Aliana was dead.

Now she knew she'd been correct. Aliana lived and breathed and Ellie knew without a doubt that she'd been on the train earlier. And possibly on the video dropping off the laced coffee and bagel.

She shook her head, aware she'd be unable to focus on work for a bit. Though she'd downplayed everything with Sean and Liam, she was a lot more shaken than she'd ever admit. Cognitive impairment was one of the first signs of ethylene glycol poisoning.

She decided to step out and visit the ER. She texted one of her friends who worked as a nurse at NYU Langone, letting her know what had happened, and that she was on her way. She'd researched and saw treatment consisted of infusion of crystalloids to enhance renal clearance of the toxic metabolites. Hopefully, she could get that done and be back at work before the end of the afternoon.

Though they'd wanted her to stay for at least a couple of hours for observation, she'd talked the doctor down to ninety minutes. As long as her vitals remained strong, the harried young doctor said she could leave.

A fan of routine and schedules, once back at the lab, she kept herself busy. If anyone asked, she'd freely admit she considered herself a workaholic because outside of the gym, work had become the center of her existence. She had no pets, though she'd occasionally longed for a cat, because she spent long hours away from her apartment. On the weekends, she made sure to meet up with friends for brunch or drinks, but beyond that the lab was where she spent the majority of her time. In fact, if she didn't love her neighborhood in Midtown Manhattan so much, she'd look for an apartment closer to work.

Again, she thought of Liam and her body's instinctive reaction to him. It had been years since she'd had any kind of relationship, mainly because she put all her energy into her career. She'd had lovers here and there, casual relationships by mutual consent. But she couldn't remember the last time she'd reacted so strongly to a man.

Her cell rang, startling her. Her mother, Violet Mathers, was a dedicated high school principal. Wondering if the woman had some kind of sixth sense, Ellie answered. "Mom! Is everything okay? You hardly ever call me in the middle of a workday."

"Everything is fine," Violet replied. "And yes, I'm

busy. I can't talk long. But I wanted to call and see if you wanted to come for dinner tonight."

"I'd love to," Ellie said. Though her mother had no way of knowing, Ellie definitely could use some parental love right now. "What time?"

"Seven. But you can come a little early, if you want to help me in the kitchen." Which was code for *if you want to talk just the two of us.*

"I'll be there around six thirty."

"Perfect." Her mother paused. "Oh, and if you're dating anyone, you're certainly welcome to bring him along."

A not-so-subtle nudge. "No, Mom, I'm still not seeing anyone."

"Oh, okay. I've got to run. See you tonight." And her mother ended the call.

Shaking her head, Ellie put the phone down. Now she had plenty of time to decide before dinner whether to tell her parents about her Aliana sighting or about the two frightening events that had occurred after.

In the meantime, work would be the best distraction. And since Ellie had a backlog of several cases, she got busy right away.

Lunchtime came and only her stomach's fierce growling made Ellie realize she needed to eat. She hadn't had anything but water since vomiting earlier. Even now, the idea of food made her feel an odd combination of slightly queasy and hungry.

On days when she didn't want to interrupt the flow of work, she always grabbed lunch at the deli across the street. A bowl of matzo ball soup would definitely do the trick. She hurried over, where the owner, Maurice, and his wife, Flo, short for Florence, greeted her by name.

"The usual?" Flo asked.

"Yes, please."

Ellie carried the soup back to her office and ate it at her desk, washing it down with a can of ginger ale. To her relief, the meal stayed down. She actually felt a lot better after eating it.

After they left the lab and headed toward Joe's, Liam braced himself. They'd gone about twenty-five feet before Sean elbowed him. "What's the deal with you and Ellie?" he asked. "I swear I could see sparks flying every time you looked at each other."

Unsurprised, since Sean had always been observant, Liam shrugged. "I don't know. Like I said, I haven't seen or spoken to her since high school. It was good to meet up with her again, even if it was under weird circumstances."

They'd turned the corner onto Humboldt Street.

"Are you going to try and meet up with her again?" Sean wanted to know. "To catch up, like she said?"

"Probably." Liam saw no reason to dodge the question. "I mean, she's a beautiful woman." He took a deep breath. "And she might be in danger."

"You never could resist the urge to protect someone in danger."

"Runs in the family," Liam shot back, which made his older brother chuckle.

"True that," Sean admitted.

Nearly at Joe's, Liam stopped and pointed to the intersection. "She was crossing there when we heard the gunshot. There were other people, just like now. No one got hit and I didn't hear a bullet ricochet off anything."

"Which is damn lucky. That's one of the multiple reasons why shooting blindly into a crowd is so unpredictable and dangerous."

Liam looked around, trying to place Ellie's exact position at the moment they'd heard the gunshot. "She'd made it about halfway through the crosswalk," he said, pointing. "Traffic was moving along on Humboldt Street. I think the shot came from a vehicle driving by, though I didn't get eyes on the shooter."

Sean nodded. "Let's see if we can find a bullet. It had to go somewhere. You take this side of the street and I'll take the other."

While working conditions weren't ideal—looking for a bullet lodged somewhere while dodging impatient pedestrians—Liam searched as best he could. When he finally admitted defeat, he looked up to see his brother had apparently done the same.

"Come on." Sean motioned him over.

Liam waited for the light to change before hurrying over. "Any luck?" he asked.

"Nope. And it's not like we can cordon off the area and have a team comb the intersection looking. No one even called in a report. I checked." Sean held the door open, releasing an instant aroma of fresh-brewed coffee. "Damn, that smells good."

"It tastes even better." Liam headed toward the counter. "Order whatever you want. My treat."

The two men took a seat. At this time of the day, Joe's was only moderately crowded, which Liam appreciated.

Lydia, one of Joe's daughters, brought their coffee over. "I included an assortment of donuts," she said, smiling. "On the house."

Liam thanked her, eying the plate with four different kinds of pastry. Lydia had made sure to include jelly-filled, since Liam ordered them every time he visited. There was also a huge bear claw, and a couple of cake donuts. Sean immediately reached for the bear claw.

"I'm worried about Humphrey," Sean said, taking a sip of his coffee. "Mmm. That's good."

"Don't tell me you've never been here," Liam countered. "This place is legendary." He took a bite of his jelly-filled, allowing himself to savor the flavor.

"It's been a while," Sean admitted. "I've been really busy. And there's a great place right around the corner from the precinct."

"Your loss." Liam finished up one donut, interspersed with sips of the strong coffee. "And yes, I'm worried about Humphrey too. Learning he and Ciara had a marriage of convenience was kind of a shock. And I'm still trying to figure out what secrets Ciara is hiding."

"Whatever they are, I still don't think she had anything to do with Humphrey's disappearance," Sean said, after washing down a bite of his bear claw. "Though maybe she did, since I remember, one of Humphrey's patients called 911 and claimed he'd seen Humphrey walking on Amsterdam Avenue by Columbia arm in arm with a woman."

"Yeah, I remember. No one took it seriously. But maybe Ciara did. The guy was Rob somebody or other, wasn't that his name?"

"Rob Widdicombe. He insisted he'd know Humphrey anywhere, even though Humphrey had a black mustache, dark plastic framed glasses, and wore a Russian type hat." Sean spread his hands. "He had to have been mistaken. Humphrey definitely would have been in touch."

"I agree." Otherwise, Liam thought, that would mean Humphrey had engineered his own disappearance.

"Why don't you ask around on the street and see if you can find anything out?"

Liam nodded. "I can do that." He'd helped a lot of ex-cons start new lives once they got out of prison, and for that he had earned their respect. Even the ones who'd been unwilling or unable to follow a law-abiding lifestyle talked to him. This made him an invaluable informant when the NYPD needed someone on the street. Sometimes, Liam found it tough to juggle both his job running the foundation, giving his scared straight seminars, and this, but so far he'd managed to make it work. He'd even helped solve a couple of cold cases.

Speaking of cold cases....

"What do you think of the possibility that Ellie might have seen Aliana Martin?" Liam asked, leaning back in his chair. "I remember how awful it was when she disappeared. She was only sixteen."

"Her parents were devastated," Sean said. "And the police were convinced she ran off with some guy she'd been seeing."

"An older guy." Liam nodded. "The thing is, she and Ellie were best friends. If Aliana was going to take off with a boyfriend, she would have told Ellie."

"Not necessarily. It could have been a spur of the

moment thing. We see it all the time with runaways. Sixteen-year-olds tend to live in the moment. They don't always consider the consequences."

"True." With a sigh, Liam pushed the plate with the remaining donuts away. "For a while there, Ellie was convinced Aliana had a secret boyfriend who forced her to go with him. But since Aliana and she were best friends, she felt she would have known about any boyfriend."

"Who knows?" Sean drained the last of his coffee. "It's been sixteen years. However, the fact that this woman, Aliana or not, appears to be trying to harm Ellie is pretty damned worrisome. No matter what happened in the past, I can't conceive of a single reason why anyone would do that. Just because what, Ellie saw her?"

"I'm going to help her look into it," Liam said. "If she wants my help, that is. Since I'm already helping you guys figure out what happened to Humphrey, what's one more case?"

With a laugh, Sean pushed to his feet. "You wouldn't say that if you saw the stack of case files on my desk. I'd better get to work. Do you want to come with me?"

Liam checked his watch. "I can't. I've got to head to Midwood High. I'm schedule to give my scared straight presentation in an hour."

"Have fun." Tossing his empty cup into the trash receptacle, Sean headed out the door. Liam got up too. When he gave his talks at the various schools, he liked to arrive early. Once he'd checked in at the office, he'd take his time heading toward the gym or auditorium, hoping to catch the students in between classes, so he could get a feeling for the mood of the place. Sometimes, he got nothing. Other times, he could feel a restless sort of angry undercurrent swirling among the kids. Either way, all he could do was speak his truth and hope he connected with somebody. Even helping one kid straighten out his or her life made everything he did worth it.

At a little past five, Ellie shut things down to head home. Some nights—okay, *most* nights, she worked late, but today had been unusual to say the least. Plus, she had dinner plans with her family. No matter how old she got, she knew she'd always find comfort just being around her parents and their unconditional love.

Growing up biracial, Ellie had often struggled to figure out who she really was. Her white father, Vincent, had always been proud of his job as a plumber and even more proud of his highly educated wife who'd worked her way up from public school teacher to assistant principal and finally principal. He'd been a vocal supporter of Violet as she earned her master's and her doctorate degree while working full-time as a math teacher. And he'd never missed an opportunity to point out to Ellie that her mother was living proof that Ellie could do anything she wanted if she set her mind to it and worked really hard.

Ellie hadn't fully appreciated the inspiration of that truth until she'd gone away to college.

As for Violet, she'd taught Ellie to appreciate her African American heritage. She'd also made sure Ellie saw beyond the narrow constraints of race and taught her to love herself for exactly who and what she was. "A perfect blend of the two of us," her mom always told her.

As soon as Ellie got home to her small apartment, a third-floor walkup that kept her legs toned, she jumped into the shower to freshen up. She got dressed, choosing a pair of comfortable leggings, boots and an oversized sweater. Again she thought over the day's events, from seeing Aliana on the train to reconnecting with Liam Colton. Though she didn't want to dwell on the gunshot or the poisoning, she had to decide if she wanted to mention these to her folks or simply keep the worrisome details to herself.

Her parents' apartment was only a few blocks away, so, since the weather was nice, she decided to walk. Fresh air and exercise would help clear her mind.

She arrived at the building's entrance around six twenty-five. After greeting Mel, one of the doormen, she took the elevator up to the tenth floor. Her parents had lived in this apartment her entire life. She'd grown up here. Most of the tenants were also lifers, as her dad liked to call them.

As soon as she exited on the tenth, she saw Mr. and Mrs. Silverstein. They hurried over, greeting her effusively. Mrs. Silverstein invited her to come in for tea, as she always did, but Ellie explained her mother was expecting her to help with dinner preparations.

Walking away, she reached to knock on 10C's door, but her father pulled it open before she had the chance. "Come here, you," he ordered, pulling her in for a tight bear hug. "Your mom is in the kitchen, waiting for you."

Ellie stepped into the living room, lovingly surveying her dad. He still wore his plumber's uniform. Seeing her notice, he gestured. "I just got home. I'm about to change." With that, he walked away toward the bedroom.

The house smelled amazing. Years ago, Mrs. Licciardoni, one of the Italian women who lived down the hall, had taught Violet how to make her old family lasagna recipe. That bit of deliciousness had long been one of Ellie's favorite meals.

"Mom!" Entering the kitchen, Ellie grinned as her mom enveloped her in a tight hug. "I can't believe you made lasagna. I know how much work that is."

"I know how much you love it," Violet shot back. "And to be honest, I wanted an excuse to have it."

"Ahh, so that's why you invited me to dinner," Ellie teased, one arm still around her mother's slim waist. "Is there anything I can help you with?"

"The lasagna's already in the oven, but I was going to make a salad."

Working side by side with her mom, chopping vegetables and chatting, helped chase the last remaining bits of tension from Ellie's body.

"I ran into Liam Colton today," she mentioned casually, bracing herself in case Violet tried to make too much of one encounter.

"Liam!" Her mother grinned. "I remember when you two were inseparable."

"Until he got himself in trouble."

"Right? But Liam's one of the few who was able to successfully turn his life around," Violet pointed out. "In fact, he did his scared straight program at my school today. He comes every year, but this time I really think he made a huge impact on the students." Violet shook her head. "A lot of the girls develop an instant crush on him. He's still got that bad boy persona going, doesn't he?"

Ellie felt herself grow warm all over. "I hadn't noticed," she lied. "But it's really nice the way he's trying to help kids that might be heading down the same path he did."

"Nice?" Violet scoffed. "That's too bland of a word to describe what he does. Inspiring, yes. Dedicated too." She grabbed her phone off the counter. "I recorded him today. Let me show you and then you can see for yourself what I mean."

Fascinated, Ellie took the phone and pressed Play on the video. For the next several minutes, she watched as Liam paced the stage, his movements charismatic, the conviction in his voice both compelling and incredibly sexy.

He talked of his youth, of focusing on the adrenaline rush, the thrill of getting away with something even though he'd known it was wrong. "I thought only of myself," he said, his rueful expression and ringing tone captivating. "Fast cars were my thing. It never occurred to me that someone could have gotten hurt, even killed. I was very lucky no one did."

Several of the kids in the audience appeared invested. But many more sat there with arms crossed and bored expressions. "Those kids right there," Violet said, pointing at the screen. "Are the ones who need to hear this the most. But watch. Their faces change as Liam goes into his full story."

Though Ellie already knew what had happened to Liam, she found it utterly captivating, hearing him talk about the way he'd finally realized to his shock that this time he wasn't going to get away with only a slap on the wrist.

He spoke candidly about going to prison at eighteen.

"Too old for juvie, and way too young to experience the things I did. It didn't take long for me to realize that this wasn't how I wanted to live the rest of my life."

One kid raised his hand. "Prison ain't no big deal," he scoffed. "I've got an older brother and a cousin doing time now."

"Do you?" Liam kept his tone conversational, though his expression got intense. "When was the last time you talked to them?"

"I haven't," the kid admitted. "But I will soon."

"Good. Make sure you ask if you can get a tour of the facility. Some places do that. If not, ask your brother how he'd feel about you getting sent there someday. I guarantee you he won't like that. At all. And I'm putting it mildly."

"My brother told me if I was that stupid, he'd beat the crap out of me," another kid said. "It sounds like it really sucks in there."

"It does." Though still on stage, Liam leaned closer, as if speaking in confidence to a much smaller audience. Keeping his word choices carefully generic, he outlined some of the horrible things that went on. "Just like on TV," he finished. "Except this is real life."

After that, he took questions, answering each one thoughtfully and concisely. When no more students raised their hands, he nodded. "I've left a bunch of my business cards on the table on the way out. Grab one if you want. I've got a fully trained group of people answering the phone lines. Call if you ever need anything or have any questions. I promise you can remain anonymous."

The applause started slowly at first, in that reluctant

way teenagers sometimes adapted toward adults. But after a few seconds, the tenor changed. One row of students stood, whistling and clapping and then the entire auditorium got to their feet.

On stage Liam appeared both grateful and moved. He bowed once, before disappearing from view.

The applause continued for a moment after he left. Then the auditorium lights came on and the video cut off.

Ellie swallowed hard. If anything, watching Liam speak, so articulate and passionate, had only deepened the attraction she had begun to feel toward him.

"I dismissed everyone after that," Violet said. "I noticed quite a few students went ahead and grabbed the cards from the table on their way out."

Ellie nodded, watching as her mother expertly tossed the salad before stowing it in the fridge. "It's interesting that he started an entire foundation."

"He's made it his life's work to try and keep as many teens out of prison as he can." The approval in Violet's voice matched the warmth in her brown eyes. She hadn't been nearly as enthusiastic about Liam back when he and Ellie had been a teenaged couple. "After his wife died, he threw himself into his foundation wholeheartedly."

"Talking about Liam Colton again?" Ellie's dad entered the kitchen. He'd changed out of his plumber's coveralls and wore a pair of comfortable sweatpants and a T-shirt. He glanced at Violet and smiled fondly. "I swear, your mother talks so highly of that guy, you'd think he was a saint."

A saint? Ellie thought of Liam, with his sexy grin

and confident swagger, and shook her head, though she kept her musings to herself.

"Silly." Violet wrapped her arms around him and kissed his cheek. "That boy has turned out well, despite his rocky start. I can only hope he's able to reach some of my students who are heading down a similar path."

The timer went off with a ping.

"The lasagna is done," Violet announced. She grabbed a couple of potholders and carefully removed the pan from the oven. "We'll let it cool a bit. We can eat our salads first."

They all took a seat at the table. Vincent poured a glass of Violet's favorite red wine for her and also for Ellie. He went to the fridge and cracked open a beer before taking his seat at the head of the table. "Dinner with my two favorite ladies," he said. "Life is good."

Lost in thoughts about Liam, Ellie could only nod. Maybe life was about to get even better. Right then and there, she decided to call him on her way home and see if he wanted to meet up for a drink.

Chapter 3

After giving his talk at the high school, Liam had answered all their questions and left a stack of his cards on a table by the exit. He then spent a few minutes talking to Dr. Mathers, Ellie's mother and the principal. Ellie had her wonderful, caramel-colored eyes, he marveled. And those high cheekbones and heart-shaped face. They looked a lot alike, though Ellie's skin was a few shades lighter than her mom's. Odd how he hadn't thought about Ellie in years and now that she'd contacted him, he couldn't stop. Seeing her across that crowded street had brought such a rush of desire he'd almost gone weak at the knees.

He said none of that to her mother, of course. Instead, they exchanged a few pleasantries, the same as they always did. They went over the high points of his talk, even though he suspected by now Dr. Mathers could recite it from memory, and he left her with yet another stack of business cards in case she wanted to hand them out to any student who might need them. Though Liam saw Ellie's mother frequently, the recent encounter with her daughter had him seeing the older woman in a new light. He couldn't help but wonder if the older woman would approve if Liam were to take Ellie out. Neither of her parents had been exactly thrilled with him back in his troublemaking younger days. The thought made him shake his head. What the heck had gotten into him? He rarely dated the same woman twice, yet he was already thinking about Ellie and wanting…more.

As he left the school building, he decided he'd stop by the 98th Precinct and see what his siblings were up to. Not only did his older brother, Sean, work there as a detective, but his baby sister, Eva, was a rookie officer. His twin Cormac, a successful private investigator, did a lot of business for the NYPD and the DA's office and frequently stopped in as well. Liam, who had a lot of connections from his brief stint in prison, even served as a consultant for the police.

"You again?" Sean looked up from the stack of papers on his desk. Though he sounded gruff, Liam knew Sean lived for his family. After all, he'd stepped up and raised Liam, Cormac and Eva when their parents had died. There'd been a bit of a rift during Liam's rebellious teenage years, and Liam had alienated his entire clan. Luckily, the love between the siblings had always remained, and they never truly turned their back on him even when he was at his lowest. Now they were all close again.

"Yeah, me again." Liam said. "I was in the neighborhood and thought I'd stop by before I went home. Anything new on Humphrey?"

"Nothing." Sean grimaced. "I have to admit I get more worried the longer I go without hearing from him."

Sean had been closer to Humphrey than anyone. In fact, the two men had put an entire plan in place to ensure Humphrey stayed safe. Liam knew that detail bothered Sean immensely. Humphrey hadn't activated any of it before disappearing into thin air.

"I hear you." Liam squeezed his brother's shoulder. "Call me if you hear anything at all."

"I will." Shuffling paper, Sean looked up and met Liam's gaze. "You do the same, you hear? Talk to your contacts on the street, see if anyone knows anything."

Liam nodded. He kept up with his contacts, which was one of the reasons the NYPD occasionally used him as a consultant on their more difficult cases. Still, he hated hearing the worry in his older brother's voice. Sean tried to hide it, but Liam knew him too well.

"I'm heading out." Looking around for his sister, Liam grimaced when he didn't see her. "I take it Eva isn't here."

"She's working a case."

"Tell her hello for me, all right?" Liam waved and turned to go.

Still thinking about Ellie and debating whether it was too soon to call her, Liam stopped at his favorite deli and grabbed a Cuban sandwich and bag of chips to take up to his apartment. Sean had invited him out to dinner with him and Orla, but Liam hadn't wanted to feel like a third wheel, so he'd declined. He'd almost called Cormac to see if he wanted to meet up at that Irish pub his twin liked so much, but at the last minute decided he'd rather be alone. Just in case he decided to go ahead and call Ellie.

Restless, he finished off his dinner and eyed his phone. Since Noreen had died, he hadn't dated much, and only then when a woman actively pursued him. He let them know up front that he wasn't looking for a serious relationship, any relationship for that matter. If they were good with that, they usually had a lot of fun. For a while, at least. Usually either the woman met someone else and moved on, or she began to make the kind of demands he'd told her up front he wasn't going to be able to meet.

Ellie was different. The kind of visceral attraction he'd felt when seeing her had knocked the air from his lungs. He hadn't felt anything so strong since he'd dated her in high school. Even with Noreen, he remembered, determined to try and be loyal to his deceased wife. He'd loved Noreen and she'd loved him—at first. While their marriage hadn't ever been especially physical, particularly toward the end, they'd both tried. Noreen had died in a car accident while visiting a friend in Rhode Island. Liam hadn't even gotten to say goodbye.

Pushing away the morose thoughts, Liam dug out his phone and stared at it, wondering why he was making such a simple thing so difficult. He and Ellie were old friends and had some catching up to do, that's all. It shouldn't matter that he found Ellie Mathers smoking hot.

As if his thoughts had conjured up magic, his phone

rang. Ellie. Immediately his heart began racing. He took a deep breath and answered. "Hello?"

"Liam, it's Ellie." The warmth in her voice brought a rush of pleasure. "I just got done having dinner with my parents and wondered if you wanted to meet up and have a drink."

When he didn't immediately respond, she continued. "To catch up, I mean. Listen, maybe this was a bad idea. Short notice and all that. If you're busy, I definitely understand. In fact—"

"I'd love to." Interrupting her, he had to smile. Clearly, he made her as nervous as she did him. "Though that depends where you want to meet. I live off 45th."

"Really? That's not too far. I'm near 53rd. Have you ever been to that rooftop place on 50th? In Times Square?"

"Cloud M?" he responded. "Sure. When?"

"I'm walking from my parent's apartment so I'm really close. I can grab a table for us."

"It's just a couple of blocks," he told her. "I'll meet you there in a few minutes." After ending the call, he picked up his pace.

Once he had the bar in sight, he forced himself to slow down. *Casual*, he reminded himself, even though he felt a rush at the thought of seeing Ellie again.

Pushing through the door, he scanned the crowded lower room. Despite the nice weather, a lot of patrons had opted to remain inside rather than head up to the rooftop with its spectacular views. Most of the people up there were likely tourists eager to make the most of their NYC experience.

Then he spotted Ellie, waving him over to a table by

the window. As before, the sight of her slender figure made his heart skip a beat. He managed to compose himself as he walked over, wondering if she had any idea how beautiful she was. Several other men clearly thought the same, because Liam couldn't help but notice them eying her with appreciation.

"That didn't take you long," she commented, beaming at him.

For the space of a heartbeat he allowed himself to bask in the warmth of her smile before taking a seat. "It's great to see you again, Ellie. You look amazing."

Their gazes caught and held. Again, he felt that flash of heat.

"You do too." I can't believe so many years have passed since we saw each other."

The waiter came over just then to take their drink orders. Ellie ordered a vodka tonic while Liam stuck to his usual beer. Once the server had gone, Liam leaned forward. "I was glad to hear your voice on the phone this morning. I'm surprised you still had my number."

"I was kind of shocked that the number I had for you was still valid," she admitted. "When I called it, I thought someone else would answer and tell me I had the wrong number." She grimaced. "Though I guess I could have always checked with my mom."

He nodded. "Sean hung on to my phone for me when I was in prison. He paid the phone bill and everything. He gave it back to me once I got out."

Ellie shifted in her chair, making him wonder if she found his talking about prison uncomfortable. "You've done well for yourself, Liam," she said, erasing his fear. "I truly admire how you've taken your experience and used it to try and keep other teenagers from making the same mistakes you did."

She leaned across the table and covered his hand with hers. Her fingers were slender and sensual. "At dinner earlier, my mother showed me a video of the talk you gave today at her school. I have to say you did a wonderful job."

Nonplussed, he shrugged. "Thanks. I consider this is my life's work. If I can help one kid not make the stupid choices I made, then I feel like I've succeeded."

Their drinks arrived then. When the waiter asked if they wanted anything to eat, they glanced at each other and simultaneously shook their heads. Once he'd gone, Liam took a sip of his beer. "I'm still curious though. Why did you really decide to call me about Aliana? I know you said I was the only person who'd get it, but still. We haven't spoken in years."

"This might sound odd, but when I saw Aliana—and I *know* it was her—you were the first person who came to mind. The only person who came to mind. You saw me through the dark days after she disappeared. And anyone else would have doubted me, said it was just a look-alike or that I've been working too much and was tired. I knew you wouldn't. I kept hearing you say—"

"Prove it," he finished for her.

"Yes." She smiled. "That used to be your motto."

"Still is."

They sat for a moment in companionable silence, while the hum of conversation ebbed and flowed around them. Unlike other dates he'd been on, Liam didn't feel the need to fill the quiet with meaningless conversation. Ellie felt somehow familiar to him, like a long-lost friend returning into his sphere.

A long-lost, *sexy-as-hell* friend, he amended silently. Around her, he felt like a kid again, with that same reckless optimism that anything might be possible. Foolish and dangerous, he told himself, even as he gazed into the warmth of her long-lashed dark eyes.

"Will you help me?" she asked. "I want to find Aliana. I've never really believed she was dead. I know it's a cold case, but—"

Shocked, he interrupted. "Do you want to find her because of your shared past or because she tried to kill you?"

"Allegedly tried to kill me," she corrected gently, taking a sip of her cocktail. "If she did, then I want to know why."

Which made sense. And working with Ellie? Naturally, he found the thought of spending more time with her exhilarating. "Of course I'll help you. Though you should know I'm already working on trying to find out what happened to Humphrey Kelly. And also keeping my foundation running, giving talks, all of that."

"Thank you." The curve of her lips when she smiled had him aching to lean over and kiss her. He barely managed to rein himself in.

"I get it. We're all busy. I'll still be reporting to my day job as well," she said, half laughing. "We'll have to meet after work and on weekends."

His pulse leaped at the thought. "I'd like that," he replied, meaning it.

"Me too," she echoed softly. "Tell me about what's going on with Humphrey's case."

"I wish there was more to tell." Liam had introduced Ellie to Humphrey back when they were teens. The prominent psychiatrist had liked her; he had felt that she was a good influence on Liam. "I can't believe there haven't been more leads. A lot of the beat cops have been talking about it."

"Sean is devastated. Heck, we all are. After my dad died, Humphrey was all we had." Liam and Humphrey hadn't gotten along too well back then, but they'd mended fences since."

"I understand." She sipped her drink. "It's been sixteen years and I never got over losing my best friend. Hopefully Humphrey will turn up."

"Hopefully so." He shrugged, then looked deep into her eyes. "I have to wonder if maybe Humphrey and your friend Aliana might both have engineered their own disappearance."

"Explain your logic," she demanded.

"Everything is simply too clean. No witnesses, no evidence of foul play, no blood, no anything."

She thought about it for a minute. "Maybe you're right. But I hope not. That theory bothers me. I can't imagine that Aliana at least would have put her parents and me through so much worry and grief. She wasn't that kind of person."

"People are capable of anything," he pointed out.

"I'm well aware." She took a sip of her drink. "I see the bad side of humanity every day in my job investigating crimes. Still, I hate to be that cynical about someone I loved like a sister."

Hearing that, he grinned. "I admire the way you're able to keep yourself from thinking bad things about someone you haven't seen in sixteen years. Especially since seeing her you were shot at and then poisoned."

Staring at him, she opened her mouth, no doubt to make some sort of witty comeback. Before she could, he leaned across the table and did what he'd been aching to do ever since he'd seen her again. He kissed her.

That grin and the kiss that followed after were the hottest damn things Ellie had ever experienced. Stunned, she kissed him back. When he finally sat back down, they stared at each other. Unbelievably turned on, she couldn't help but wonder if the kiss had affected him the same way.

One corner of his mouth kicked up in the beginnings of another smile. Still holding her gaze, he took a long drink of his beer. Heart racing, she forced herself to do the same with her vodka tonic.

Ellie had never been an impulsive person. Almost everything she did was the result of careful consideration, often using her beloved list-making technique. This methodical temperament served her well in her occupation as a forensic crime scene investigator.

But right now, sitting across from the sexiest man she'd ever met, with her entire body tingling, she was about to do something completely out of character.

That is, if she didn't lose her nerve.

Liam had finished his beer. She glanced down at her own glass, picked it up and took a long drink. "Let me see if I can get the check," she murmured, hoping she didn't sound as nervous as she felt.

"I'll do that." He glanced around, located their waiter,

and caught his attention. A moment later, he had the check.

Ellie got out her wallet to pay, but Liam shook his head.

"Let me take care of this," he said. "You can get the next one if you want."

The next one. She loved the sound of that. "Sounds good," she said, managing to sound casual.

By the time Liam had paid, she'd finished her drink. Standing, she smoothed down her skirt with one hand and took his arm. "Are you ready?" he asked, the warmth of his eyes igniting the simmering spark already inside her.

"I am." They headed toward the door.

Once they were outside, Liam tugged her closer. "Do you want to go someplace else?" he asked. "I'm not ready for the night to end yet."

Snuggled into his side, she looked up at him, hoping he'd read the invitation in her eyes. As he turned to her, she stood up on tiptoe and pressed her mouth to his.

She heard his harsh intake of breath. Then he made a sound low in his throat and it was on again.

Everything vanished but the sensual movement of his mouth on hers. The traffic noise, the pedestrians who had to move around them, all gone. There was only this man, his strong body, and the raging desire his kiss brought to life inside her. A desire that was achingly familiar, despite the years that had passed since he'd first kissed her.

"Why don't you get a room," someone said, startling her right back into the present. Heat suffused her as she realized they'd just had a very public display of affection surrounded by complete strangers. Not like her at all.

"That's not a bad idea," she murmured. Slipping her hand into Liam's, she tugged him along with her. "Come with me."

He didn't question her. Not there, not yet. Not even when they reached the front of her building. "Come up?" she asked, every fiber of her being hoping he'd agree.

He stood stock-still, looking down at her, the desire in his expression clear. "Ellie, are you sure?"

Instead of answering, she was tempted to tug him close again. Only the knowledge that any of her neighbors could see them stopped her. She nodded and then, with her hand still in his, she led him inside and straight to the elevator.

They got off at her floor. Though her apartment was about halfway down the hallway, she had to force herself not to walk faster. Heart hammering inside her chest, she unlocked her door and they stepped inside.

She opened her mouth to speak, but before she could utter a sound, he crushed her to him and kissed her again. *This*, she thought, dazed and aroused all at once. *This* was what she'd been missing. All this time.

Hungry. More than that—*starving*. And she'd never even realized how empty she'd felt inside. They kissed with a sort of reckless abandon, devouring each other, burning with their mutual need. He pressed the hard length of his body into her, until she had her back against the wall. His arousal was evident, both making her melt and thrilling her with its strength and size. Exactly as she'd remembered.

Knees weak, she clung to him, gasping out loud as his lips seared a path down the curve of her throat. She fumbled with the buttons on his shirt but managed to unfasten them. Finally, she let her hands roam, caressing his bare chest. When she reached his abdomen, he sucked in his breath. The belt buckle came next, his jeans strained by his powerfully aroused body. Mouth dry, she made quick work of that, eager to see him naked.

As she stared, his body even more magnificent than she could have imagined, he reached into his discarded jeans, located his wallet and removed a condom. Heart pounding, breathing ragged, she watched as he pulled it over the impressive erect length of him. The boy she'd known, she thought, had become a heck of a sexy man.

"I could have helped with that," she managed.

"Maybe, but then I might have lost what little remains of my self-control," he said.

This statement made her entire body throb. Damn.

"Now it's my turn," he rasped, skimming his fingers up under her shirt and lifting it over her head. Her skin prickled, though she managed to hold herself still as he deftly unfastened her bra freeing her aching breasts. When he lowered his mouth to taste them, she couldn't stifle her moan.

Breathing ragged, she squirmed, her body warm, already pulsing. Ready. "I want you inside me," she gasped. "Now."

Her entreaty made him flash a savage grin. "Now?" he asked, rubbing the full length of himself against her but not yet entering her. She caught her breath, unable to breathe as heat suffused her entire body. His hardness electrified her and melted her at the same time.

"Now," she ordered, on the verge of shattering. "Now!"

This time, he complied. With one swift movement, he shifted, possessing her with a single deep stroke, again and again and again until she lost all capacity for rational thought.

The peak came almost instantly, shattering her. She cried out, back still against the wall, her core vibrating. The release of her passion appeared to drive him wild, making him take her deeper and faster, until she felt the swell of ecstasy rising again.

This time, they were moving as one; when she shuddered around him, he answered in kind.

Spent, he collapsed against her. If not for the wall supporting them, she knew she would have slid to the ground.

"That was…intense," he finally said, stepping back and taking himself out of her. Turning his back to her, he removed his condom and then made his way toward her bathroom, despite not ever having been inside her place before. As she straightened, wondering what to do with herself, the bathroom door opened and Liam emerged with a washcloth. "Come here," he invited. "Let me help clean you up."

Mystified, since she'd never had a man offer to do that before, she went with him, standing still as he used the warm washcloth on her. "There," he said. "That should do for now."

She nodded, feeling awkward. As if he sensed this, he pulled her close to him and kissed her again. A slow, but thorough kiss, making her dissolve into a puddle of desire once more.

"I'm sorry about that," he finally told her. "We should have at least tried to make it to your bed."

This brought a smile. "I don't know. I liked that. I've seen that happen in the movies, but never to me. It was wild."

"Wild." Nuzzling her neck, he chuckled when she shivered. "I still want to cuddle though. Bed or couch?"

Cuddle? Mystified, she took his hand and led the way into her bedroom. Since she always made her bed, she had to pull back the comforter before sliding under the sheets. A second later, Liam joined her.

Another man might have acted awkward or hurried away now that the sex had happened. Not Liam. He slid next to her and pulled her into his arms. "You're magnificent," he murmured.

Magnificent. Now that was a word. She liked it. "You too," she finally said, though for her the lovemaking had been something different. More earthy, more real, it had been like coming home, she thought, then blinked at her own foolishness. Glad she hadn't let herself speak her thoughts, she nestled her face into his chest and closed her eyes.

They lay like that for a good while, long enough for her to doze.

"I should go." His voice rumbled against her ear.

Loath to move, she sighed. "I know."

With a chuckle, he kissed the top of her head and gently rolled away. She eyed his naked back as he went into the other room, picked up his clothes and brought them to him. Watching him as he began to dress, she marveled that already she'd grown hungry for him again.

Finally, he'd gotten everything back on and turned to face her. "I brought your skirt and blouse," he said, holding it out to her.

She let the sheets fall as she stood, unabashedly naked, and watched the desire once again darken his gaze.

"Ellie…" He glanced at the clock. "We've both got to work tomorrow. I have to go."

She wanted to pout, but of course she did not. She knew she could entice him, by arching her back just so, thrusting her breasts out, making it clear how badly she desired him. But she'd never been that type of woman and damned if she'd start now.

Grabbing her skirt from him,, she stepped into it. "I understand," she said, her voice quiet. "And you're right."

"Hey." He cupped her chin with his big hand. "I'd make love to you all night long if I could." Then he kissed her, a slow, thoughtful kiss that made her body hum.

When he broke away, she sighed.

"I'll let myself out," he said. "Make sure and lock up behind me."

Slowly, she nodded. Something about this entire situation made her feel exposed and vulnerable, not at all like the confident, capable woman she considered herself to be.

At the bedroom doorway, Liam turned. "I'll be in touch," he promised. "We should both get some rest. I'll talk to you tomorrow."

Only once she'd heard her front door close did she

pad over to it to turn the deadbolt. Then she headed to her bathroom to wash up before bed and brush her teeth. She put on her satin hair wrap and adjusted it, before returning to her bed to slide under the sheets.

Closing her eyes, she tried to stop the flow of carnal images. She should have been sated; after all, she'd been well loved. Instead, she craved him again, wanting more.

It was then she realized she'd made a horrible mistake. She knew better than to let her emotions get involved. Great sex was one thing. They were both healthy adults with their own separate lives. A coldness settled over her, all the way to her bones. Long ago, she'd determined to dedicate herself to her career. This had worked well for her and she saw no reason to think it wouldn't continue to do so. She had no room for a romantic entanglement.

Reflecting on Liam's quick and careful exit, she figured he most likely felt the same way. With mutual agreement, they could keep this—whatever this was— casual. It would be all right.

Somehow, she managed to fall asleep, her empty arms wrapped around her spare pillow, inexplicably missing someone she shouldn't.

Chapter 4

Leaving Ellie's apartment, Liam decided to walk home instead of trying to snag a cab. It was late enough that the sidewalks weren't as crowded and despite the distance, he needed the time to collect his thoughts.

He'd been alone a long time, though that didn't mean he lacked female companionship. The women he'd spent time with before, while beautiful and interesting, couldn't hold a candle to the exotic and sensual creature that was Ellie.

Each step he took seemed to echo her name. *Ellie*. He hadn't thought of her in years, not since he'd spent the first ten months of his two-year stint in prison wishing they hadn't broken up.

After sentencing, he'd done his time and moved on, resolutely focusing on the future and making himself a better person. He'd met Noreen and after a whirlwind courtship, they'd married. At first, she'd believed in him and his dreams. Her wealth had opened a lot of doors that might have stayed closed. However, the more he'd dedicated himself to the foundation, the more distant Noreen had become.

In fact, the night she'd died as the result of a horrific car accident, he'd wondered if she'd been leaving him. Even thinking this had been more painful than he'd expected, and he'd walled off his heart and shut himself down.

Now, after making love with Ellie, he felt those walls crumbling. His chest actually hurt, his stomach aching as if he'd been mortally wounded. Ellie. Intellectually, he knew he should be worried. After all, he'd taken great care to avoid emotional entanglements since Noreen had died. Trying to navigate the ups and downs of a marriage turned rocky had been confusing and draining, so much so he'd decided never to put himself through that again.

Since then, he'd kept an iron control on his love life, spending time only with women who understood up front that things would be casual. He'd never even had that discussion with Ellie. Heck, they'd only decided to meet for a drink and catch up on the past. He'd never expected them to go so far, so fast.

Like a match to gasoline. Explosive and quite honestly, dangerous. He'd need to be careful, or he'd find himself severely burned.

All the analogies made him shake his head at himself. His life, while staid, was satisfying. He wasn't certain he felt up for any kind of emotional upheaval. He didn't want to upend his life. He hoped he could manage this, whatever this was. Because honestly, he doubted he could make himself stay away.

Casual. At the earliest opportunity, he and Ellie needed to have a discussion. Surely, she'd agree. After all, she was a busy professional. They'd agreed to work together to try and solve Aliana's disappearance. As long as they focused on that, things should be all right.

He still had two blocks to go when his phone rang. His heart actually skipped a beat as he pulled it out, checking the screen to see if it was Ellie.

Instead, it was his twin brother, Cormac, who worked as a private investigator. He'd recently received the joyful news that he was going to be a father. Since he and the baby's mother-to-be, Emily Hernandez, were clearly in love, these days Cormac exuded happiness.

"Hey, bro," Liam answered. "What's up?"

"I just talked to Sean. He said you were hanging out with Ellie Mathers. Talk about a blast from the past."

Liam sighed. "I was surprised to hear from her, that's for sure. But we just finished meeting up for drinks and catching up. It's been really great." Talk about the understatement of the year.

"Yeah, I'm glad to hear that. I'm disappointed we haven't found any more clues about what might have happened to Humphrey."

"I know. Me too." As he continued to walk, Liam waited for his brother to get to the point. He knew Cormac's small talk would eventually give way to the reason for his call.

"Emily and I are going to do it," Cormac finally blurted out. "We've decided to get married. She's planning the whole thing out now."

Liam stopped in his tracks. Cormac was going to

be a husband as well as a father? "Congratulations," Liam said, meaning it. "I'm really glad for you, man."

They talked for a few minutes more before Cormac cleared his throat. "I did want to ask you something," he began. "I've already talked to Sean and he's cool with it. Would you be my best man?"

Stunned, Liam stopped walking. Once, before his wild teenage years, he and his twin had been inseparable. The choices Liam had made, which had culminated in Liam being sent to prison, had driven a wedge between them. Since his release, Liam had worked hard to rebuild their relationship. The fact that Cormac thought highly enough of him to ask Liam to stand up beside him in his wedding, brought tears to Liam's eyes.

"I'd be honored to," Liam choked out. "Thank you for asking."

"Of course," Cormac spoke with a smile in his voice. "Since you and Noreen got married at City Hall without inviting the family, I hope you'll return the favor someday."

Though Liam had no plans to ever remarry, he agreed. Cormac laughed and they ended the call.

Once Liam made it back to his building, he took the elevator up to the top floor, feeling oddly pensive. Seeing Ellie again had brought feelings rushing back. He wanted her, he craved her, he couldn't stop thinking about her. Once, she'd been a teenaged boy's dream. These days, he thought his younger self had been on to something.

Ellie Mathers.

The next morning, he woke up in an excellent mood. He'd dreamed of Ellie, naturally. And today, he had no speaking engagements booked, so he'd planned to spend some time at the 98th Precinct to help his siblings. Humphrey's disappearance was driving everyone crazy, and before that they'd all been working on an unsolved murder.

After jumping on his treadmill and running for thirty minutes, he took a shower, got dressed and headed to the kitchen to make a protein shake. When he'd bought the large apartment a few years ago, he'd had a complete renovation done before moving in. He loved the large windows that provided an abundance of light.

Briefly, he considered taking a day off and staying home today. That was something he never did, unless a rare cold felled him.

He'd just finished his shake when his phone rang. Ellie, he couldn't help hoping, but the caller ID showed it was his sister.

"Shocking news," Eva said without preamble. "How soon can you get down to the crime scene lab in Greenpoint?"

His first thought was Ellie. It shouldn't have been, so he pushed it away. "Can't you just tell me on the phone?" he asked, not bothering to hide his annoyance, even though it was directed at himself instead of his sister.

"I could, but I'm not going to. I just happened to be here when Ellie got the test results, so I called Sean. He wants all of us to meet at the lab to discuss."

Which made sense. They were a team, after all.

"I can be there in half an hour," Liam said. "I'm leaving now."

"Good. Please hurry, because this is huge." And she hung up.

Intrigued, he hailed a cab, deciding the expense would

definitely be worth the ease of travel. For the first time in what seemed like forever, he got one to stop on the first try. He recited the address from memory and then settled back into his seat, closing his eyes in hopes of better enjoying the ride.

Which turned out to be a huge mistake. All he could see was Ellie, naked and sensual, stretched out next to him on her bed. His body immediately responded, making him shift in his seat and turn to look out the window. Watching traffic hopefully would help him regain his balance and put his mind back where it needed to be.

He and Ellie had kept things casual. Surely they could both pretend that night had never happened.

Arriving at the lab, he paid the driver and got out. When he entered, he saw Sean, Eva and Ellie all waiting for him in the conference room. Curiosity piqued, Liam hustled over, flashing Ellie what he hoped was an impersonal smile. She nodded in response, her gaze flitting from him to the others.

Sean motioned at him to close the door. Once he had, Ellie cleared her throat. "We've gotten some preliminary results from DNA found near Humphrey's in the courthouse closet."

Liam froze. Noticing, Eva nodded and mouthed at him to just wait.

"It belongs to a relative of Wes Westmore," Ellie continued. "We're running analytics on it now, trying to get an exact match. I know Wes is the primary suspect in the Lana Brinkley murder."

A case Sean and Eva had been working on until Humphrey's disappearance had taken their complete focus.

Sean cursed. "That make zero sense. What's the connection?"

"Unfortunately, neither I nor the DNA can answer that question," Ellie responded. "All I can do is give you what I've found."

Liam couldn't help but notice the way she refused to look at him.

His baby sister, Eva, apparently caught that as well. "Are you okay?" she asked Ellie. "I heard someone tried to poison you the other day."

"I'm fine." Flashing a brief smile, Ellie went back to shuffling her papers. When she looked up again, she directed her attention at Sean. "I'll leave these results here for you. They're copies, so feel free to take them with you. If anyone needs anything else, I'll be in my office."

Head held high, she exited the conference room without a backward glance.

Liam couldn't help but stare, tracking her with his gaze until she closed the door behind her. When he returned his attention back to the others, he found both his older brother and younger sister staring at him.

"What did you do?" Eva demanded. "I know you and Ellie met up the other night to catch up. And I heard about the shooter and the attempted poison."

"I don't know what you're talking about." His protest sounded weak and he knew it. And judging from the looks Sean and Eva exchanged, they knew it too.

"Spill." Crossing her arms, Eva glared at him. "I really like Ellie and I swear if you did something to hurt her..."

"As if I would." That alone should have been enough. But his sibling's skeptical expressions indicated it wasn't. However, what had happened between him and Ellie was private and personal. Even if he were inclined to spill those beans, he'd never do so without obtaining Ellie's consent.

"I promise you, nothing bad happened," he continued, spreading his arms. "Just two old friends playing catch-up."

"Funny, that's almost exactly what Ellie said." Eva shook her head.

Finally, Sean apparently took pity on him. "Ah, Eva, give him a break. Let's get back to the case."

Relieved, Liam agreed. "First up, we need to figure out the connection between Wes Westmore and Humphrey. Did Ellie say who the relative is?"

"No." Sean glanced down at the stack of papers. "DNA only identified him or her as someone related to Wes, not specifically who. She's working on identifying that."

"We just need to figure out how and why." Animated, Eva focused her attention on the paperwork. "Sean, can I get a copy of those too?"

"Of course." Smiling fondly, Sean slid the papers across the table toward her. "Take these. When you get back to the precinct, go ahead and make me copies and leave them on my desk."

"Will do." Eva scooped up the papers, practically vibrating with energy. "I hope you don't mind, but I'm going to head out. I want to get to work on this right away."

"I'll call you when I hear from Ellie with more details," Liam promised.

"Roger that." She waved. "If I come up with anything, you two will be the first to know."

"Go for it," Sean said. Together, he and Liam watched as Eva rushed out the door, forgetting to close it behind her.

"I wish I had half her energy," Liam commented.

"And enthusiasm. I will say this, I'm proud of her. She's got the makings of a good cop," Sean said. "Now all BS aside, please tell me you didn't do anything stupid with Ellie."

Liam shook his head. "Did I badger you about your relationship with Orla?"

This earned a fierce glare from his older brother. "Oh, is it a relationship now? You've barely known Ellie again for forty-eight hours."

"You know what I mean," Liam interjected. "And Ellie and I are both adults. I'm reasonably sure we can figure out how to handle ourselves around each other."

"Yes, we can." Ellie spoke from the doorway. "Sorry, but I couldn't help overhearing. Sean, I appreciate your concern, but you need to—"

"Back off," Liam finished for her.

Grinning, Sean raised his hands in surrender. Looking from one to the other, he began to slowly back away. "I think that's my cue to exit," he said. And then he left.

"What was all that about?" Ellie wanted to know. Even with her arms crossed and her aloof expression, she still looked drop-dead gorgeous. He figured it would be best to keep that opinion to himself.

"Both my brother and sister are observant," he said. "They could tell something happened between you and me, but they don't know what. Naturally, they decided I must have done something to hurt your feelings. That's what Sean was busting my chops about."

She cocked her head, her dark eyes cool, her gaze appraising. "Why would they think that? Do you normally go around hurting women?"

Though she had no way of knowing, the ridiculousness of the question made him laugh. "Not hardly," he said. Then, growing serious, he regarded her. "Though maybe we need to have a discussion about the other night."

At his words, she winced. "I'm not looking for a relationship right now."

"Neither am I," he said, feeling both relieved and, oddly enough, peeved.

"Okay, good." She thought for a moment. "As long as we're both in agreement about keeping things casual, I'm definitely up for getting together again."

His pulse immediately leaped at the thought. "Me too," he managed to say, hoping he sound as nonchalant as she had.

Ellie nodded once, then turned on her heels and walked out.

Liam stayed where he was, heart in his throat. What the hell was wrong with him? He couldn't figure out how Ellie managed to affect him so strongly.

With his body still partially aroused, he managed to make it to the door. Hopefully, the walk over to the precinct would help him get his head on straight.

Though she didn't watch him leave, somehow Ellie knew the moment Liam had left the building. She sat back in her chair, staring blindly at her computer screen, and wondered what the hell had happened to her. Great sex, she told herself. Nothing more. And they'd both agreed to keep it that way, so everything should be fine. Her life wasn't going to change.

Then why did she feel so bothered? It had to be because after a long dry spell, her body had been brought back to life. That must be the reason she couldn't stop thinking about Liam, and aching to feel him inside of her again.

Ellie believed in dealing with her life in a logical fashion. Now that she knew the *why*, she needed to come up with a solution. The answer seemed relatively easy. Relax and let herself enjoy the unexpected bounty that was Liam Colton.

So simple. But was it? As long as she could manage to keep herself free of emotional entanglements, she could manage.

Relieved, she clicked on a file on her desktop and tried to lose herself in work.

The DNA evidence from the courtroom closet had been a complete surprise. Someone had noticed a stray strand of hair and thankfully, instead of trying to clean it up, they'd notified NYPD. Almost everyone, including Ellie, had figured the hair would belong to the missing psychiatrist Humphrey Kelly. Instead, learning it was a close match to a suspect in another murder investigation had brought more questions than answers. What was the connection between Wes Westmore and Humphrey Kelly and how did this case tie into the Lana Brinkley murder?

Luckily, her job was only to analyze the evidence, not solve the crimes. She happily left that to detectives like Sean Colton.

Except for Aliana's disappearance. The case had

long ago been marked a cold case and disappeared in the huge backlog of other, similar cases. For sure that wouldn't happen with Humphrey Kelly. Not only did he have a high profile, but there was no way the Coltons would let his case go unsolved. They were all old family friends.

Which was why Ellie had never forgotten about Aliana. She still considered herself like family. She wouldn't rest until she found out what had really happened to her friend. Even if, she thought, someone didn't want her to know.

The rest of the day passed quickly, as it always did when Ellie got immersed in her work. Her lab had been set up as a kind of overflow lab for the main NYPD Forensic Crime Scene Lab in Queens. Like them, her lab handled cases from all five boroughs.

Over the years, Ellie had developed a reputation for not only being thorough, but also providing exactly the right piece of evidence to crack each case. Detectives in precincts all over the city requested her by name.

Since she couldn't possibly work them all, she was given a lot of the higher-profile cases. Humphrey Kelly's disappearance being one of them.

Speaking of that case… She went to her computer, which she'd set to running analytics on the DNA sample that had been found in the courtroom closet. The closest match she'd been able to get so far had been a marker showing the hair was related to Wes Westmore, but so far whoever it belonged to wasn't in the system.

A few more tests had indicated the person was female, but that was it. Hoping to get something a little more concrete, she hadn't yet shared that information with Sean and his team.

Tapping a few keys on the keyboard, she opened the program. It had finished the analysis and only come up with *results inconclusive.*

She picked up the phone to call Eva and tell her, then thought better of it. She couldn't rid herself of the niggling feeling that she was missing something. Until she'd figured that out, she'd keep this last bit of information to herself.

Now that she'd finished her assigned work for the day, she decided she'd once again go over the information she'd collected on Aliana. She'd filled a three-ring binder with copies of news stories, police reports and old photographs. Every month like clockwork, she checked the database to see if she got any hits on drivers' licenses issued to anyone named Aliana Martin, and she also checked the DMV for vehicle registration. Not once in sixteen years had she gotten a single hit.

Despite that, she ran the search again today. Both times, the search came back as *No Matches.* Of course not. She hadn't really expected otherwise. That would have made things way too easy.

But she *had* seen Aliana on the subway. Which would mean either Aliana had made herself vanish, or she'd managed to escape from whoever had taken her. The second option, while the most palatable of the two, left more questions than answers. For example, if someone had held Aliana captive all these years, and she'd finally been able to break free, why wouldn't she go to the authorities?

She tapped her pen on the desktop, wishing she had someone to brainstorm with. Tossing ideas back and forth always helped her think of new possibilities.

Immediately, she thought of Liam. Would he think it

weird if she called him and asked if he'd run over some thoughts with her?

Most likely he'd think it was a booty call.

Shaking her head at herself, she realized she wouldn't be averse to that either. In fact, just thinking about it made her body tingle.

Her desk phone rang. Caller ID showed NYPD. Possibly another case, which would be great since she needed a distraction.

Once she'd answered, the man on the other end identified himself as Detective Kaprowski, who worked in the 98th Precinct along with Sean and Eva. "Someone called and left a message for you," he said. "Even though I tried to give them the number to the crime scene lab, they insisted on leaving it with me. I'm calling you to pass it on."

"Male or female?" she asked.

"A woman."

Grabbing a pen and a piece of paper, she told him to go ahead.

"Okay. I'm going to read it to you exactly as it was left, even though it doesn't make sense." He cleared his throat before continuing. "Tell Ellie to leave the past alone. Otherwise, she's going to regret opening a can of worms."

Ellie froze. "That's it?" she asked. "That's all she said?"

"Yep. I'm assuming it's related to some case you're working on?"

"Probably," she replied. "Thank you for calling."

Once she'd replaced the phone in the receiver, she shook her head. "Aliana?" she wondered out loud. It had to be. Except if Aliana had been the one to drop off the poisoned breakfast, she knew Ellie worked at the crime scene lab, not at the 98th precinct. Why call there and leave a message?

Mentally, she reviewed her current load of active cases, on the off chance the caller might have been referencing one of them. As vague as the message had been, it could have been any of them—or none. Except in her gut, she felt sure the caller had been Aliana, warning her to back off searching.

But why? Like every unsolved case, the answer almost always came back to that. The *why*.

She picked up her phone again and then put it back down, shaking her head at herself. Once again, her first impulse had been to contact Liam. Her decision to call him the other day had come out of the blue, and she could still hardly believe she'd done it. Though honestly, she was glad she had. Connecting with him again had made her feel more alive than she had in years.

Leave the past alone, the caller had said. Let Aliana stay missing? Which, if not for that chance encounter in the subway, she'd still be.

For the first time, she had to consider the possibility that Liam's theory might be correct. What if Aliana had made herself disappear and wanted to stay that way? So much so, she'd taken desperate measures to make sure she wasn't found. Like have Ellie shot at and then try to poison her breakfast.

Though Ellie's first instinct was to dismiss those thoughts—after all, she couldn't prove the gunshots had been directed at her—she couldn't dispute the scientific evidence. Someone had tried to poison her. Even though her heart cried out in protest, she had no choice but to consider Aliana a prime suspect.

Checking her logs, she decided to go through her caseload, both open investigations and ones she'd recently completed. Maybe somewhere in one of these she might find someone else who had a reason to want to kill her. In all the years she'd been working forensics, no one had ever threatened her before. But that didn't necessarily mean Aliana was the only person who could be wishing her harm.

Her mother called as she was midway through her online cache of case files. Startled, Ellie glanced at the clock, surprised to realize it had gotten so late. "Hi, Mom," she said. "What's up?"

"Are you working on the Humphrey Kelly case?" Violet asked, even though she knew Ellie couldn't talk about an ongoing investigation. Luckily, Violet didn't wait for an answer before she began to read aloud from an article she'd found.

Ellie waited patiently for her mom to finish. None of the information the reporter had garnered was news to her, of course, but the general public likely found the great air of mystery fascinating.

"Did you know all that?" Violet asked once she'd wound down.

"Yes. But you know I can't comment. That's an active case."

Violet sighed. "I know. It all just seems so deliberate. I'm aware you are highly skilled at what you do and that you don't need my help, but I really think the police need to look at this from another angle."

Intrigued, since Ellie valued her mother's insight and intelligence, Ellie prompted her to go on.

"Well, it seems to me everyone is looking at this man's disappearance in the light of something happening to him. Instead, maybe what should be looked at are what reasons he might have for wanting to disappear."

"I'm sure they're checking out all possibilities," Ellie said, making a mental note to ask Eva about that the next time they talked. Since Sean Colton was lead detective, and he had a reputation as an excellent one, she figured they were already on it.

Violet changed the subject, talking about her weekend plans. Ellie braced herself, well aware of how her mother operated. No matter how hard she tried, Violet could not accept her daughter's single status. She used to constantly try and set Ellie up on blind dates, usually with the sons of some of her church friends. When Ellie had begged her to stop, Violet had begrudgingly done so, though she'd never given up hope. While her mother celebrated her daughter's career success with pride, she wanted Ellie to have the same kind of loving, supportive relationship she had with Ellie's father. And a couple of cute grandkids wouldn't hurt either.

Bracing herself, Ellie decided to change the subject instead. "I saw Aliana Martin in the subway the other day," she said.

Violet's shocked intake of breath proved the distraction had worked. "You what?"

"I saw Aliana. And before you ask, I'm absolutely sure it was her. I'd know her anywhere."

"You've never given up on her disappearance," Violet mused. "You know she's not the same sixteen-year-old best friend she was back then. Assuming that she's even still alive."

Which meant that her mother didn't believe Ellie had truly seen her. Though she'd expected this, it still stung. Which was exactly why she hadn't mentioned it before now.

"I'm aware," Ellie murmured. "Either way, I wasn't able to catch up with her."

"Maybe that was a good thing," Violet said, the relief in her voice palpable. "There's no sense in dredging up the past." She sighed. "I don't know how her parents survived all that."

For months after Aliana's disappearance, Violet had kept Ellie close. Ellie and Aliana had done everything together, and Violet couldn't help but worry that whatever had happened to one, could happen to the other.

"I know, Mom. But how amazing would it be if I found her?"

"I think you're setting yourself up for a world of hurt," Violet cautioned. "Just be careful, okay?"

Ellie promised she would, glad she hadn't mentioned the gun shots or the attempted poisoning. Of course, she knew better. Her mother considered Ellie's laboratory job safe, so she never worried. Ellie didn't want to make her start now.

Chapter 5

When Liam walked into the 98th Precinct, no one in the bustling main space even noticed him at first. Of course, he was around so often, it felt like he worked there sometimes. The low hum of voices, numerous telephones ringing and all the other accompanying sounds of a busy police station acted like a familiar balm on his troubled soul. Even when he had no official police business, he often stopped by the precinct just to calm his restless nature.

The 98th represented stability. And more importantly, family.

Though the relationship between him and his older brother, Sean, had once been tumultuous, that had all changed the day Sean showed up to bring Liam home after his stint in prison. Liam had gone in a brash eighteen-year-old and emerged two years later a completely changed man. He'd wanted to emulate his brother, but due to his criminal record, he could not become a police officer. Instead, he'd found his true calling, starting his scared straight foundation and working with his connections on the street to help NYPD as a consultant when necessary. The bonus part of the second gig was he got to spend more time with his siblings.

These days, Liam would lay his life down for Sean and vice versa. He had no doubt all his siblings felt the same way. Their family had grown tight. Sean, Liam, Cormac and Eva.

"Just who I wanted to see!" Eva sauntered over. She wore her police uniform well, with an attitude to match. Over the past several months, she'd gained confidence in her abilities as a police officer and that showed in her demeanor.

Liam heaved an exaggerated sigh. "What do you need?" he asked, giving her a quick hug, which she enthusiastically returned.

"Thanks for asking." Her contagious grin had him smiling. "I need someone to go with me to have another chat with Ciara Kelly."

"I'm surprised you're not wanting Sean to go," he replied, secretly flattered.

"Sean was supposed to, but he got called away on another case at the last moment." She shrugged. "It happens."

"What about your partner?" he asked, looking around. No one in the family was particularly fond of Eva's partner, Detective Mitch Mallard.

"He took a personal day off," she replied. Glancing to the left and right as if to make sure she wasn't overheard, she leaned closer. "It's been kind of nice with him gone."

"I imagine."

"Yeah. So can you go with me or not? We can take the patrol car. Which will also be a treat, since Mitch always insists on driving."

"I can do that." Liam squeezed her shoulder. "Lead the way."

"I'm on it." Moving toward the door, she stopped when he didn't immediately follow. "Are you coming?"

Her impatience had him shaking his head.

Once they'd gotten into the patrol car, he settled back to watch his sister drive. Growing up in the city, none of them had learned to drive as teenagers. With public transportation and taxis always at the ready, there was no need. Liam himself hadn't until after he'd married Noreen. Then and only then had he gotten his first car, because only then did he have a place to park it.

Eva drove with a cautious kind of competence.

"Does Ciara know you're coming?" he asked.

"Yes. I texted her to ask if it was all right if I stopped by. She agreed, though she said she didn't have a lot of time."

He thought for a moment. "I'm guessing she knows she can't throw out a statement like she did the last time we were there and not expect us to follow up on it."

"Most likely." Eva sounded positively cheerful. "Though none of us think she was involved in any way with Humphrey's disappearance, now is not the time to keep secrets, even if they're personal."

"*Especially* if they're personal," Liam agreed. "We have no way of knowing what information might be tied to his disappearance. Ciara said she and Humphrey hadn't married for love, but for secret reasons. Those reasons, whatever they are, might help give us valuable clues."

They reached Ciara's duplex. Eva lucked into a parking spot right out front, pulling in just as another vehicle pulled out.

"This location," Eva mused. "I'd kill for this view."

Liam agreed. "The proximity to the Museum of Natural History would be convenient when entertaining guests."

They walked up the front stairs. Ciara opened the door before they even reached it. "Come in," she said, her expression solemn. Her dark hair hung down her back in a neat braid.

Once they'd stepped inside, she closed the door and locked it. Though she smiled, her green eyes remained shadowed. "Would either of you like anything to drink?"

"No thank you." Eva shook her head.

"Oh, then go ahead and sit," Ciara said, twisting her fingers nervously. "Please, make yourselves comfortable."

Eva immediately dropped onto the couch. Following his sister's lead, Liam took a seat next to her. Ciara chose a large armchair.

"I imagine you wanted to speak to me so I could clarify what I told you the last time we spoke." Crossing her legs, Ciara sighed. "This was something Humphrey and I hoped we'd never have to make public. Before I give you the details, I'm going to have to ask for your promise to be discreet."

Both Liam and Eva nodded. "You have our word,"

Eva said. "Whatever information you give us today will be confidential."

"Thank you." Ciara looked from one to the other. "I don't imagine you've gotten any new leads on Humphrey's whereabouts?"

"No, we haven't. That's why we need you to explain what you meant about your marriage. You never know what might help us."

"I see." Taking a sip of water, Ciara carefully put the glass back down. "I desperately needed money to pay for my ill mother's cancer treatment. My grandfather had just passed away and left me a small fortune, but he was an ornery old cuss and he put a stipulation in the will that I couldn't inherit unless I was married."

Eva nodded, but she didn't comment. Liam kept quiet too, not wanting to interrupt Ciara's clearly painful retelling.

"I'd been taking care of my mother, so I had no social life," Ciara continued. "Humphrey was a family friend and he wanted to help. He offered to marry me, keeping things strictly platonic. We planned to divorce after five years, since the will stipulated the marriage had to last that long. Since I needed the money immediately, Humphrey gave me a loan. I signed a contract to repay him once I came into my inheritance."

If this had been a romance novel, Liam thought, Humphrey and Ciara would have fallen in love. Apparently, that hadn't been the case.

When neither Eva or Liam said anything, Ciara took another sip of water before continuing. "Humphrey and I were friendly, but we lived as roommates. That's it. My big secret." She took a deep breath, her eyes glistening with unshed tears. "I'm sorry I didn't tell you sooner. However, I want you to know that I am truly worried for Humphrey's well-being and I have no idea what happened to him."

"Thank you." Eva stood. "I realize this was difficult for you. We appreciate you taking the time to share your story."

"You're quite welcome." Clear-eyed, Ciara stood and led them toward the door.

Once they were out in the hall, they didn't talk at all until they gotten back in the car.

"Let's call Sean and fill him in," Eva suggested. Without waiting for Liam to agree, she handed him her phone. "Put it on speaker," she ordered.

Sean picked up on the second ring. He listened while Eva repeated what Ciara had told them.

"I don't think this adds anything as to motive toward Humphrey's disappearance," Liam interjected. "But it does open up the very real truth that Humphrey had secrets he kept from us. Maybe it really *was* him that his former patient spotted on Amsterdam Avenue with a woman. She might have been more than a friend, too."

"I agree," Sean said. "We all need to start looking into the possibility that Humphrey didn't vanish after all but engineered his own disappearance."

"My first question is why," Eva mused.

"The most likely reason I can see is for his own safety," Liam said. "Maybe one of his clients came after him or is blackmailing him. Something like that."

"That's a possibility," Eva agreed. "Except it doesn't feel right."

Both Sean and Liam agreed with her.

"If that was the case," Sean said. "He would have reached out to one of us. At the very least, he would have triggered his alarm system. He's well aware we Coltons will always have his back."

"That leads us right back to the all-important *why*," Eva mused. "If we can figure that out, then I have a feeling we'll know exactly what happened."

Like with Aliana Martin, Liam thought, thinking of Ellie and her determination to find out what had happened to her friend. Suddenly, he wished he could call Ellie, talk over what he'd learned from Ciara and get her input.

Right then, he decided he would, later. When Eva and Sean weren't listening to his every word.

They had just ended the call with Sean and Liam had handed her cell back to her when her phone rang again. "It's Ellie," she said, smiling as she went to answer.

Despite himself, Liam's heart jumped.

"Wow," Eva said into the phone. "Let me put you on speaker. Liam's here with me. Would you mind repeating what you just told me?"

A moment later, Ellie's lilting voice filled the interior of the car. "Hi, Liam. As I was telling Eva, I got a little bit more information on the DNA that was found in the courtroom closet. While we do know that person is related to Wes Westfield, I've also been able to determine it belonged to a female."

"Who?" Liam asked.

"That I wasn't able to find out. Whoever it is, she isn't in our system."

"We need to let Sean know," Eva said. "Hey, I have an idea? How about we all get together after work and eat?" She glanced at Liam. "There's this little Italian place on West 47th that we all love."

"Definitely. Trattoria Trecolori? I adore that place," Ellie responded. "What time?"

"How about seven? That should give us all enough time to get home after work and clean up." For the first time, Eva appeared to realize she hadn't consulted Liam. "Would that work for you, Liam?"

"Sure." He didn't bother to pretend he had other plans. "We'll see you there."

Once Eva had ended the call, she grinned. "Do you want to call Sean or should I? I'm sure he'll want to bring Orla."

"Since we're on our way back to the precinct, why don't we just invite him along in person?" Liam suggested. "He might already have other plans."

"If he does, he can just cancel them," Eva said firmly. "Or change them. I've been craving chicken Parm."

This made Liam laugh. What his baby sister wanted, she usually got. As for him, all he could think about was seeing Ellie again.

"Will you call Cormac?" Eva asked, intent on driving too. "I'd like to include him as well."

"Great idea." Liam got his phone out. He loved seeing his twin so happy, so in love. Cormac and Emily were eagerly anticipating the arrival of their baby, even though Emily was barely showing. And now they had a wedding to look forward to as well. Cormac didn't pick up and the call went to voicemail, so Liam left a detailed message with time, place and letting his brother know the entire family would be there. He ended with a hint that they'd received new information on the Humphrey Kelly case, aware that would for sure pique Cormac's curiosity.

Eva shook her head when Liam ended the call. "I guess you made sure he'll come tonight."

He grinned. They all knew each other very well. "I'll go ahead and make the reservation right now. Hopefully we can still get in tonight."

"It's not a weekend, so that shouldn't be a problem. Make it a table for eight, just in case."

Pulling up the website, he lucked out and was able to book a slot at seven for their party. After he'd done that, he glanced up at his sister. "Are you bringing a date?"

To his astonishment, Eva blushed, though she continued to stare straight ahead at the road. "Maybe," she admitted. "It's no fun being the odd person out. Sean will be there with Orla, Cormac and Emily, and you and Ellie. That leaves me."

"Ellie and I won't be there together," he pointed out.

The sideways look she shot him made him laugh.

Back at the precinct, Eva carefully parked the police cruiser.

Once he'd gotten out of the car, Liam hugged his sister. "I'm going to head home," he said. "I'll see you later tonight."

"Sounds good." With a quick smile, she turned and strode away.

Once he made it back to his apartment, Liam showered. He spent the next fifteen minutes rummaging through his closet, trying to figure out what to wear, before he stopped pacing. "This is not a date," he reminded himself sternly, glaring into the mirror. "It's a family get-together, related to a case."

Except that Ellie would be in attendance. He couldn't wait to see her.

He felt like his sixteen-year-old self again, a bundle of nerves and lust and anticipation.

Somehow, he managed to get dressed, though he found himself ready way too early. Which might be a good thing, as he'd definitely need to get himself in the right frame of mind. His family would spot even the slightest sign of weakness and make his life hell. He didn't want that, especially in front of Ellie.

Checking his smart watch for what felt like the tenth time, he decided to walk to the restaurant. Fresh air and exercise would do him good.

The beautiful spring weather had apparently given everyone else the urge to get outside and enjoy it too. The sidewalks were crowded and everyone appeared to be in an upbeat mood. He saw numerous couples out strolling, some hand in hand, others with their arms linked.

When he reached the restaurant, the crowd waiting outside made him glad he'd arrived a bit early. He shouldered his way toward the host stand. "Reservation for Coltons," he said. "Though the rest of my party isn't here yet."

The tall, dark-haired man jerked his head toward the back. "Actually, they are. I just seated several members of your group," he said. "Follow me."

Liam spotted Sean and Orla and Cormac and Emily sitting on the same side of two tables that had been pushed together. Both women looked up at his approach. Sean grinned, gesturing to one of the empty chairs across from him. "Sit, sit."

Since Eva had hinted she might be bringing a date, Liam made sure there were two empty chairs together. He sat down, leaving the last chair for Ellie.

The waiter came to take his drink order, making him realize the others had already gotten started. He ordered his favorite Italian beer just as Eva strolled in, alone.

"Hey!" she greeted everyone, taking the single seat on Liam's right. "Yes," she murmured, leaning into Liam's side. "I came alone. Deal with it."

His beer arrived. Eva ordered a glass of Pinot Noir. Though Liam tried not to be obvious, he couldn't help but keep glancing at the door for Ellie.

"Wow," Sean muttered, earning an elbow in the ribs from Orla. Liam followed the direction of his older brother's gaze and sucked in his breath. Ellie, wearing high heels and a short black dress displaying legs that went on forever, made her way toward them. Her long hair swirled around her shoulders. Everyone else in the restaurant faded into the distance as Liam watched her approach.

"Get your eyes back into your head," Eva whispered. "Be cool, big brother. Be cool."

Rising to his feet, Liam pulled out the chair on his left. Once Ellie had taken her seat, he helped push her back in. When he looked up, he realized both his brothers were staring.

"Hi, Orla," Ellie said, smiling. "It's good to see you again." Cormac introduced Emily, and they all began talking at once. The menus that had been placed in front of everyone were barely opened. But then again, most of the family had been here often enough that they already knew what they wanted.

When the waiter came to take their orders, Ellie quickly glanced at the menu, ordered lobster ravioli and a glass of Pinot Noir.

Meanwhile, Liam struggled to carry on a conversation with Cormac, who clearly took pity on him and started talking about a particularly interesting case he'd just wrapped up. This got Ellie's attention too, and she leaned forward, her thigh brushing against Liam's, which sent his heart rate skyrocketing. He swallowed hard and took a large gulp of his beer.

Catching his eye, his sister slowly shook her head. "Who knew?" she mused in a quiet voice. "Exactly how long has this been going on?"

He kicked her lightly under the table, which made her grin. Meanwhile, Cormac had gotten so engrossed in telling his story that he didn't notice.

One of the things Liam loved about his family was the way they included all guests and made them feel welcome. They'd done so with Orla and Emily, and did so now with Ellie. With its wood-paneled walls and dim lighting, the restaurant had a quiet, dignified vibe, so they tried to keep the noise level down. However, a couple of times when laughter rang out, it got kind of loud. None of the other diners appeared to mind. It was a beautiful spring evening in New York City and all the diners appeared intent on enjoying themselves.

Their food arrived, their waiter and two assistants carrying plates and setting them down on the table with great fanfare. After admiring each other's food, everyone dug in. Liam watched as Sean shared some of his manicotti with Orla, and the way she reciprocated with her lasagna, tenderly feeding a forkful into Sean's mouth. He felt a quick stab of envy, which surprised the heck out of him.

"That looks good," Ellie said, eying his plate. Since he'd barely gotten started on his chicken piccata, he politely asked her if she'd like to sample it. It made him far happier than it should have when she cut a piece off with her fork and tried it. "That's amazing," she enthused. "Would you like to try a taste of mine?"

Aware of his siblings watching him, he declined. Determined to focus on eating his meal, he dug in. He didn't realize he was actually shoveling food into his mouth until his sister leaned over and whispered, "Slow down."

Once the plates had been cleared away and desserts ordered, cannoli for everyone except Orla, who ordered cheesecake, Sean tapped his half-empty wineglass. Everyone quieted, giving him their full attention. "I wanted to make sure everyone had been updated on Humphrey's case. Cormac, did anyone get a chance to fill you in?"

"Not yet."

Sean relayed everything they'd learned, deferring to Ellie to talk about the DNA results she'd gotten from the courtroom closet. Liam enjoyed watching the animation light her beautiful dark eyes as she spoke. Sean finished up, summarizing the fact that they basically knew nothing.

By the time he'd concluded, Cormac sat back in his seat, arms crossed, his frown making him appear thoroughly disgruntled. "That's not much to go on," Cormac said.

Eva and Ellie nodded their agreement.

Liam eyed his twin. "You're the PI. Why don't you dig around and see what else you can turn up on Wes Westmore's relatives? I'm going to be asking around my contacts on the street."

"Great idea," Ellie enthused, beaming at him. "And while you're at it, Cormac, I could use a little help with my case too." She told her story concisely, starting with the disappearance of her best friend sixteen years ago and culminating with spotting her on the subway. She completely left out the fact that she'd been shot at and that someone had attempted to poison her. Liam, Sean and Eva all exchanged glances. Why was she omitting such important information?

Meanwhile Cormac now leaned forward, completely engrossed. "Are you absolutely certain it was really her you saw?" he asked. "It might have been a look-alike."

Ellie nodded. "I'm positive."

"Tell him the rest of it," Liam drawled.

"We don't know for sure that those things were tied in any way to me seeing Aliana," Ellie said.

"We don't know that they weren't either," Liam countered.

"What are you two talking about?" Cormac looked from one to the other.

Clearly reluctant, Ellie told him about the gunshot and then the poisoning. When she'd finished, Cormac whistled. "Damn. And I thought I led an exciting life."

"Exactly," Liam said.

Next to him, Ellie shook her head. "There was nothing exciting about any of this. First off, the gunshot might have been completely random. It could have been aimed at anyone."

"Then what about the poisoned breakfast?" Liam asked. "What's your explanation for that?"

Ellie thought for a moment and then shrugged. "Like Sean mentioned, I've worked on a lot of high- profile cases. Who knows how many enemies I might have running around the city?"

"True," Liam grudgingly admitted.

She waited a moment, until the others' attention had left them and gone on to something else. "I got a weird message today," she told Liam, speaking quietly. "Someone called the 98th and left it there. Not sure why. Basically, the gist of it was that I should leave the past alone."

Liam's gaze sharpened. "Aliana?"

"I think so, yes. Though the detective who called me said she didn't leave her name."

Liam bit back a curse. He didn't have a good feeling about any of this. Though Ellie didn't seem to understand, he couldn't shake a gut feeling that her life might be in danger.

The check came and everyone started talking, trying to calculate how much they owed. One by one, they sent their money, including a generous tip, to Sean via Venmo.

Liam stood up to leave. Next to him, Ellie did the same. The entire family stared, not bothering to hide their interest.

Ignoring them, Liam held out his arm to Ellie. Without hesitation, she took it. Neither looked back as they headed out the door.

Once outside, Ellie tugged on his arm, making him stop. "You know they're all talking about us, right?"

"Let them." He grinned down at her. Then, unable to help himself, he bent down and kissed her. If any of his siblings happened to be watching, now they'd really have something to talk about.

Chapter 6

The instant Liam kissed her, Ellie nearly melted into a puddle of desire right there on the sidewalk. When they broke apart, they were both breathing heavily.

"My place?" she asked, still clinging to him.

"Definitely." Even the deep rumble of his voice turned her on.

Hand in hand, they speed walked, weaving through the crowd, in too much of a hurry to talk.

Back at her building, she thought about jumping him in the elevator, but managed to restrain herself. But when they made it to her apartment, the instant the door closed behind them, they fell on each other as if they were both starving.

"The bed this time," he managed, though they were shedding their clothes in between kisses and caresses.

By the time they reached her bedroom, they were

both naked. She pushed him back onto her mattress, then climbed on top to straddle him.

Fast and furious, she rode him, pushing herself to a shuddering completion. When her tremors subsided, only then did he take control, rolling them over and beginning a serious of slow, sensual movements that soon had her frantic for more.

"Shhh," he told her, nuzzling her ear. "I want to take my time now."

She tried, oh, how she tried, to let him, but every deep stroke drove her mad. Arching her back, she tried to urge him faster. When he finally lost control, plunging his body into her with mindless intensity, she shattered again. A moment later, he cried out and did the same.

They held each other while their breathing slowed and the perspiration cooled their skin. She felt complete and happy, in a way she never had before. It should have worried her, she supposed, but for now she wanted to simply enjoy the feeling.

What is this? she wondered silently, lying in his arms, the sound of his strong and steady heartbeat under her ear. Then, as her eyes drifted closed, she realized she didn't really want to know.

When she woke a few hours later, Liam was gone. Though she found it unsettling that he'd snuck out while she slept, it worried her even more that her front door would have been left unlocked.

Padding naked up the hallway, she reached the door and was surprised to find it still locked.

"Looking for me?" Liam asked, startling her so badly she let out a small scream as she spun around.

He stood in the entrance to her kitchen, as naked as she, eying her with interest.

"Where'd you go?" she sputtered. "When I woke up, I thought you'd left."

"I needed some water." He held up a glass. "And then I saw your bowl of apples and decided some midnight carbs might not be a bad thing. I might need more energy, you know?"

Swallowing hard, she realized he was once again fully aroused. And also again, her body responded with a rush of warmth, then heat.

They made love again, this time with her tucked under him.

After, he made sure she was awake when he pushed back her sheets and got out of her bed. "I'm going to run," he said, kissing her softly. "I've got a busy day scheduled tomorrow."

She sighed, watching as he dressed. "Me too."

After locking the door behind him, she went into her bathroom and did her normal nightly preparations. Then, she climbed into bed, anticipating a wonderful night's sleep.

The next morning, she struggled with the urge to text Liam immediately after waking, just to let him know she was thinking of him. She knew better, so she didn't. That was the kind of thing people in a relationship did. Since they weren't, she wouldn't.

While sipping her coffee and toasting an English muffin, she turned on the news. The two anchors were taking about Humphrey Kelly's mysterious disappearance and the fact that NYPD had no new leads.

"Ouch." She grimaced. Judging by what she knew

about the chief of police, he would not take kindly to the media making the NYPD look like fools. She imagined he'd be on the phone to the lead detective in the Humphrey Kelly investigation, demanding results. Since Sean Colton headed that up, she knew this morning wouldn't be a pleasant one for him.

Sure enough, her phone rang just as she was about to walk out the door. It was Sean.

"Ellie, do you mind if we stop by the lab this morning and discuss the Humphrey Kelly case?" he asked. "The police chief is breathing down my neck wanting results."

"I saw the news report this morning, so I figured," she said.

"Yeah. I wasn't sure of your schedule, so I thought I'd see if any certain time worked best for you."

We? She checked her watch. "I'm leaving for work now. How about you meet me around nine? Will that give you time to gather your team?"

"Sure," he replied. "And our team is just family. Me, Eva, Liam and Cormac. I'm hoping we can toss around some ideas and maybe come up with something new."

"Sounds great," she said, trying not to get too excited at the prospect of seeing Liam again so soon.

She made it to Greenpoint without any issues, though these days she constantly searched the subway terminal for a second sighting of Aliana. As usual, she didn't see her, though she refused to give up hope.

Grabbing a coffee on the way in, she reached her office with a few minutes to spare. She'd barely powered up her computer when the receptionist buzzed her to let her know her guests had arrived and she'd be sending them back.

Sean led the way, his confident stride at odds with his grim expression. Behind him, Eva, Liam and Cormac all crowded into her small office. Of course, she had to struggle not to focus on Liam. He looked great, she thought, trying to be dispassionate. And naturally he caught her looking and sent her a sexy grin.

Clearing his throat, Sean began talking about the news report and his subsequent call from the chief of police. "Meanwhile, I had to tell him that at the moment, we've got nothing. Absolutely zero." He took a deep breath before continuing. "To say he wasn't happy would be an understatement."

"I can't say I blame him," Eva said, her voice glum.

Privately, Ellie agreed. She kept her mouth shut for now, mainly because while this might be an informal meeting, it was being held at her job. Therefore, technically, she was at work.

"I'm really getting suspicious of how people vanish into thin air without a trace," Liam said, his arms crossed. "Like Aliana Martin sixteen years ago, and now Humphrey."

Ellie nodded, though she remained quiet.

"But what about the courtroom coat closet?" Eva asked. "There were definite signs of a struggle." Since she was only six months out of the police academy, she took nothing for granted. Which could be a good thing, sometimes.

Still, Liam clearly felt he had to point out what to him seemed obvious. "Signs of a struggle? Come on. There were a few knocked over supplies? It could easily have been staged." He glanced at Ellie, almost as if he hoped she would chime in. When she didn't, he continued. "The more I work the Aliana Martin case, the more I wonder about Humphrey's disappearance. Nothing adds up in either one."

Sean's gaze sharpened. "Are you really working on the Aliana Martin case? That file went cold years ago."

"He's helping me with it," Ellie interjected, trying not to bristle. "Unofficially, that is. And for the record, I agree with Liam. Nothing adds up."

Eva shook her head. "Evidence, not emotions have to guide our judgment. You know that."

"We have no evidence," Cormac reminded her.

"But we do," Eva insisted, looking to Ellie for confirmation. "The DNA. We know a couple of things. It belonged to a female. And that female has family ties to Wes Westfield. That's something. I plan to dig deeper into that."

"Good luck," Sean said. "I really hope you find something, though with the way it's been going lately, that'll likely turn out to be a huge waste of time."

His older brother's comment had Liam shaking his head. "I'm keeping an open mind," he said pointedly. "We all should."

Narrowing his eyes, Sean studied him. Then he slowly nodded. "Possibly, you're right."

Glancing at Ellie, Liam took a deep breath. "I hate to say this, but maybe we need to start looking into the possibility that Humphrey is dead."

"And that someone related to Wes Westmore killed him?" Ellie added. "Is that what you're thinking?"

Before Liam could respond, Eva made a frustrated

sound. "That would mean it wasn't Humphrey on Amsterdam and 114th. This is all so damned confusing."

Ellie agreed.

"Just keep in mind," Cormac interjected, "that Humphrey Kelly's case and Wes Westmore's have nothing to do with each other. Their cases are not connected."

"Except for the ADA working on both of them," Sean pointed out. "Why don't you call Emily and double-check?"

Cormac nodded and dug out his phone. His soon-to-be bride, Emily Hernandez, worked as an assistant district attorney.

They all listened as he spoke for a few minutes, thanked her and then ended the call. "She says the DNA is the only connection. We just need to find out who the female relative is."

"At least Mitch can't get on my case about me working on Humphrey's disappearance now," Eva said. "Since our priority is the Lana Brinkley murder and Wes Westmore is the prime suspect."

Sean grimaced and glanced at Ellie. "Her partner, Mitch, is a blowhard, but he's a good cop."

Instantly contrite, Eva nodded. "He is. I'm still getting used to him, I guess. Though to be honest, I hate to even clue him in on anything we've learned."

"Wes is still in jail awaiting trial, right?" Liam asked.

"Yep," Cormac answered. "He's considered a flight risk."

Watching the back and forth, Ellie realized she truly enjoyed seeing the way they all worked together. When she looked over at Liam, she was surprised to find him watching her. The instant their gazes connected, she felt a flush of warmth.

"Either way," Sean added, "we've still got very little to go on. Maybe we should think about bringing in our cousins."

"Your cousins?" Ellie asked, genuinely curious. They seemed like such a tight-knit family, she was surprised these cousins hadn't been around before now.

"Second cousins," Sean elaborated. "But they're still Coltons. Deirdre Colton is an FBI agent. And Aidan Colton is a US Marshal. They definitely have more resources than we do."

"True." Liam's expression revealed how little he liked the idea. "How about we give it a couple more weeks first and see what we turn up."

Sean, Cormac and Eva all agreed.

"Ellie, what about you?" Liam asked, meeting her gaze. "You've been awfully quiet."

Struggling not to feel like an outsider, she shrugged. "I'm sorry. You all work so well together. I'm just taking it all in. I'll go with the majority on this one."

"Then that's settled," Sean said. "We'll only call in reinforcements if we continue to come up blank."

Ellie's desk phone rang. She glanced at the number and sighed. "Work beckons," she said and picked up the phone. As she listened to the detective from a precinct on the West Side, she watched the Colton family file out of her office. The last out of the door, Liam caught her eye and blew her a quick kiss before making the *call me* gesture with his hand. She nodded, her heart skipping a beat, before returning her attention to her call.

Sean waited for Liam, while Eva and Cormac had gone on ahead. His frown might have given anyone pause, but Liam knew his brother well. He knew Sean struggled to hide his frustration and definitely understood that feeling, the sense of spinning your wheels and going nowhere. While Liam didn't actually work in law enforcement, he'd helped out NYPD on enough cases to understand how investigations worked. This one, in additional to being high-profile, had personal ties to the Colton family, and it was going nowhere fast.

"What the hell was that?" Sean demanded, keeping his voice low.

Surprised, Liam glanced at him. "What exactly do you mean?" he asked cautiously.

"I saw you blow Ellie a kiss. I'm not sure if the others did or not."

"So?" Liam shrugged.

"The last time we talked, you claimed you and Ellie were just two old friends, catching up. Clearly, that's no longer true. Are you two taking it public now?"

Liam didn't bother to hide his exasperation. "What's it to you, Sean? Ellie and I are both adults. What we choose to do—or not do—in our private lives is really none of your business."

"Except you promised not to hurt her," Sean pointed out. "And like I've already mentioned, Ellie is one of our best crime scene investigators. Not to mention I consider her a friend. I don't want to see her hurt."

"That stings," Liam admitted. "I'm astounded that you'd ever believe I'd do anything to hurt such a special woman. I like Ellie." He swallowed. "Actually, I like her a lot."

"I get that," Sean said, giving Liam a friendly punch

on the arm. "But ever since Noreen died, you've been a love 'em and leave 'em type guy."

While Liam couldn't deny that, he also didn't want to make a big deal out of his burgeoning relationship with Ellie. He shrugged and said nothing.

But Sean, who knew his younger brother well, must have read something in Liam's expression. His frown softened and he squeezed Liam's shoulder. "Be careful, okay?"

"Roger that," Liam answered. "I always am."

Eva and Cormac waited up for them at the subway entrance. Cormac planned to head to his office, while Sean and Eva needed to go back to the 98th. Liam decided to tag along with them. He wanted to take a deeper look into the Aliana Martin case. After all, he'd promised Ellie he'd help her.

As the three siblings waited for their train, Liam glanced around the crowded platform. There were hundreds of people here, random people from all over the city. Some were going to work, others school or running errands. The chances of Ellie seeing Aliana in such a situation had to be astronomical.

Yet she said she had and Liam believed her. Ellie wasn't the type of person given to flights of fancy. She never had been. Her practical, analytical nature served her well in her job. If she was convinced she'd seen Aliana, then Liam had no doubt she had.

"Are you okay?" Eva asked, elbowing him. "You seem awfully quiet."

"Just thinking," Liam answered. "I'm going to hang out in the precinct this afternoon. I'd like to use a computer, if that's okay. I want to review the Aliana Martin case."

"Seriously?" Eva's eyes grew huge. "Why?" Then, before he could reply, she answered herself. "Because you're helping Ellie. She has been fixated on that case lately."

"Lately?" Sean snorted. "Sometimes I forget you've only worked here for six months. Ellie's been working that case for years."

"And even before then," Liam put in. "All through high school and I bet while she was in college."

A loud rumble announced the imminent arrival of their train, preventing anyone from commenting further. After the lead car pulled into the station, brakes squealing, and stopped, the crowd surged forward the instant the doors opened. Liam allowed himself to be swept inside with the others.

Back at the precinct, Sean motioned for Liam to follow him to his office. "Come on. You can use my computer."

"Thanks. I appreciate that."

Sean went ahead and logged in. "I've pulled up all the Aliana Martin case files for you," he said. "There's likely nothing in there that Ellie hasn't gone over a few hundred times, but knock yourself out."

Liam nodded. "I just want to refamiliarize myself with the case. All I know right now is what I remember from when it happened and what little Ellie has told me."

"I get it." Pausing, Sean glanced around to make sure he wasn't overheard. "Honestly, I don't think that case was taken seriously enough. Back then everyone assumed she was a teenaged runaway. They issued an Amber Alert, just in case. But nothing came of it. No ransom demands, no sightings, nothing. Aliana Martin disappeared as completely as if she never existed."

Like Humphrey, Liam thought, though he didn't say it out loud.

"I'll check in on you later," Sean said, and left Liam alone.

Soon, Liam lost himself in the past. To his surprise, he found a transcript of his own interview sixteen years ago, when the police had questioned all of Aliana's friends. He remembered that day all too well—how he'd stood with his arm around Ellie's slender shoulders, wishing he knew a way to make her stop shaking. Ellie had cried while answering the police officer's questions. When she'd finished, she'd begged them to please find her best friend.

Liam remembered feeling helpless. As if there had to be something he could do to help bring Aliana home. Not for him, but for Ellie. He'd have done anything at that moment to see Ellie smile.

Sitting back in Sean's chair, Liam rubbed his temples. He'd forgotten all about that day somehow. He decided to go get a cup of coffee before reading any more.

Once he'd done that, he sat down and took a sip of the bitter brew. Wincing because he'd honestly forgotten how bad the precinct coffee was, he turned his attention back to the case files and continued reading.

He almost missed it. In fact, he had to go back and read the entry again. Someone had come forward, another kid named Eric Campbell who'd been Liam and Aliana's age, and he had demanded money to report what he'd seen. Liam recognized the name as one of his current contacts on the street.

Because Eric had been a known drug addict at the time, the police had hesitated to pay him, but Aliana's desperate parents had stepped up and given over the money. Eric had then reported he'd seen Aliana with an older dude, probably early twenties, on the day she disappeared. This had been noted but dismissed as non-credible evidence.

Finally. Liam sat back. Something that might have been missed. Eric Campbell had eventually done prison time for possession, though he was out now. He shouldn't be too difficult to find.

Looking around for Sean, Liam saw his brother engaged in a serious-looking conversation with two other detectives. Instead of bothering him, Liam made sure to catch Sean's eye before waving.

Outside, Liam headed toward a dive bar a few blocks away. Eric and some of his buddies were regulars there and even though it was still early, Liam suspected he'd find them day drinking.

Entering the bar, he looked around and spotted Eric, sitting alone at a table near the back, nursing a tall beer. Liam sauntered over, smiling broadly. "Hey there, Eric. How's it going?"

Eric looked up, blinking. "Okay, I guess. How are you?"

Without waiting for an invite, Liam slid into the seat across from the other man. He signaled the bartender to bring two more beers. Seeing that, Eric gulped down the rest of his glass.

"Thanks, man," he mumbled, wiping his hand across his mouth.

The beers arrived right away, the bottles sweating. Liam handed over a twenty, telling the bartender to keep the change.

Once the man had gone, Liam slid his beer partly over toward Eric. "You can have this one too. But first, I need to talk to you about something."

Looking from the beer to Liam, Eric licked his lips. "Okay," he said. "But if you're looking for crack, I don't do that stuff no more. I'm clean, man."

"Congratulations," Liam responded, meaning it. "But I'm here to ask you about a statement you gave about Aliana Martin sixteen years ago. You said you'd seen her on the day she went missing, with an older guy. Do you remember that?"

"Yes, I do." Eric grimaced and shook his head. "I'll never forget it. I had a huge crush on Aliana. I was trying to work up the nerve to ask her out. Seeing her with that guy just about killed me." He sighed, then took a long drink of beer. "Later, when I found out she'd disappeared, I knew he had something to do with it. I told the cops too, but they blew me off."

Liam decided not to mention that he knew Eric had demanded payment. Instead, he nodded and said nothing, hoping Eric might elaborate.

Instead, Eric chugged half his beer. "Did they ever find her?" he asked. "I never heard whether they did or not."

"No."

Eric winced. "That sucks. I guess what I saw didn't help then. I always kind of hoped me coming forward made a difference."

"You did good," Liam said. "It's been a long time,

so I just want to ask you one last time. Had you ever seen the man before? Did he look at all familiar? Can you give me a brief description?"

"No, I'd never seen him at all, before or since," Eric replied. "And from what I remember, he looked pretty ordinary. Average height and build, light brown hair."

Which is about what Liam had figured. Still, it never hurt to ask. "One last question. You're absolutely positive about what you saw?"

"I am." Eric looked at him with a sort of quiet dignity. "That's kind of one of those moments you don't ever forget."

"Thanks, man." Liam slid the other beer all the way over to Eric before pushing to his feet. "I appreciate you."

"Right back atcha," Eric replied. "Thanks for the brews."

Back outside, instead of returning to the precinct, Liam found himself walking toward Ellie's lab. When he realized where he was heading, he'd already gone halfway there.

He could have told himself that he needed to see Ellie because he had something new to share. Which was true. He wasn't sure if she'd noticed Eric's statement in the mountain of notes about the case. If she had, which he doubted, she hadn't investigated it. He could visualize her excitement once he'd told her what he learned. Even if the fact that Aliana had been seen with an unknown guy sort of echoed the Humphrey Kelly sighting where he'd been spotted with a strange woman.

In fact, the similarities between the two cases really bugged Liam. Sixteen years had gone by since Aliana

Martin vanished. If she'd made herself disappear, she'd definitely succeeded—until a chance spotting in the subway by one of the few people in New York who'd never forgotten her. She'd been sixteen, young, possibly in love. She might have simply run off with the older guy she'd been seen with.

Even if that had been what happened, it still didn't answer the question of how she could let her family and her best friend believe the worst for so long. If she truly was alive and well—and in the city—why not reconnect with her loved ones?

Humphrey on the other hand, was a successful professional. Sure, his life wasn't at all what it appeared to be on the surface, but what actual reason would he have for disappearing? Liam knew if they could find the answer to this question, they'd likely find Humphrey.

He couldn't wait to discuss this with Ellie. In fact, he had one block left to go when he made himself stop and reassess. Ellie was at work and while she likely wouldn't welcome an interruption in the middle of her day, he knew she'd truly want to hear the new info he'd gathered.

Still, he had to take a minute and consider. Because most of all, he knew he was on his way to see Ellie because he ached for her.

This alone gave him pause. He and Ellie had agreed to keep things casual. However, this yearning was anything but.

Liam had never considered himself to be a self-indulgent sort of person. But in that moment, he picked up the pace and continued on toward the lab.

Entering, he didn't like how there didn't seem to be

much security precaution. Sure, the woman seated at the front desk likely had a panic button under there. And he spotted the security cameras trained on the front door and reception area.

"Can I help you?" the woman asked, her smile slightly frosty.

"Liam Colton. I'm here to see Ellie Mathers," he said.

"Do you have an appointment?"

He debated how to respond for a second, settling on replying that Ellie was expecting him. This earned him a raised eyebrow and skeptical look, but at least she picked up her phone and called Ellie.

"Ms. Mathers will see you now," she announced. "I'll buzz you in."

She pushed something on her desk, generating a loud buzz as the door to the left of her clicked open. Good. He smiled at the receptionist as he strode past. That meant people couldn't simply walk in.

Remembering the way to Ellie's office, he headed down the hall. To his surprise, she came halfway to meet him. At the sight of her, the intense buzz of pleasure that hit him made his mouth go dry.

"Liam!" Her smile lit up her dark eyes. "What brings you here this afternoon?"

It took him a second to gather his thoughts. "I was looking over the Aliana Martin case files." And then he told her what he'd seen and who he'd talked to.

When he'd finished, she could barely contain her excitement. "I don't know how I missed that," she said. "And I can't believe you were able to track the witness down and talk to him. Or that he even remembered it after all these years."

"It was Eric Campbell. I'm not sure if you remember him, but we went to school with him. He said he'd always had a crush on Aliana, so he's positive about what he saw."

Slowly, she shook her head. "But Aliana and I were best friends. If she'd had a new boyfriend, especially one who was older, she would have told me."

"Maybe he convinced her to keep their relationship secret." While he hated what he had to say next, it only made sense. "Especially since she was only sixteen. If he was older, like say twenty-one, he'd have been dating a minor."

Ellie cursed under her breath. "You're right. And that would mean he might have had something to do with her disappearance. Like what if they ran off together?"

"Exactly. And I'm guessing at some point the relationship didn't work out."

"Or it did and they're still together." Ellie frowned. "Either explanation still doesn't answer the main question. Why'd she stay away? Why not at least let her family and friends—me—know she was all right? She has to know how badly her parents suffered."

Jamming his hands into his pockets to keep from touching her, he nodded. "That's the million-dollar question. And one I've started asking myself about Humphrey Kelly too."

She opened her mouth to speak, but just then one of her colleagues came out from the main lab and called her name. "Ellie! Can you come in here? We could use your assistance."

"On my way." Giving Liam an apologetic look, she

sighed. "Work calls. Thanks for following up on that lead. We'll touch base again later, okay?"

"Definitely." He watched her walk away, managing to hide his disappointment. But then what had he honestly expected?

Turning, he left the restricted area, waved at the unsmiling receptionist and exited the building. He felt better when he hit the street, striding along as if the physical movement could help clear his head.

Except his head wasn't the problem in this particular situation. He refused to let it be his heart.

Chapter 7

After Liam left, Ellie found it difficult to concentrate on work. Another investigator had needed her help reassembling some bone fragments, so having something to occupy both her hands and her mind helped her settle down.

Aware she could only focus on one task at a time, she pushed the new information Liam had gathered into the back of her mind. She'd examine it later, starting with taking another look at the case file records to see how she had missed it.

When Eva called and asked Ellie to meet her after work, Ellie immediately agreed. She had always liked Liam's younger sister, even though she'd never paid much attention to her when they'd all been younger.

"Perfect." Eva hesitated. "Are you okay around dogs?"

"Dogs?" Ellie frowned. "I thought you were a cat person."

"I am. But we'll be working with a K9 electronics detection dog named Bing. He's a yellow Lab," Eva replied. "I'm borrowing him since it's after hours."

"Working with a police canine?" Ellie asked. "Now it sounds like this night is going to be really interesting."

"Only if you're okay around dogs. Someone owes me a favor, so I'm borrowing Bing for a couple hours."

"I'm good with dogs. They usually like me. But now I'm really curious. What exactly are we going to be doing?" Ellie asked.

"I thought we'd start with searching Humphrey Kelly's office. I'm looking for thumb drives, or any kind of electronic storage. There's got to be something we're missing."

Though Ellie wondered why Eva didn't ask Sean to accompany her, she didn't want to interfere with the family dynamic, so she kept quiet.

"I'm also going to need your help," Eva continued. "I want to see if we can get into Humphrey's email accounts on his work computer." She grinned. "I know I've got skills, but your reputation as a master problem solver precedes you."

"*My* reputation?" Brow raised, Ellie shook her head. "I've heard about you. You're the one everyone goes to when they need to get into a phone or a computer."

"Maybe so." Eva shrugged. "But I can use all the help I can get. Are you in for tonight, then?"

"Do you have a search warrant?" Ellie hated to ask, but she was a stickler for rules. Also, even though Eva was relatively new to police work, she had to know any information obtained illegally would be inadmissible in court.

"We don't need one," Eva replied. "Humphrey's wife gave me permission. She's listed as a silent partner in his psychiatry business. She also said it's okay if we want to search their house, which we might do if we don't run out of time. She really wants Humphrey found."

"I'm in," Ellie said. "This is shaping up to be one of the most interesting nights I've had in a while. I love field work."

"Perfect." Again, Eva hesitated. "Liam will be coming also. I needed someone with a car so we could bring the dog. We can pick you up around six thirty."

Ellie caught her breath. "That's fine," she said, hoping her voice didn't reveal her sudden excitement at the prospect of seeing Liam again.

After ending the call, she rushed through the rest of her tasks, one eye on the clock. This wasn't like her at all. Usually she relished every moment of the work she did, but now she couldn't wait to get out of the lab. Not only because what Eva had planned sounded both fun and exciting, but because it would give Ellie an excuse to see Liam again.

She felt like a teenager with a crush. Weird, but also kind of wonderful.

Once she made it home, she took a quick shower, careful to keep her hair dry. She put her hair in a neat French braid, pleased with the results. Then she reapplied her makeup, taking extra care to ensure her face looked as artlessly natural as possible.

This done, she spent way too long trying to decide

what to wear. In the end, she settled on her favorite pair of jeans, high-top sneakers and a casual t-shirt.

After grabbing an apple to snack on, she'd barely finished it when Eva texted, announcing that they were parked out front.

They. After taking several deep breaths to calm herself, Ellie texted back to let Eva know she was on her way down.

The instant Ellie stepped out onto the sidewalk, she spotted Eva, leaning against a sleek silver Tesla. Smiling, Eva waved. "You can have shotgun," she called out. "I'm in the back seat with Bing."

Heart racing again, Ellie went around to the passenger side, opened the door, and slid in. "Nice vehicle," she said, trying not to visibly react at the sight of Liam, who had his hands resting on the steering wheel. Owning a personal car in the city was prohibitively expensive, not just because of the insurance, but because parking was at a premium.

"Thanks." Liam smiled at her, sending a flush of heat zinging through her body. How he could do this, with only a smile or a look, mystified her.

To distract herself, after buckling in, Ellie turned around to check out the yellow Lab, who wore a back harness, also buckled in. The dog seemed friendly enough, wagging his tail and appearing to smile as he looked around.

"He's a good boy," Eva enthused. "Even if he was a little too interested when he caught the scent of my cat on my clothes."

Luckily for Ellie, Eva kept up a running flow of conversation as they drove to Humphrey's office. Since it was right smack in Midtown Manhattan, Ellie knew parking would be extremely limited. But when Liam pulled into a covered parking garage and typed in an access code, she realized some of the successful psychiatrist's patients must live in a different stratosphere.

Eva must have noticed Ellie's expression, because she laughed. "I'm sure he validates his patients' parking. Or did," she corrected.

After parking, they all got out of the car. Eva seemed comfortable handling the dog and Bing stayed in the heel position at her side.

Eva used an access card to unlock the exterior door. "Humphrey's wife, Ciara, let me use this," she said. "It will also work on his office door."

At this hour, the elegant office building was mostly deserted, which was good as she imagined most people might question the dog's presence. The security guards must have been busy elsewhere, as they didn't come into contact with them at all.

They walked through the lobby to the elevators and rode to the third floor. Once there, they easily located Humphrey's office suite and Eva let them inside.

"Okay, guys. Spread out and look, but try to stay out of Bing's way. He's a pro at this."

"What exactly are we looking for again?" Liam asked. He appeared uncomfortable now, shifting his weight from one foot to the other and glancing around. "I've got to be honest, this is really weird to me. Being inside Humphrey's inner space without him present feels like…sacrilege, somehow."

Ellie couldn't help herself. She crossed the room and

hugged him, hoping to wipe the tormented expression off his handsome face.

The instant she wrapped her arms around him, he responded in kind, bringing her in close. Only the sound of Eva clearing her throat awkwardly kept Ellie from pulling him down for a kiss.

"Sorry," she said, stepping back. Breathless, she walked over to the floor-to-ceiling windows, gazing blindly out at the lights of the city while she struggled to regain her composure.

"It's okay," Eva said, her voice gentle. "But I brought you two here because I need your help. We've got to figure out what happened to Humphrey."

"I agree." Tone brisk, Liam turned to the wall of full bookshelves. "I'll start here."

"I'll put Bing to work on Humphrey's desk," Eva announced. "He's trained to locate electronic storage devices. A desk would make the most sense for that type of thing."

Fascinated, Ellie watched Bing work. "What does he do to alert you when he finds something?" she asked.

"He'll sit." Just as Eva said that, the Lab sat, staring fixedly at one of the desk drawers. "Ah-ha?" Eva exclaimed. Opening the drawer, she began rummaging inside. "I don't see anything, but if Bing says it's here, I believe him. I've just got to find it."

Even Liam paused his search of the bookcase to watch.

A moment later, Eva held up a flash drive. "Here we go!" She reached into her pocket, retrieved a dog treat and rewarded Bing. "Good job, boy."

"Do you think there might be more?" Ellie asked.

"Since I have Bing here, I'm going to keep looking. You guys do too."

Ellie stepped forward. "Why don't you two continue to search. I want to see if I can find anything on the computer."

Immediately, Eva nodded. "Good thinking. Let me know if you need any help getting in."

"I will. I don't suppose either of you have any ideas of what password Humphrey might use?"

Liam and Eva exchanged a glance. "No," Eva finally answered. "But you might try turning over his desk calendar. Some people write their passwords there."

Ellie did, but found nothing. "I'll keep poking around," she said. "Go ahead and get back to what you were doing."

"Let us know if you need anything." That said, Eva turned away and once again gave Bing the command to work.

Since Humphrey had been a psychiatrist, at first Ellie tried passwords related to his field of work. When none of those worked, she began a thorough search of his desk, just in case he'd been the type to write things down. In the back of the large middle drawer, she found a small notebook. Inside, a veritable treasure trove of passwords.

"Jackpot," she muttered, earning a sharp glance from Liam.

One she logged into the computer, she went to Humphrey's email. However, there was absolutely nothing there. She checked the trash, the sent folder, even spam. Nothing.

"His email accounts have been wiped clean," she announced.

Eva groaned. "Great."

"Let me try his social media accounts." Ellie consulted the notebook. "I've got all the passwords right here."

But Humphrey's Twitter, Facebook and Instagram accounts had all been deleted. Ellie even tried Snapchat, since Humphrey had listed a password for it. Nothing. Even LinkedIn showed nothing existed under Humphrey's professional bio.

An internet search revealed several hits when she typed in Humphrey's name. But they were all news articles related to his recent disappearance.

Next she moved on to what Humphrey kept offline. His client list and appointment schedule. But the folder titled Client List was empty. She checked the recycle bin on the off chance that whoever had deleted everything might have left info there, but it too was empty.

When Ellie looked up, she realized Liam had come to stand behind her and look over her shoulder.

"Nothing?" he asked.

Slowly, she shook her head. "Someone took great pains to make every aspect of Humphrey's life a blank slate. It's almost as if he never existed."

Liam swore. Eva had finished taking Bing around the room and returned, holding out the thumb drive. "Try this," she said. "Maybe he moved everything to this."

Privately, Ellie figured if Humphrey had done that, he would have taken the thumb drive with him. It made no sense to go through all this trouble and then turn around and leave an incriminating thumb drive.

She plugged it in, then clicked to find out what might be on it. "Nothing," she said out loud. "Absolutely nothing."

"What the hell is going on?" Liam wondered. "I need to call Sean and have him patch in Cormac."

Once both his brothers were on the line, Liam put the phone on speaker and filled them in.

Sean waited until Liam finished before he spoke. "It's looking like you were right. Now it really seems like Humphrey Kelly might have engineered his own disappearance."

"But why?" Ellie interjected.

"That's what we're all wondering," Liam said. "And since one of his patients claims to have seen Humphrey with a woman over by Columbia, it's not too much of a jump to guess that she could be the female relative of our high-profile murder suspect, Wes Westmore. Especially since her DNA was found in the courtroom supply closet."

"Finding out who she is has just moved to the top of my list," Eva declared. "Let's shut this place down. I've got to get Bing back to his handler."

Ellie powered off the computer and stood. Liam went around turning off lights and they moved toward the door. One hand on the knob, Liam slowly looked around the room. "Just when you think you know somebody…" He sighed.

"I hear you. But I have to say, this has suddenly gotten very intriguing," Ellie mused, earning sharp glances from both Liam and Eva. Shaking her head, she shrugged. "Most of my cases are fairly routine. This one just keeps getting stranger."

Bing barked, as if agreeing with her. This made them all smile.

Finally, they stepped into the hallway. Liam double-checked the door to make sure it locked behind them. Once he'd done that, he glanced around him.

"What's wrong?" Ellie asked.

"I can't shake the feeling like we're being watched," he said, scratching his head.

"Odd. Because I feel the same." Then she realized why. "Liam, Eva." When they turned, she pointed at the camera mounted near the end of the hall. "Look."

"Security cameras," Eva said. "We'll ask to review the footage. It might not have anything helpful, but then again…"

"You never know," Ellie finished for her. "Any little clue might help."

"I think we should take Bing and check Humphrey's apartment too," Liam mused. "I'm sure Ciara wouldn't mind."

"That's a great idea, but we'll have to do it another time," Eva said, patting the dog. "I've got to return Bing to his handler. I had to call in a huge favor to even get him to let me borrow this dog."

"Understood," Liam replied. "If need be, we can get Sean involved next time."

"Of course." Though Eva nodded, Ellie could tell by her tone that she wasn't keen on the idea.

"He's always so busy," Eva mused. "Trying to do it all. I wanted him to get some alone time with Orla."

"Good thinking," Liam grimaced. "He does tend to be a workaholic. So, I'll let you decide whether or not to speak to Sean," he added, earning a smile from his baby sister. "Come on, you two. Let's get that dog back to his handler. And then how about we go get something to eat."

"Sounds like a plan." Good mood restored, Eva led Bing ahead of them down the hall.

Liam eyed Ellie. She nodded. "Good job," she said, and then held out her hand for him to take.

"I feel like I won the lottery," Liam murmured, capturing her fingers with his.

Hand in hand, they followed Eva down the hall.

Liam's remark made Ellie feel as if she was walking on air.

When they reached Liam's car, Liam opened the back door for Eva, then the front passenger side for Ellie, before he went around to the driver's side.

"You're glowing," Eva murmured to Ellie, loud enough for Liam to hear, before using a hand signal to direct Bing to jump into the car.

Ellie glanced at Liam, as if to see if he'd heard. When he shrugged, she exhaled before getting into the passenger seat and closing the door. "Thanks," she said, apparently deciding to accept the remark as a compliment.

"Where to?" Liam asked Eva, once they were all buckled in.

"Back to Brooklyn," she replied and gave him an address, which he promptly plugged into the car's GPS.

Eva kept up a steady stream of chatter as Liam navigated the evening traffic. Grateful, Liam drove while Ellie leaned back in her seat and closed her eyes. He liked that she felt comfortable enough to doze off.

When they arrived, Liam pulled up to the curb and parked.

"We're here," Liam said softly, waking Ellie. He then turned toward the back seat. "Do you need me to come with you, Eva?"

"No," Eva replied. "I'll be right back. I just need to drop Bing off and thank his handler for letting me borrow him."

After Eva and the dog got out of the car, Ellie covered her mouth with her hand and yawned. "I'm sorry I fell asleep. I must have been more exhausted than I realized."

About to ask her if that was her way of hinting she wanted to go home instead of grabbing dinner, he caught sight of Eva hurrying out to the car.

Eva came over, appearing flustered. Instead of getting into the back seat, she tapped on Liam's window. Once he'd rolled it down, she asked if they'd mind going on without her. "I'm going to hang out here for a while."

Liam shrugged, carefully casual. "I'm good," he replied. "What about you, Ellie?"

Slowly, she nodded. "Are you sure, Eva? What about food? I know you haven't eaten."

"We'll grab something from the deli." The two women exchanged a long look, making Liam wonder what he was missing.

"Well then, have fun," Ellie said.

"Thanks. You too." And Eva turned and walked away without a backward glance.

"Is she trying to be a matchmaker?" Liam asked.

"Maybe." Ellie didn't sound at all concerned. "The

other possibility is she's attempting to have her own social life."

This made him laugh.

"Point taken. Where to?" Asking it this way would give her the opportunity to tell him if she wanted to go home instead of out to eat.

She glanced at him. "How about somewhere in your neighborhood? You could park your car wherever you normally do, and then we could walk. I'd love to see where you live."

Unexpected joy flashed through him. "Really?"

"Yes. That is, if you don't mind."

He liked her directness and the fact that she didn't play games. Though in the past, he had always made it a practice never to take dates to his home, he realized he wanted Ellie to see his apartment. He'd bought it after selling the brownstone he and Noreen had shared.

"I don't mind at all," he replied. "I even have an outdoor space."

"Seriously?" Her beautifully shaped eyebrows rose. "Is it shared, or your own private area?"

Her question made him grin. Since private outdoor spaces were rare in Manhattan, he'd paid dearly to purchase a place with his own. "You'll just have to wait and see," he told her.

As usual, the heavy traffic made for slow going as dusk changed to dark and the night settled in. But as Liam navigated the drive, changing lanes when he could, he couldn't help but notice a dark blue Prius staying right behind him. If they were deliberately following, the driver made no attempt to stay hidden. Which mean it was probably all in his imagination.

Still, Liam hadn't gotten ahead by ignoring his instincts. Though it would take him several minutes out of his way, he made an unnecessary right turn, just to see if the Prius would do the same.

When it did, he cursed.

"What's wrong?" Ellie asked.

"I think we're being followed." He kept his tone even. "I'm not positive, but until we lose them, we're not going anywhere near my place."

She nodded. "That makes sense. Maybe we should pull up in front of the precinct. I can call ahead so a couple of uniforms will be waiting for us outside."

Once more, he glanced at his rearview mirror. "That's a great idea, but let's give it a few minutes. Maybe they're just going the same way we are."

As he spoke, he yanked the wheel hard right, making a completely unannounced right turn. The headlights behind him did the exact same thing.

"That's it." Hands tight on the steering wheel, he glanced at Ellie. "Go ahead and call the police."

Just then, their back windshield shattered sending a shower of glass all over them.

"They're shooting at us." He shoved her shoulder. "Get down and stay down."

Doubled over in her seat, Ellie frantically tried to use her phone. But her hands were shaking so hard, she dropped it.

Liam changed lanes again, trying to put a few vehicles in between them and the Prius.

A large box truck had stopped in the middle lane of traffic. Though he nearly hit the SUV behind it, Liam maneuvered in between the two, angling to get on the other side. Their pursuer, unable to make the lane change, took another shot at them, taking out the back passenger side window.

"Damn it." Liam laid on his horn, then edged his car over despite the refusal of a white Lincoln to make room. At this point, he would have taken out the front quarter panel of the other car if he had to. Luckily, the Lincoln slammed on his brakes and laid on his horn, but Liam was able to make his move. Once on the other side of the box truck, he tried to keep it between them and the Prius. Finally, as they inched along, keeping the box truck in between, a green light gave Liam the opportunity to turn left, leaving the Prius stuck in traffic and unable to follow.

He kept going, periodically checking to make sure they weren't being followed. He made it to Midtown, driving blindly until he somehow reached his parking garage. Pulling in, he went to punch in the code that would allow him entrance, but realized he was shaking so badly he couldn't.

"Deep breaths," Ellie said, laying her hand across his arm. "We're both okay. That's what matters."

She was right. But still. Finally, he managed to do the code. Once the red gate went up, he pulled in and drove to his spot and parked. Turning to face Ellie, he exhaled. "We need to notify the police."

"I agree." She looked around. "I know not anyone can get in here, but I still don't feel safe. Can we go inside your apartment before we call?"

"Yes." Opening his door, he brushed glass off him and went around to her side to help her out. Tiny pieces of glass were everywhere, though neither of them had been cut.

He took her arm, steadying her as she stood. The florescent overhead lights gave them both a sickly glow. As she met his gaze, he saw a reflection of his own shock in her eyes.

"Come on," he said. "Let's get inside and call Sean."

She nodded but didn't move. "Why is someone trying to kill me?"

"How'd they know you would be in my car?" he pointed out. "Maybe this time, I was the target."

"Possibly." Though she didn't sound convinced. "But they always say things happen in threes. There was the shot when we were meeting up for coffee, then someone tried to poison me, and now this. I have to believe it's all related."

"To Aliana?" he asked, even though he figured he already knew.

"Who else would it be? No one knows about any of the cases I work on. And if someone was targeting me for one of those, it would have happened long before now." She took a deep, shaky breath. "I have to think that someone must be watching me."

"Or me. Come on." Keeping her arm tucked firmly in his, he led her toward the elevator. Once there, he once again punched in his code.

"This seems like a very secure building," she commented. "I assume they have a similar setup before you can access the stairwell?"

"They do." He didn't tell her that those safety measures came at a high price. His monthly HOA fee was more than double most people's mortgage payment. He knew she'd figure that out soon enough.

Inside the elevator, he punched in the code to allow them access to the top floor.

Eyes narrowed, Ellie noticed. "The penthouse? You live in a penthouse apartment?"

He nodded. "I do. My wife was very wealthy. She owned quite a bit of high-value property in the city. I sold most of it and reinvested a lot in this apartment."

"Your wife?" She frowned. "That's right, I'd heard you were married. I'm sorry for your loss."

The elevator doors opened. Again, he took her arm, guiding her out into the short foyer just outside his polished mahogany double front door. "Here we are," he said. Once again, he had to punch in his code to unlock his door.

"Wow!" She shook her head. "No one's getting in there without permission, are they?"

Nope. He actually hesitated opening the door. He never brought women into his personal space. Ellie would be the first. And to his surprise, he realized he really wanted her to like it.

Swallowing, he pushed the door open, flipped the lights on, and gestured to her to precede him inside. He made sure to lock up behind them.

Ellie took a few steps, silent as she took in his long corner walls of floor-to-ceiling windows. One side looked out over the city lights and the other, his large balcony and outdoor garden. He'd had a pavilion built, with a hot tub installed inside. It was his absolute favorite space in the entire city.

But Ellie didn't know any of that. She walked into his

impersonal, professionally decorated apartment, drawn to the view. "This is amazing," she said. "I imagine you never get tired of seeing this."

"I don't," he replied. "Would you like something to drink? I have a nice bottle of Pinot Noir, if you want wine. I also have sparkling water."

"Wine sounds great," she said, without turning around. "I need a glass of wine to calm my nerves after being shot at."

"Okay." Though she kept her back to him, he could see she was still shaking after what they'd gone through. Trying for normalcy, he continued. "I know we never got to eat, so I can rummage around in the refrigerator and see what I could make."

Finally turning, she blinked. "You cook too?"

This comment made him laugh. "Occasionally. Let me go get us some wine."

Instead of waiting in the living room, she followed him to the kitchen. "Wow. This looks like something out of a magazine article. White cabinets, country sink, quartz countertops and high-end appliances. Did you choose all this yourself?"

"No." Gesturing around, he shrugged. "I had the entire apartment professionally done before I moved in."

Walking around the room, she nodded. "I like it." Looking at the living room, she smiled. "I like that too. But why didn't you add any personal touches?"

"Such as?" he asked, meaning it. "I mean, the designer even chose the artwork and the pillows on the couch. I wouldn't know what else to add."

He opened the bottle of wine and poured them each a glass.

"Thanks." Accepting the glass, she took a sip. "I was incredibly rude, and I apologize. I certainly should never have criticized the way you choose to decorate your apartment. It's beautiful and well done. Ignore me."

As if he ever could. "I don't spend a lot of time here," he finally admitted. "Other than to sleep."

Her lovely eyes widened. "This place is amazing. Why wouldn't you hang out here? If I had an apartment like this…" She shook her head, clearly bemused.

"Come with me." Picking up his wineglass, he crossed to the door that led to his balcony. "This is where I spend time, weather permitting. My own private oasis."

"Now you've got me curious," she said.

Opening the door, he motioned for her to precede him. He rarely brought people to this spot. Even though it was perfect for entertaining, he'd only allowed his siblings here. He'd never felt comfortable having women here and to be honest, none of them were around long enough for him to want to share a place he considered as close to heaven on earth as he could get in the city.

But Ellie was different. Not only was she an old friend, but his high school girlfriend, and his…first love.

Brushing past him, she brought the faintest hint of her perfume. As she stepped outside, she let out an audible gasp.

"I see what you mean!" she exclaimed, eyeing the redwood hot tub enclosure, the teak lounge chairs and the abundant potted plants and flowers. "How do you keep these alive in the winter?"

He pointed to his greenhouse, an eight-by-ten glass

structure he'd had built against one side of the brick building. "They go in there. It's heated."

"Are you kidding me?" She went over to check it out. He watched her go, but didn't follow. Instead, he walked to the railing and gazed out over the city he loved.

This was his home. Completely different than the house he'd shared with Noreen. Old money, he'd often thought, versus new.

Once such excess would have embarrassed him. These days, after months of therapy, he'd learned to allow himself to enjoy his life and the various perks his wife's fortune allowed him. It wasn't as if he didn't give back to others. The foundation he'd created should have been enough to alleviate any lingering guilt. After all, he spent much of his time attempting to make sure teenagers didn't blindly follow the wrong path the way he had.

But it still existed, deep inside. Often, he felt like an imposter, living in a place where he didn't belong. He hadn't been born to this kind of life. His people, the Colton family, were solidly middle-class. Comfortable, salt-of-the-earth types. Each and every one of them claimed to be envious of his amazing apartment. Liam suspected each and every one of them was lying.

Ellie returned, her expression animated, her eyes sparkling. "You have got to be one of the luckiest people in Manhattan," she said. "And I can see why you prefer to spend your free time out here."

Finally, her trembling appeared to have stopped and the stark terror had receded from her eyes. Though the danger was still high, he'd done his best to shift the focus to something ordinary, to help Ellie.

They still needed to call Sean and report the shooting. That would be top priority. After, they also needed to eat. But as Liam locked gazes with Ellie, he did what he'd been aching to do ever since he'd seen her come sauntering out of her building. He gently tugged her close and covered her mouth with his.

Chapter 8

Damn, this felt good. If Liam hadn't kissed her, Ellie suspected she might have backed him into the wall, cupped his face in her hands and kissed him herself. Truth be told, she'd been buzzing with desire ever since they'd dropped Eva off. Having someone shoot at them, taking out the rear window of Liam's car, had only heightened her need, amplifying every shaky breath, every look, everything. Her heart, which had still been racing from the adrenaline surge, rocketed into overtime the instant his mouth claimed hers.

Somehow, they made it back inside, all hands and mouths and passion, shedding clothes as they went. They made it all the way to the living room, only to stumble over the huge sectional.

"Here," she gasped, not sure whether she meant it as a question or an order.

Instead of responding with words, he lowered her onto the cushions and covered her body with his.

Later, sated and content, she allowed herself to cling to him. Only for a little while, she told herself.

"Stay," he said, nuzzling her neck. "I can take you home in the morning."

Tempting as that sounded, she shook her head. She had a hard and fast private rule to always sleep in her own apartment, in her own bed. "I'm sorry, but I'd better not. And you don't have to drive me. I can walk or call an Uber."

"Do you really think that little of me?" His hurt expression might have been feigned, but somehow she suspected it was real.

"I…"

He silenced her with a kiss. "I'm taking you home," he declared. "After what happened earlier, there's no way I'm letting you wander the streets unprotected."

She thought about telling him he wouldn't be able to monitor her 24/7, but she figured he already knew that. And if she were honest with herself, the shooting had made her a bit nervous. "Okay," she conceded. "We can ride home in your car with the busted-out windows."

"No, we won't," he said. "We'll just take my other car."

"You have more than one car?" She stared.

"Yes." He pushed himself up off the bed and began gathering up his clothes. "It's older and not as nice, but it'll do. Plus, if anyone is watching for us to leave, they won't notice a black BMW with dark-tinted windows."

Luckily, he'd already walked off toward the bathroom, so didn't see her mouth fall open. Two cars and the second one a BMW? She quickly closed it, grabbed her own clothing and headed toward another bathroom she'd noticed earlier.

Once she'd cleaned up and dressed, she emerged to find him perched on a barstool, scrolling through his phone while he waited for her. Looking up, he smiled. She felt the warmth of that smile all the way to her toes.

"Are you ready?" he asked.

Unable to find her voice, she nodded.

"Let's go. We'll call Sean on the way and fill him in on what happened."

Which made her realize she'd completely forgotten about the need to make some sort of police report. More proof of how much of a distraction she found Liam.

Out in the foyer, she waited while he locked his front door. Though she felt the urge to tap her foot or make other restless movements, she forced herself to remain still.

They rode the elevator down to the parking garage with her arm still tucked into his. Surprisingly, she still felt a bit jittery. Of course, she supposed that was normal. After all, someone had clearly shot at her. Or them. Either way, going outside felt more dangerous than she'd expected.

"Are you all right?" Liam asked, as if he knew her internal struggle.

Taking a deep breath, she slowly shook her head. "I'm more nervous than I thought I'd be."

"Me too," he responded, surprising her yet again. "But it's all going to be okay. This old BMW is built like a tank."

He led her past his poor Tesla to a boxy black car parked a few spaces away. "Here we go," he said, unlocking the doors. "I guarantee no one will notice this thing."

"I hope not," she replied.

Once they'd left the parking garage and headed toward her apartment, she pulled out her phone to call Sean. "It's kind of late," she said, glancing at Liam. "Should I wait to call until the morning?"

"It's barely ten," Liam responded. "Sean will still be up. And he needs to know about this. If we call NYPD and not him, he'll be furious."

Still, she hesitated. "I'm not sure how I feel about your brother knowing we were together tonight."

After a quick, sharp look, Liam laughed. "We were with Eva, so he's going to know anyway. Believe me."

Grimacing, she scrolled through her contacts and when she located Sean's cell phone, she took a deep breath before tapping the connect button.

"Ellie?" Voice crisp, Sean seemed instantly alert. "What's wrong?"

She told him what had happened earlier as concisely as possible. "I'm just glad Eva decided to make other plans," she added. "Luckily, neither I nor Liam were hurt."

"Have you filed an official report?" Sean asked.

"No. We were hoping you could do that." She thought for a moment. "Otherwise, I can make another report in the morning."

"No, that's fine. I'll take care of this." Sean cleared his throat. "Is Liam with you now?"

"Yes."

"Let me have a word with him, please," Sean requested.

She handed Liam the phone. Listening to his side

of the conversation, it sounded as if Sean made him go over every detail. Once he'd finished, Liam told his brother he would be happy to call it in to NYPD. Sean must have reiterated his plan to do that, because Liam sighed and said "If that's what you want to do."

"I'll talk to you later," Liam finally said, quickly ending the call and handing the cell back to Ellie.

Putting her phone back into her purse, Ellie shook her head. "Clearly, my phone call interrupted Sean's social life. I feel terrible. It might be okay to you, because you're his brother, but I shouldn't have called a work colleague this late."

"He'll survive," Liam reassured her, his tone unconcerned.

They were coming up on her block.

"It's up ahead," she said. "And since parking is really scarce, it's all right if you drop me off."

"Absolutely not," he replied. "Even if I have to drive around the block a few times, I'm not sending you up there alone."

"I'm sure I'll be fine," she protested. "Unless you really just want to try and finagle a sleepover."

This brought another smile. "Maybe I do."

"Remember, we agreed to keep things casual." She lifted her chin. "While I do appreciate you being kind enough to see me home, it's really not necessary."

"Yes, it is." The finality of his tone told her he wouldn't hear any further argument.

Just as they passed her building, a parking spot opened up and Liam pulled into it.

"What luck," she said. Maybe this was how things happened for Liam. Parking spots magically opened up as he drove by. The notion made her smile. Seeing this, he smiled back as he turned off the ignition.

They got out and she waited while he used the phone app to pay for the meter.

"This really shouldn't take too long," she promised, suddenly nervous about bringing him into her home, even though he'd been there twice before. This just felt more…intimate, somehow. Worse, she had no idea why.

"Relax," he said, taking her hand. "Nothing has changed. I just want to make sure you're safe. After that, I promise I'll get back in my old tank of a car and leave."

Not sure how to respond to that, she settled for nodding.

Still hand in hand, they waited for the ancient elevator. When it finally arrived, with a great deal of noise, Liam squeezed her hand. "Are you sure this thing's safe?" he asked.

"No," she replied, only half joking as she stepped inside, pulling him with her.

Once they'd arrived at her floor, the elevator shuddered to a halt and the doors creaked open.

"Come on," she said, her fingers still intertwined with his. Down the hallway, they were nearly to her unit when she realized something was wrong and stopped.

"What is it?" Liam asked, then followed the direction of her gaze.

"My door's open." Swallowing past the lump in her throat, for a heartbeat she wasn't sure how to react. "I locked up when I left earlier. I always do."

He nodded. "Wait here while I go check it out."

While she appreciated the way he didn't question her about locking up, no way did she plan on standing in the hallway while he assessed a possible break-in of her apartment. "Shouldn't we call the police first?"

"You can. I'm not waiting around for them to show up," Liam replied.

"No. I'm going too."

Again he simply nodded. At her front door, slightly ajar, she took a deep breath before pushing it all the way open and stepping inside. Flicking on the lights, she gasped.

Her small apartment looked like it had been hit by a tornado. The sofa cushions and decorative pillows had been tossed on the floor. Her side table pushed over, resulting in her glass lamp being broken.

Chest aching, she tugged her hand free of Liam's and forced herself to continue toward her bedroom. She stepped over broken picture frames, shredded pillows, barely glancing at the wreck that had been made of her kitchen. Somehow, she suspected her sleeping area would be much, much worse.

And she wasn't wrong.

Every morning, she carefully made her bed. She took pleasure in the colorful comforter set with the matching sheets and the decorative pillows. Whoever had broken in had pulled everything off the mattress, cutting the comforter to ribbons, slicing up the sheets and pulling the stuffing from her once cute pillows.

Standing in the doorway surveying the mess, she wanted to cry. Instead, she kept her emotions under control and turned to look at Liam. "Why?" she asked. "Why would someone do this?"

Though he reached out and quickly squeezed her shoulder, he seemed to understand that she was hanging on by a thread. "I'd say they were looking for something."

The instant he said that, she realized he was likely right. "But what?" she asked, more to herself than anything else.

"What did you have over there?" he asked, pointing.

In the corner of the compact bedroom, she'd placed a small desk. There, she kept her laptop and any files she brought home, along with the one containing her extensive research on Aliana Martin's disappearance. That area too had been thoroughly tossed. Hurrying over, she realized immediately that both her computer and her Aliana case file were missing.

"Was it your personal laptop or the NYPD one?" Liam asked, once she told him.

"Personal. It's old, but still works. And it's password protected, so I doubt it'll be of much use to anyone. I use two-factor authentication on my banking apps and anything sensitive. Even so, I'll be changing all my passwords tonight as a precaution." Luckily she didn't have too many to deal with, just three or four.

Liam nodded, still frowning.

"What?" she asked.

"You aren't going to like what I'm about to say," he warned. "But I think Aliana herself might have paid your apartment a visit."

"I know." Much as she hated to admit it, why else would someone have taken that file? "Which means you've been right all along. For whatever reason, she isn't happy I saw her in the subway. The shooting, both on the crosswalk and tonight, plus the attempt to have me ingest antifreeze, all have to be her doing." She took a deep breath. "And remember, I got that mysterious phone call, ordering me to stop. That's it, nothing more."

"It now seems serious, after all this," he said.

"I agree," she sighed. "Honestly it didn't seem threatening at the time, since the caller didn't actually go into specifics and I didn't really think it could possible be Aliana."

"From now on, you need to be more careful." Grimacing, he shook his head. "And saying she isn't happy is the understatement of the year. Clearly, she's willing to kill in order to make sure the sighting ends with you."

Looking around at the wreckage of her apartment, she had no choice but to agree. "But we still don't have any idea why. I think if we can figure that out, we'd be a lot closer to solving the case."

Solving the case. Liam wasn't sure if he should be relieved or worried that Ellie had moved her former friend's long-ago disappearance out of the realm of intensely personal into something more like work related. Since she was a crime scene investigator, he supposed that was only natural. And he couldn't help but believe that she'd be a lot safer if she made herself put more distance between herself and Aliana.

"She's amping things up," he commented out loud.

"I disagree," Ellie promptly responded. "She started out trying to kill me. Breaking into my apartment and trashing it seems more like a step down."

Put that way, she had a point.

"I don't think Aliana is a murderer," Ellie continued. "She tried and failed, three times now. So this must be her attempting to frighten me off."

"That's convoluted logic," he pointed out. "Granted,

neither of us really knows Aliana Martin, but this had to happen either right before she shot out my rear windows or right after. It seems more like someone giving in to a fit of rage."

Eyes wide, Ellie stared at him while she considered his words. "That's a possibility," she finally admitted. "I just wish she'd talk to me. A few minutes of conversation would go a long way toward helping me understand."

"You expect her to explain herself?" He shook his head. "I think it's clear she has no intention of ever doing that."

"Maybe not. But I've spent sixteen years refusing to give up hope. Even if I knew how, I'm not sure I could start now."

Reluctantly, he nodded. He couldn't help but admire that about her; her absolute refusal to give up on a friend. Even if the person she remembered from the past bore no clear relation to the person apparently trying to kill her now.

He saw no need to point out the obvious. Ellie was an intelligent woman. If she hadn't already come to understand this, he knew she would soon enough.

"Are you going to be okay here by yourself?" he asked. "Honestly, I don't feel good about you staying her alone under the circumstances."

"I'll be okay," she insisted. "Though I wish I had access to a fingerprint kit just for my own knowledge. Though collecting them is a time-consuming process and since there was no murder, I know the police won't do it."

Liam nodded. "I can help you clean everything up before I leave if you'd like."

Her shoulders sagged as she looked around her destroyed home. "Thanks, I appreciate that. If you don't mind, you can start on the living room and I'll take the bedroom and kitchen."

"Sounds good."

He waited until she'd disappeared into her bedroom before getting started. He put the cushions back on the couch, careful to put tears or rips on the bottom side so they'd be hidden. Some of the decorative pillows were okay; others could be repaired, so he put as much of the stuffing as he could back in them. The broken lamp might be a goner, but he picked up all the glass shards and deposited them in her trash bin. Picture frames and the occasional decorative knick-knack for the most part had survived the wreckage.

Once he had the living area in order, he opened the coat closet, looking for the vacuum cleaner. He lucked out, and plugged it in, carefully vacuuming the area rug and the wood floors. When he'd finished, he looked up to find Ellie standing in the doorway, arms crossed, watching him.

He hit the off switch. "Do you need me to do the bedroom too?"

"Sure." She stepped aside, motioning him past her. "I'll clean up the kitchen while you do that. And thank you."

"Don't mention it," he said. "I don't mind at all."

She summoned up a smile, more defeated than anything. "There's nothing sexier than a man doing housework," she said, before heading toward the kitchen.

"At least you kept your sense of humor," he responded, and then switched the vacuum back on.

He finished her bedroom, noticing she'd stuffed the

ruined comforter into a large plastic trash bag. She hadn't remade the bed, no doubt planning to toss everything the intruder had touched.

Once he'd stowed the vacuum back in the coat closet, he went to the kitchen to see if Ellie needed any help. She looked up and smiled again. "This room wasn't too bad," she said. "I've put everything back. Her gaze searched his face and she swallowed hard.

He went to her and pulled her in for a hug. "Are you sure you're all right?"

After holding on for a moment, she stepped back, and shook her head. "I'm not comfortable being here right now. If it's still all right with you, I'm going to take you up on that offer to stay at your place tonight."

"I didn't know how I was going to convince you, but there was no way I would have let you stay here alone after this. Go pack a bag. I'll wait right here until you're ready to go."

She only took a few minutes before emerging with an overnight back. "Let's get out of here."

Once she'd locked up, they headed down to the street where he'd left the BMW. He opened the passenger door for her and after stowing her bag in the trunk, went around to the driver's side. "I'm sorry this happened to you," he said.

Grimacing, she nodded. "Me too. I know I need to make a police report, but we've already bothered Sean once tonight, so I'm going to wait until tomorrow."

"Or you could just call the main number and let them take a report," Liam suggested as he eased out into traffic.

"I could. But I think Sean might take offense to that. I'm just going to wait and make the report directly to him in the morning. Even though he's a detective and doesn't usually take the initial reports, since he considers me part of the team, I know he'd want to be involved."

Preoccupied with trying to ease over into the left lane, Liam waited a moment to comment. "Interesting. It seems I learn something new about my older brother every day. I didn't know he was so protective." But he did. At least where family was concerned. Sean took his job as eldest Colton seriously. Apparently, he felt the same way about his team. Which only made sense.

When they pulled into his parking garage, Liam noticed the way Ellie glanced at the Tesla and tensed up. "I'm sorry that happened to your car," she said. "If I hadn't been with you, that never would have—"

"Don't." Turning off the ignition, he faced her. "You can't blame yourself for something you had no control over. Come on, let's get inside."

She didn't move. "I should have asked this already, but do you have a guest bedroom I can use?" She bit her lip. "I know that might sound weird, but…" Though she didn't finish her sentence, he got her meaning loud and clear.

"It's okay," he reassured her, wondering why it hurt. "We did agree to keep things casual, after all."

Her relieved smile made his chest ache even worse. Mentally chiding himself, he got out, opened her door and took her bag from the trunk. Setting it down, he snapped a few photos of his damaged rear window and the bullet holes in his car body, before grabbing her bag again. "I'll need these for the insurance company," he said.

Back inside his place, he told her to make herself

comfortable while he got the guest bedroom ready. Since his cleaning service kept fresh linens on the bed, there wasn't really anything for him to do. But he needed time to compose himself.

For whatever reason, he'd thought they'd spend the night wrapped in each other's arms. Foolish of him. Despite the way his body stayed half-aroused whenever he was near her, he knew better than to act on that. After all, she'd just been through a very traumatic night.

Still, he turned down the bed for her and then double-checked the guest bathroom to make sure she had fresh towels and new toiletries. Satisfied that everything was in order, he returned to see her sitting on the couch, her head in her hands.

"Are you all right?" he asked.

Clearly startled, she looked up. "I'm starving," she admitted. "We never did get to eating dinner. I was going to scrounge something up once I got home, but then…"

"Your place was trashed." He thought for a moment. "I can't believe we forgot to eat."

This coaxed a small smile. "In our defense, we were busy. But maybe we should eat something? Even if it's just cheese and crackers?"

"Cheese and crackers?" He pretended to be horrified. "I can definitely do better than that. How about a BLT?"

Her smile widened. "That sounds perfect. Is there anything I can do to help?"

"Just come keep me company in the kitchen."

After pouring them each a glass of wine, he got busy making the sandwiches. He didn't tell Ellie this, but BLTs were one of his go-to meals when he found himself short on time, so he always had the ingredients on hand. His butcher kept him supplied with a high-quality, lower-fat cut of bacon, and it fried up perfectly.

They ate at the bar, sipping wine and concentrating on the food. Ellie made no pretense of eating slowly. She inhaled the sandwich, polishing off every crumb with gusto. "Thank you," she finally said, pushing her plate away. "I needed that."

Looking at her, his heart skipped a beat. She had a tiny crumb on her lower lip. Somehow, he managed to suppress the urge to lick it off. Instead, he told her about it, and then watched with regret when she used her napkin to blot at her mouth. He felt as if every time he looked at her, his burning desire must be plain for her to see.

Apparently not. They watched what was left of the evening news. Then, stifling a yawn with her hand, Ellie stood and stretched. "If you could point me in the direction of where I'm going to sleep, I think I'd like to go to bed."

Liam thought about tempting her with a kiss. But seeing the exhaustion she didn't even try to hide in her beautiful dark eyes, he didn't. Instead, he showed her both the guest bedroom and bathroom, wished her a quiet good-night and left her alone.

Too restless to sleep, he poured himself the last of the wine and carried it outside to his patio. He stretched out on one of his chaise lounges, gazing at the sparkling lights of his city below, and tried to figure out what the hell had happened to him.

Ellie Mathers was part of his past, part of the time before his life had gone off the rails. With her by his side, he could have done anything. Instead, he'd taken to hanging out with the wrong crowd and after several wrong choices, ended up in prison.

Scared straight, they called it. And Liam knew that had been exactly what had happened to him. When he'd gone away to prison, he'd been far more innocent than he'd realized. By the time he'd gotten out, he had experienced things that had come close to breaking him.

Never again, he'd vowed. And now he dedicated his life to attempting to make sure other teens didn't choose the wrong path like he had.

Noreen had seen the good in him. When they'd met, shortly after Liam had started working at the only place that would hire an ex-con, a local bar, she'd soon started coming in every night. To see him, she'd later told him. They'd become friends, then lovers, and by the time Liam had learned she was a very wealthy heiress, she'd already accepted his marriage proposal.

In the beginning, things had been good. She'd bankrolled his foundation, a dream born during his time behind bars and which he'd shared with her early in their relationship. But over time, as he'd thrown himself into the work he felt called to do, she'd begun to complain and call him boring. She'd started going out and partying without him and begun acting secretive, and he'd suspected she was seeing another man.

But before he could confront her, Noreen had wrapped her car around a tree and died.

Pushing away the dark thoughts, Liam swallowed the rest of his wine and closed his eyes.

He must have dozed off, because when he opened them again, his watch showed it was nearly five in the morning. He headed on inside, deciding to stay up, take a hot shower and down several strong cups of black coffee.

The shower first. After drying off and getting dressed, he headed toward the kitchen. Despite the lack of sleep, he felt surprisingly alert. He took care to move about as quietly as possible, not wanting to wake Ellie.

Coffee in hand, he carried it out to the patio to drink while he watched the sky continue to lighten and the sun rise. One of life's best little pleasures was the taste of that first sip of coffee in the morning.

Shortly after seven, right after the sun had begun to clear the horizon, his phone pinged, indicating an incoming text message. Sean. As was his habit, he texted from the lobby, asking if it was okay to come up. Liam had long ago given both his brothers and his sister their own electronic cards to get into the building, with one stipulation. They weren't to show up unannounced.

Kind of early, isn't it? He texted back, heading inside for more coffee.

Yeah, I got called in early. Thought I'd stop by on the way.

Liam glanced back toward his guest bathroom. A minute ago, he'd heard the shower start up, which meant Ellie would be occupied for at least a few minutes.

Come on up, he texted Sean. Hopefully, he got get his brother in and out before Ellie ever emerged from the bathroom.

A few sips of coffee later, and he heard Sean knock on the front door. After opening it, he led the way back to the kitchen. "Want some dark roast?"

"I already have some." Sean held up a disposable cup.

"I stopped on the way over. I thought I'd take a look at your car, if you don't mind. I can take a few pictures to put with my report."

"I took some last night. Let me transfer them to you." Once that was done, Liam told his brother about the break-in at Ellie's apartment.

Sean's expression grew thunderous. "Why didn't you call me last night?" Without waiting for an answer, he dug out his phone and made a call.

A moment later, they both could hear Ellie's phone ringing in the other room. Shaking his head, Sean ended the call before she answered.

"Ellie's here? I thought I heard the shower. Did you forget to mention that? Or did you think I wouldn't find out?" Sean demanded, the fierceness of his glare letting Liam know what he thought of that idea.

"Of course not," Liam responded. "We've only been reconnected for a few days. After what happened, Ellie wasn't comfortable staying there last night, so she stayed here. Do you have a problem with that?"

Since Liam was usually easygoing and nonconfrontational, Sean eyed him as if he'd suddenly grown two heads.

"No," Sean finally said. "No problem."

Chapter 9

Ellie heard Sean and Liam arguing before she even finished getting dressed. She hadn't gotten to her phone in time, because Sean had clearly ended the call when he'd realized she was right there in Liam's apartment.

Shaking her head, she finished doing her makeup before getting dressed. Then she took the shower cap off her hair, carefully brushed it out and put in her earrings. Satisfied that she looked polished and put together, she opened the door and sauntered out into the living room. The click of her heels announced her arrival.

Both men stopped talking the moment she emerged.

"Good morning," she said, walking past them toward the kitchen and heading straight for the coffee pot. While she waited for her cup to brew, she turned and eyed Sean. "I take it Liam told you about what happened to my apartment yesterday?"

"He did. Why didn't you call it in?"

"Because I knew you'd want to handle it personally." Her coffee finished and she headed toward the fridge to grab the milk. Once she'd finished doctoring it, she looked up to find Sean staring at her. as if he couldn't understand why she was there.

"What?" she asked, realizing he'd noticed how comfortable she felt in Liam's kitchen.

"Nothing." Sean took a long drink of his own coffee. "When you get in to work today, call the precinct and make a report, okay?"

"I will," she promised.

"Good. I'll give them a heads-up to expect your call." Sean took a few steps back and then glanced at Liam. "No need to show me out. I know the way. Talk to you later."

A moment later, they heard the front door close and he was gone.

"What's up with him?" she asked, though she sort of already knew. "Why is he acting so weird?"

"He's not sure how to handle the idea of the two of us together," Liam said. "He can be overprotective with people he really cares about."

Not quite sure how to take that, she frowned. "Does he think I'm going to hurt you or something? I know you're his younger brother, but you're also a grown-ass man."

To her surprise, her comment made Liam laugh. "It's not *me* he's worried about," he finally said. "It's you. I've already been given a stern talking to about that. He doesn't want you hurt."

Strangely relieved, yet also intrigued, she eyed him.

"Why would he worry about that? Do you make a habit of hurting women?"

"Of course not."

The promptness of his answer reassured her.

"I always have an understanding with the women I date," he continued. "Going in, they know up front it's not going to be serious. No one gets hurt."

She nodded, though she had no idea why hearing about him with other women stung. They certainly had never even discussed an exclusive relationship, nor did she want to. Not serious meant exactly that.

When she didn't comment, Liam shrugged. "Sean doesn't get it. He thinks it's all me, that I'm a love 'em and leave 'em kind of guy."

"A regular heartbreaker then," she said dryly. "Do you want me to set Sean straight?"

"Of course not. What you and I do is none of his business." Eyeing her, his gaze softened. "Unless of course, you feel otherwise."

Since she wasn't sure how she felt, she settled on drinking more coffee rather than answering. "Well, I'd better get going," she finally said. "Thank you for letting me stay here last night."

Turning, she went back to the guest room to collect her overnight bag. When she returned, Liam waited by the front door, car keys in hand.

"I can drive you," he offered. "If you'd like. I really don't think it's safe for you to go out on your own. Plus, it'd be easier for you since you have that bag."

Though she liked that he asked, rather than insisted, she shook her head. "You've already done enough. But thank you for offering. I refuse to let these threats turn me into a hermit, scared of my own shadow. I'll talk to you later."

Then, unsure whether to hug him or not, she decided to simply head for the door.

As she rode the elevator to the lobby, she wondered why she suddenly felt like crying.

Since Liam didn't live too far from her neighborhood, she went to her usual subway station and rode the train to the lab. Once there, she went directly to her office, called the precinct and filed a police report on the break-in. She elected to give her statement over the phone rather than ask for an officer to come out. Once that was done, she got to work and tried her best to put last night out of her mind.

Except when quitting time came. One by one, her coworkers started leaving. Most of them popped in to tell her good-night. Since she often worked late, no one seemed to find it odd when she made no signs of shutting things down. As long as she had work to do, she figured she'd stay. Until she realized she wasn't sure she could make herself go home.

Ellie considered herself a strong woman. She'd worked hard to get where she was and she didn't frighten easily. But having someone break into her apartment, go through her things, destroying as they went, and steal her laptop and her files was personal. Especially since the intruder had likely been her former best friend.

While she wondered why, when it came right down to how she felt, the why didn't matter. Her privacy had been invaded. Not just invaded, but destroyed. She refused to let Aliana make her feel that way about the city. *Her* city.

Ridiculous, she told herself. She straightened her spine, organized her desk and prepared to leave for the evening. Even if the thought of going home made her stomach knot up, she didn't know where else she could go. If she went to stay with her parents, she'd have to fill them in on what had been going on, which would only worry them.

Her only other option was Liam. And, since they'd had that brief conversation about keeping things casual, the last thing she wanted to do was impose on him.

Nope. It looked like she was on her own. She just needed to get herself together, go home and see what she could do to make her place more secure.

Nerves jangling, she rode the train back to Manhattan, glad for the evening rush hour crowd. When she reached her stop, she got off, lugging her overnight bag along with her. Up the subway stairs she went, trying not to think about anything until she made it to her building.

Inside, she took a minute to catch her breath before getting into the elevator to ride to her floor. The creaking sounds that she used to find reassuring now sounded ominous.

When the doors opened on her floor, she got off and marched herself down the hall until she stood in front of her door.

That's when the panic attack hit. It came on out of nowhere, sucking the air from her lungs and turning her legs to rubber. She leaned against the wall, gasping for air and telling herself to get a grip, even as the edges of her vision grayed and she thought she might pass out.

A neighbor got off the elevator and eyed her curiously as he walked by. Somehow, she managed to offer a casual wave. Once he'd gone, she swallowed, realizing she couldn't stay out there in the hallway forever. This was her home, damn it. She couldn't let some lowlife take that away from her. Time to force herself to face her fear and go inside.

Trembling, she managed to get her door unlocked and stepped into the place that had once been her sanctuary. She flipped on the light switch and hurried from room to room, unable to keep from looking in every possible hiding place to make sure no one hid in wait.

Once she'd satisfied herself that her apartment was secure, she stood in her living room and looked around. Everything—from her colorful area rug to the eclectic artwork on her walls—looked the same. Yet it also appeared different. She wondered if she'd ever feel safe inside her home again.

Overwhelmed, she tried to figure out what to do. Usually, on a Friday night like this, she'd order take-out and binge watch some TV until she fell asleep on the couch. Boring? Maybe. Predictable? True. But after working a sixty-plus-hour week, she rarely had energy for anything social until she'd had a chance to recharge.

Tonight however, with her nerves a jangly mess, she knew she couldn't relax.

Her phone pinged, alerting her to a text. Liam.

Are you ok? If you need some company, let me know and I can stop by. Or if you just want to talk, you can give me a call. And if you'd rather be left alone, just pretend you didn't see this text.

After reading it, she found herself smiling. Some of the tension leached out of her shoulders. While Liam's offer was tempting, this was something she knew she had to conquer on her own.

I appreciate the offer, she texted back. But you've already done so much. Then, deciding she might as well be completely honest, she continued. Honestly, while I'd love your company, this is something I've got to do on my own. I've got to reclaim my apartment. I hope you understand.

She eyed the black dots that meant he was responding and held her breath.

Yes, I get it. Promise you'll call me if you need anything.

Letting him know she would, she put the phone on the coffee table and leaned back on her couch. She felt better now. More settled, the uneasy jangling of her nerves quieted.

Because of Liam? Maybe so.

She decided to do a deep clean of her apartment. Keeping busy would keep her thoughts at bay. And maybe by the time she'd finished getting her place spic-and-span, it would feel like her home once more.

After streaming Q104.3, the classic rock station, from her phone to her wireless sound bar, she poured herself a glass of wine and got started.

An hour later, she took a break, just as the Rolling Stones' "Wild Horses" came on. Eying the gleaming kitchen counters, the freshly mopped floor, she breathed in the scent of her favorite pine cleanser and smiled. During the process, while singing along to songs she knew by heart, she'd almost managed to forget about the intruder.

Almost.

After pouring herself a second glass of wine, she made herself a sandwich and ate it standing up. Then she headed into the bedroom to get started there.

The sight of her small corner desk brought her up short. Though she'd picked up all the papers and books that had been knocked to the floor, the absence of her laptop served as a stark reminder that a stranger had been in her private bedroom. A stranger. Maybe. She shook her head. The longer this went on and the more attempts that were made against her life, the less she believed this was the work of a stranger. As awful as it seemed, she now believed that Aliana Martin was after her. Simply because Ellie had recognized her former best friend in a crowded subway station.

But why? Why go to such lengths to take Ellie out? Aliana clearly knew Ellie worked with the NYPD. Did she honestly not understand if Ellie was killed, her police officer friends would not leave any stone unturned in the hunt for her killer?

Ellie shook her head, glad when the music changed to something more up-tempo. Any rational person might have simply disappeared again, hoping to be forgotten once things had died down.

Which meant that Aliana clearly wasn't rational. Ellie had no choice but to believe her former best friend had something big that she was trying hide, and she was willing to kill to make sure whatever it was stayed hidden.

Naturally, this only increased Ellie's determination to get to the truth. She hated that for sixteen years she'd been searching for someone who didn't want to be found, a woman who clearly had never been the person Ellie had believed her to be.

Ellie remembered Aliana's parents and their desperate anguish when their only child had disappeared. She'd visited them weekly, sitting with Mrs. Martin and listening to her talk about her daughter. They'd continued to celebrate birthdays, and milestones, carrying on with an ironclad belief that Aliana was still alive and would return home one day. For her senior prom, Ellie had worn a second, smaller, wrist corsage in honor of Aliana.

Aliana's mother had died a year after Ellie graduated high school. Some claimed her broken heart had killed her. Ellie believed that. Aliana's father had drifted into alcoholism and Ellie had no idea what had happened to him.

If, Ellie thought grimly, Aliana truly had disappeared on purpose, knowingly allowing her friends and family to believe she'd been abducted, she had a lot to answer for. And Ellie was determined to make sure that she did.

The next morning when Liam woke, all he could think about was Ellie. He'd worried about her the night before, well aware she likely felt uneasy staying in her apartment after the break-in. He'd meant what he'd texted her—he'd been perfectly willing to spend the night there with her if she'd wanted him to. More than willing, actually. But when she'd declined, he'd understood that too. Ellie's fierce independence was one of the things he admired most about her.

His phone rang, startling him. Though his first thought was Ellie, caller ID said otherwise. His older brother, Sean.

"Good morning," Sean said. "What's on your agenda

for today? I'm wondering if you can make time to stop by the precinct for a quick meeting with the team."

"Just a sec." Liam checked his phone calendar just to be safe. While he knew he wasn't giving one of his scared straight talks until next week, he needed to make sure he didn't have anything else scheduled. Since he frequently helped NYPD at other precincts by working his contacts on the street, sometimes he had briefing sessions scheduled. "As it happens, since it's Saturday, my entire day is wide open," he admitted. "What time do you want to meet?"

"This morning?" Sean suggested. "Eva's shift starts at ten, so it has to be before then. Otherwise, I'd have to include that annoying blowhard of a partner she has."

Sean's description of Mitch Mallard, while accurate, made Liam grin. He checked his watch. "I can be there at eight thirty or nine," he said. "Do you guys want to meet up for a bagel or something?"

"I'm off today, so that's fine by me. But we'll need to check with Eva. Since she has to work today, I'm not sure if that'll give her enough time."

"Fair enough. How about we all meet at the precinct and go from there?"

"Sounds good. I'll let you know if that changes." Sean paused. "How's Ellie?"

"I haven't talked to her this morning," Liam admitted. "But she wanted to stay at her own place last night. She said she needed to reclaim it."

"I get that. And admire her for it." Someone spoke in the background and Sean responded, saying he'd be right there. "I've got to go," he told Liam. "See you at the precinct in a few."

After ending the call, Liam toyed with the idea of

inviting Ellie. But Sean hadn't mentioned that, and in the end, Liam knew Ellie needed some time alone to decompress and get her apartment back in order. He knew she'd reach out to him if she needed him.

A few hours later, Liam walked up to the precinct. The place had a different vibe on the weekend. Though crime never stopped, the day shift peeps on Saturdays and Sundays always seemed more relaxed and easygoing. Though a few were seasoned officers, many rookies drew weekends and nights, at least until they'd gained some experience.

Before he could walk in the door, Eva's voice behind made him turn.

"Good morning," she exclaimed, hugging him. "I heard about what happened after you dropped me off."

"Yeah, the Tesla is toast," he admitted. Already in uniform, Eva carried a bag that most likely had her breakfast.

Noticing him eyeing it, she smiled. "Bagels," she said. "Enough for all of us. Come on. We can hang out in Sean's office until he gets here."

But when they got there, Sean greeted them, already seated behind his desk. Just as Liam and Eva were sitting down, Cormac walked in with a cardboard carrier and four coffees. He put them down on the desk, so they could each grab one. Eva passed out the bagels and they all dug in.

Once they'd gotten started, Liam filled them in on what had been happening, though he figured they mostly already knew since he'd told Sean. Apparently not, because when he got to the part about the gunshots shattering his rear window, both Eva and Cormac exchanged horrified looks. "I knew the Tesla was damaged," Eva said. "But geez."

"You're damn lucky you weren't hit," Cormac grumbled. "And you really think this is tied to Aliana Martin's disappearance sixteen years ago?"

"I'm certain it is," Liam replied. "Because right after that, someone broke into Ellie's apartment. Not only did they trash the place, but they stole her laptop and the Aliana Martin case file she'd been building up over the years."

Eva pushed to her feet. "You're right," she exclaimed. "The theft of that case file in particular leaves no room for doubt."

"Yeah." Trying not to sound as glum as he felt, Liam took a bite of his bagel and washed it down with a gulp of coffee. "We just haven't been able to figure out why. I talked to one of the witnesses the police interviewed back when Aliana disappeared—he's someone I've had contact with a few times on the street—and he was insistent that he saw her with an older guy the day she vanished."

"The police knew this?" Eva asked. "Why wasn't that documented? I've reviewed the case file several times with Ellie and never saw anything following up on that."

"Because he asked for money," Liam replied. "Because of that, and a few other things, he wasn't considered a reliable witness."

"Well, they still should have followed up," Eva declared. "That's sloppy police work."

"I agree," Sean said. "But if this guy went missing along with Aliana, I think we would have heard about it by now."

"Right?" Eva nodded. "It sounds like maybe you're

getting too close to the truth for someone's comfort. Since no one has been asking about a missing guy, like relatives or friends, it's possible this man might have killed her."

"Except Ellie saw her," Liam pointed out. "She's one hundred percent certain about that."

"Okay, okay." Eva thought for a moment. "If he didn't kill her, then maybe they broke up and went their separate ways."

"Or maybe Aliana killed him," Cormac drawled. When everyone stared at him, he shrugged. "Hey, it's possible. I see stuff like this all the time in my business."

"Good point." Taking a drink of her coffee, Eva considered for a moment before turning back to look at Liam. "Here's an idea. Why don't you do a search for unclaimed bodies that weren't DNA tested for one reason or another. There's a huge backlog and if no one pushes, like family members, a lot of them just don't get identified. Or if they were, they might have had no family, so they weren't ever claimed. I'd start back sixteen years ago and move a year or two up from there."

"That's a great idea." Liam high-fived his sister. "You're going to make a great cop."

"I *am* a great cop," she corrected, and then laughed. "But seriously, you can narrow down your search for young males, aged from sixteen to say, twenty-six. Then, once you have a couple of those, if they've been identified at all, you'll have something to go on."

"You'd also make a good private investigator," Cormac said. "I wish I'd thought of that."

This comment made Eva beam. "I can show you where to start looking," she told Liam.

"Thanks," he told her, meaning it. "I plan to start right away. The sooner I can figure out why Aliana is after Ellie, the better."

Eva nodded. "What's going on with the two of you?" she asked. "The other night, I literally could see the sparks flying."

Sean almost choked on his bagel. Meanwhile, Cormac looked from Eva to Liam, his expression mildly curious. He knew better than to get involved.

"None of your business," Liam answered promptly. "If anything happens between me and Ellie that I think you all need to know about, I promise to keep you posted."

Eva frowned, but she must have decided not to comment further.

"Anything new on Humphrey?" Cormac asked. "The media has been all over his disappearance, but lately they haven't mentioned it at all."

"Which is a huge relief," Sean said. "The pressure to figure out what happened has been relentless. Maybe it'll ease up a little."

"I wouldn't count on it." Eva shook her head. "Somebody that prominent can't just up and vanish."

She stood, brushing off a few bagel crumbs from her uniform, and checked her watch. "Liam, I haven't got much time before I have to report for my shift, but if you want to grab one of the empty workstations, I can show you where to look for unclaimed bodies."

Liam glanced at Sean, who shrugged. "I can't let you use mine today," he said. "I have too much of my own work to do. No one will mind. You're around here so much, everyone thinks you work here anyway."

"Truth." Liam followed his sister out of Sean's office, turning to wave goodbye to his brothers.

"Over here," Eva said, pointing to an unused cubicle. "This one's clean, so no one has claimed it yet. Let me log you in to the system and pull up the database."

"Can you refine the search as well?" he asked.

"Sure." All business now, she typed away. "Here you go," she said, stepping away from the computer. "You're in. I've filtered your search for males between the ages of sixteen and twenty-six and set the date parameters to start at sixteen years ago."

"Thank you," he said, taking a seat.

"You're welcome. There will likely be a lot to sift through," she warned. "And what you're looking for might not even be there."

"I know. But it won't hurt to try."

Glancing across the room, Eva groaned. "There's Mitch. I'd better go. Good luck."

Once she'd gone, Liam settled in and got to work. Though Eva had set filters, the occasional unidentified male, *age undetermined*, added to the seemingly endless list.

The first three pages were all right around the time Aliana had vanished sixteen years ago. Midway through page four, the year changed.

Liam drank the last of his now cold coffee, sat back and rubbed his eyes. He'd had no idea so many unidentified or unclaimed bodies existed, though in a city as large as New York, he supposed he shouldn't have been surprised. The youngest ones really bothered him. How awful to be sixteen or seventeen years old, with no family coming forward to claim you.

On page six, one entry caught his eye. A young male's

body had washed ashore fifteen years ago. Cause of death, a gunshot wound to the stomach. Dental records had identified him as John Dobby, age twenty. Liam clicked on the file and printed out the faded black-and-white photo.

He continued to scroll, saving this John Dobby as a potential. By the time he'd made it to thirteen years ago, he'd printed out two more potential matches before deciding to call it a day.

After leaving the precinct, he found his informant, Eric Campbell, in the same dingy bar, already drinking even though it was not yet noon.

Liam sat down beside him and slid all three of the photos over, with John Dobby's on top. "Are any of these the guy you saw leave with Aliana Martin?" he asked.

Eric didn't even blink. He took a long swallow of his beer before picking up the first picture and studying it. "What's it worth to you?" he asked, the glint in his red-rimmed eyes letting Liam know his expectations.

"Here." Suppressing a flash of anger, Liam slid a twenty over. "Don't ask for more. This is simply to satisfy my own curiosity, nothing more."

Eric grabbed the money and dipped his head. "I think this is the guy I saw leave with her," he said, stabbing John Dobby's photo. "I don't know who he is, but he's the one who looks closest to what I remember."

Just to be sure, since he didn't consider Eric an entirely trustworthy witness, Liam showed him the other two photos again. "What about these guys? I need to be absolutely sure. Is there any chance it could have been one of them?"

Picking up each picture one at a time, Eric gave each

one a cursory glance. "Nope," he said, putting that one down. And then after looking at the other, he shook his head. "No way. That day and what I saw is forever etched in my memory. I'm positive it was the first guy." He took a deep, shaky breath and reached for his beer. After another deep swallow, he met Liam's gaze. "Is that guy the one who abducted Aliana?"

"I don't know," Liam answered, gathering the photos back up. "But thanks for your time."

Eric had already gone back to his beer. "No problem," he said.

After leaving the bar, Liam knew he had to relay the news to Ellie. Since it was Saturday, he figured she'd likely be at home, still trying to straighten out her apartment. The rush of energy he got from just the thought of seeing her worried him. Casual relationships never felt like this. Ever.

Pushing his fears aside, he texted her to ask if she'd mind if he stopped by.

Chapter 10

Now that she had the apartment super clean, Ellie should have had a lazy Saturday morning, complete with sleeping in. However, despite all the energy she'd expended making her place spotless, she'd had a restless night. tossing and turning. Bad dreams had plagued her. Twice she'd woken up terrified that an intruder stood over her bed with a knife. Every time she rolled over, she checked her nightstand clock, hoping it would finally be late enough to get up.

The instant the sky lightened, she shot out of bed, hating how her nervous jitters warred with her bone-deep exhaustion. Saturdays were usually her day to run errands and clean, but she'd already done one, and as far as the other, she was loath to leave her apartment. She couldn't help but feel as if the instant she left, someone would break in and trash her place again.

Not healthy, definitely not normal, but until she'd worked through her feelings, she didn't plan on going anywhere. She made herself a cup of strong coffee, briefly lamenting that she didn't have an outdoor space like Liam did. She had laundry to do, and dry cleaning to drop off, plus she needed to buy groceries, but all of that could wait. Instead, she drank her coffee, watched videos on her phone and finally made herself an omelet before she took a shower and got dressed.

That done, she stared at herself in the mirror and tried to inspire herself to get out and accomplish things. But once again, just the idea of leaving the apartment brought a round of fresh anxiety. Since she'd never been a nervous person, she wasn't sure what to do about this. Would it be best to try and ignore it, pretend she felt fine and go about her business even if her heart pounded and her hands shook?

Or should she attempt to ride it out, allowing herself to give in to the feeling for now, and hope it would go away on its own?

Uncertainty was also new to her. Usually, she considered all her options, started a listed, and methodically reviewed all the possibilities before she made her decision and acted on it. Now she found herself wavering, which infuriated her.

Liam's text came at just the right time. For the first time that morning, she smiled as she texted him back to let him know it was okay to drop by.

As soon as he responded with On my way, she rushed to her bathroom to fix her hair and put on mascara. She eyed her comfy T-shirt and joggers and decided they were okay. She doubted he'd care what she wore. After all, Liam had seen her naked.

Just the thought made her body heat. Feeling significantly better, she considered the possibilities. Spontaneous sex. As distractions went, she couldn't think of a better one. And wasn't that the very definition of a casual relationship?

Immensely cheered and partially aroused, she waited impatiently for him to arrive, picturing all the carnal things they could do.

Her buzzer sounded, startling her out of her fantasies, despite expecting it. She pressed the button that would unlock the entrance into her building, all jangly nerves and conflicting emotion mixed with desire.

Finally, he knocked to let her know he was there.

Taking a deep breath, she opened the door, hoping she had a pleasant smile on her face. However, the instant she saw him, she crumpled, falling apart inside. Struggling to retain her composure, she stepped aside and motioned him in, closing the door behind him.

"Come here," he told her, and gently pulled her into his arms. He held her tight, not speaking, just offering physical comfort. The strength and warmth emanating from his powerful body were exactly the thing she craved.

She hadn't realized how badly she needed to be held. To her shock, she realized tears were streaming down her face. As she went to wipe them away with the back of her hand, she started trembling. In response, he only tightened his embrace.

"This isn't like me," she managed, before burying her face in his shoulder.

"It's okay," he told her, his deep voice a rumble against her ear. "You don't have to be strong all the time."

Strong all the time. Stunned that he understood, she exhaled in relief. She *was* strong and would continue to rely on her strength once she got past this. Which she would. But for now, she figured maybe, just maybe, she needed to allow herself to work through things.

"Thanks," she muttered. "Sorry I'm soaking your shirt."

This made him chuckle. "I'll survive."

With anyone else, she would have been embarrassed. But this was Liam, and she realized in addition to the crazy, intense, sexual attraction, she actually *liked* him.

Once the tears had stopped, she sniffled and realized she needed to blow her nose. "Excuse me," she said, keeping her head down as she moved toward the bathroom. The instant she saw herself in the mirror, she realized the mascara had been a mistake.

After washing her face and deciding not to reapply any mascara, she emerged. Liam had taken a seat on her couch to wait for her.

"Hey," he said, his voice gentle. "Do you want to get out of here for a while? We can go for a walk, grab some heroes, whatever you want."

Considering, she sighed. "I'm struggling, as you can tell. I have this irrational fear that if I leave, someone will break in here again."

He nodded. "That's understandable. But unlikely. I think they got what they came for. Your laptop and your file on Aliana."

They. He should have said *she*. Ellie guessed he was trying to spare her feelings.

"You may be right." She glanced at the window, aware it was a beautiful spring day. "It looks like it's sunny. A walk might not be a bad idea." She brightened. "We could even go to Central Park. Hanging out there always reminds me of when I was little. My parents loved to take me for picnics there."

"Sounds good. It's beautiful outside." He hesitated, his expression serious. "But before we go, there's something I need to tell you."

Instantly on alert, she eyed him. "About the Aliana Martin case?"

"Yes." He patted the couch next to him. "Sit."

Reluctantly, she did. Near enough that she could reach out and touch him, but not so close that their legs touched. "Go on."

"After learning about the slightly older guy seen with Aliana the day she vanished, Eva suggested I search a database of unidentified or unclaimed bodies."

"Good thinking. Did Eva have a hunch?" she asked, intrigued.

"I think she might have. We put in search parameters, figuring he'd have been between sixteen and twenty-six years old at the time. Turns out, a body washed ashore fifteen years ago and while unclaimed by any family, he was identified by his dental records. Does the name John Dobby ring any bells with you?"

"John Dobby?" Unable to tear her gaze away from him, she thought for a moment. "No," she finally admitted. "But I'm assuming you think this guy was the one your witness saw with Aliana?"

"More than think." Expression intense, he dragged his hand through his hair. "I know he was. I printed out a picture and took it to the witness, along with a couple others to make sure. He positively identified John Dobby as Aliana's escort the day she disappeared."

"Finally. A lead. May I see the photo?" she asked. Once he'd handed it over, she studied it intently. Though she tried, she was unable to find anything familiar.

"Aliana was my best friend," she said. "You'd think I'd have known about any guy she was seeing. We shared everything. Or so I thought."

"I take it you don't recognize him?"

She looked again, desperately trying to see if anything jogged her memory. "Unfortunately, no. I keep thinking there's got to be something familiar, but honestly I've never seen this guy before."

As she handed the picture back, she sighed. "So, we're thinking this might be the guy who abducted Aliana?"

Judging by the way he looked down at his hands rather than answering, she suspected she wouldn't like whatever he was about to say next.

"If he abducted her, he's dead now," he finally said, meeting her gaze. "Either she killed him and escaped, or…"

"He died naturally, like from drowning," she said, even though she figured that wasn't likely from the way Liam was acting. "Was there a cause of death listed on the police report?"

Mouth set in grim lines, he nodded. "Yes. He was killed by a gunshot wound to the abdomen. His death was ruled a homicide. Whether Aliana pulled the trigger or not, we don't know. But there's a very strong possibility she was involved."

Evidence. Circumstantial at best. But still…it kept coming back to the fact that this John Dobby was seen with Aliana on the day she vanished. It didn't take much sleuthing to figure out something awful had happened after that.

Crushed, Ellie swallowed. "It just keeps getting worse and worse. Clearly, Aliana is not who I thought she was."

"Sixteen years is a long time," he said, reaching over and covering her hand with his. "People change."

She squeezed his fingers back. "Thanks, but that's not it at all. Aliana had to have been like this even sixteen years ago. I just didn't see it. Now that I do, that would explain a lot."

Liam simply continued to hold her hand wrapped in his larger one, his expression neutral. She loved that he didn't push. He just simply offered his support while she struggled with her own conclusions.

"Aliana might have murdered this guy," she said, her throat aching. "And as a crime scene investigator, I have to say *might*, because we have no evidence."

"Yet," he interjected. "We have no evidence yet."

She gave him a long look, all the while trying to figure out a way to convey why this bothered her so much. "I feel like a fool. For all these years, I've continued to look for her. I never gave up hope. And now it turns out she might be a murderer. And if that is the case, it's likely that she is really the one trying to kill me."

Though he'd been saying that exact thing all along, he simply nodded. "I know."

Accepting the inevitable might be difficult, but it

wasn't impossible. "You can go ahead and say *I told you so*," she said.

"I won't, I promise." Though the words might have been sincere, she knew him well enough to detect a spark of humor in his blue eyes.

"You had no doubts, did you?"

On corner of his mouth rose in the beginning of a smile. She saw both compassion and humor in his ruggedly handsome face, which made a different kind of warmth blossom inside. "Not since someone tried to poison you with breakfast. You have to admit, that was a major clue right there."

Damned if he wasn't sexy as hell. The muscles rippling under his T-shirt made her mouth go dry. How she could want to jump his bones while they were in the middle of discussing the fact that the best friend she'd been missing for sixteen years was trying to kill her boggled her mind.

"Are you okay?" he asked, making her realize she'd gone silent for too long. "I know it's difficult adjusting your thinking, especially after so long."

With a wry smile, she met his gaze. "I'm not usually so gullible."

The warmth of his full-on smile made her entire body hum. Focus, she reminded herself.

"I know," he replied. "It's completely understandable. She was your best friend."

Was being the operative word. Where Aliana was concerned, she'd been wearing rose-colored glasses for far too long.

Liam shifted his weight, drawing her attention back to him. With their eyes locked, she knew she had to kiss him. She scooted closer, her heart thudding in her chest. "I know something else we can do instead of walking," she murmured, hoping she sounded suggestive.

She must have, because his expression darkened. "You do?"

Instead of answering, she leaned over. He met her halfway. The instant their mouths came together, she ignited.

This. This man, his kiss, the rightness of his embrace. Desire ignited her, shattering her. Emotions whirling, she clung to him, the tremors that shook her no longer from fear, but from need.

He matched her desire with his own.

After, still on the couch with their clothes strewn all around them, they cuddled. Ellie didn't know if this sort of thing was common in casual relationships, but she thought not. Inhaling deeply, she made herself push out of his arms, get up, scoop up her clothes, and take herself into the bathroom to clean up. And, she thought wryly, she needed time to get a grip on the emotions threatening to turn this into something it wasn't.

When she emerged, Liam had also gotten dressed. He stood with his back to her, looking out her window. Turning as she approached, he smiled. Something had changed in his face, she noted. The smile not only didn't reach his eyes, but he seemed more distant. Remote.

Which stung. But only for a moment. She realized he'd probably somehow figured out that she'd begun to get too attached. She knew she'd have to fix that, or this amazing, casual relationship would be over. But she had no idea how. Maybe they both needed to take a step back from this, collect themselves and reassess.

Decision made, she took a deep breath while she tried to figure out the best way to tell him.

Liam heard Ellie return. He turned slowly, steeling himself at his inevitable punch in the gut reaction to the sight of her. He liked everything about this vibrant, beautiful woman. Far too much.

That alone gave him pause. If he wasn't careful, he'd find himself wanting more. Much, much more. And after what had happened with Noreen, he knew that would only destroy what was currently a really good thing.

For him, he'd like to keep it that way.

"Liam? Are you okay?" Ellie asked, watching him, a peculiar expression that he didn't recognize on her face.

She appeared sad, he realized, fear mingled with worry stabbing his chest. Was she that terrified about staying in her own apartment, he wondered. Should he consider inviting her to stay at his place for as long as she wanted? Or might she consider doing such a thing too intrusive, even if he made it clear he'd asked her as a friend? He opened his mouth to ask, and then closed it.

"What is it?" Clearly noticing, Ellie watched him closely.

What the hell, why not? He hadn't gotten this far along in life without taking chances. "I've been thinking," he began, trying to sound as casual as possible. "Why don't you hang out in my guest bedroom for a while until all of this blows over?"

Eyes wide, she stared. "Why?" she finally asked.

"Because you'd be safer there," he replied. "You know it's the truth. And you wouldn't have to worry about someone breaking in here while you're home and hurting you."

With her gaze still locked on his, she swallowed hard. "Do you really think she'd do that?" she asked.

Which meant he'd managed to frighten her. "It's possible," he acknowledged. "I'm not trying to scare you, but I just wanted to give you another option if you don't feel safe."

Slowly, she nodded. "I see."

"Do you?" he asked gently. "Because despite your earlier acknowledgement, you didn't seem to understand the danger you're in. For whatever reason, Aliana Martin is gunning for you."

"I know," she admitted. "But she hasn't been very successful. I was kind of hoping she'd give up."

Now it was his turn to stare. "You're a crime scene investigator," he pointed out. "Have you experienced many crimes where the instigator just gives up?"

Though her jaw tightened, she shook her head. "No."

The haunted look in her eyes made him feel like a monster. Still, he continued, because he needed to do whatever it took to keep her safe. "I'm guessing Aliana's attempts to silence you forever will only escalate."

Now she crossed her arms. "Okay. Say that does happen. I can't hide out forever."

"I agree," he replied. "I've got to come up with a way to neutralize the threat and protect you. Which means I need to take a more active role in helping you locate her."

She narrowed her eyes, considering him.

"We're friends," he pointed out. "I'll help you in whatever way I can. You let me know what you want to do. You're welcome to stay at my place if you'd like. If not, that's fine too."

When she didn't immediately reply, he wondered if she'd seen through him, if he might have gone too far, too fast. He mumbled some excuse and made his way to the bathroom. Only when he'd closed the door behind him did he allow himself to exhale. He'd never been socially awkward, but at this very moment, he felt like a bumbling fool.

Dragging his hand across his chin, he grimaced at his reflection in the mirror. What the hell? Had his protective instincts now made him vulnerable? After the hell he endured watching his marriage crumble and then losing Noreen, he knew he never wanted to go through that kind of heartbreak again. The pain had been unbearable. It had colored every aspect of his life, turned everything dark and bloodless.

And now, when his life had finally gotten into balance, Ellie had come along and knocked him off his axis. He tried not to care, but she inspired feelings inside him that he'd considered dead and buried.

If he allowed himself to continue down this path, to care for Ellie, the inevitable breakup might ruin him.

Yet he knew he couldn't stay away. Even if he wanted to. Whether Ellie admitted it or not, she needed his help, his protection. And he told himself that might be the reason he couldn't quit her, even if he suspected that might only be a partial truth.

He had always been a champion of the underdog. Growing up, he'd been scrappy, always getting into fights on the playground. What no one knew or cared about was the reason for those fights, since Liam had never told. If he'd seen a smaller kid getting picked on, he'd step in and stop it by whatever means necessary. This usually meant physical violence.

Even in prison, while he was a newcomer and thus fresh meat by the other inmates' standards, as soon as he'd established that he wasn't to be messed with, he began looking out for others. Smaller, less robust or strong, he protected so many that word went out in the prison erroneously saying he'd formed his own gang.

Nothing could have been further from the truth. Liam figured out early on that he didn't belong behind bars and that his brief stint with a life of crime would forever be over. He'd used the prison library to learn as much as he could, figuring he might as well better himself. Though that hadn't been his intent, his example had inspired numerous others to do the same. Several men had even thanked him.

That was when he'd gotten the first glimmer of the idea that later became his foundation. Noreen had believed in it—and him—then. Later, he hadn't realized that the thing that defined him would be what broke his marriage apart.

Over the years, Liam's certainty in what he considered his life's work deepened. He believed he'd been put on this earth to do what he did, to help others avoid following the wrong path. Noreen had seen otherwise, claiming he spent too much time at the office and not enough with her. In the ruins of his crumbling marriage, and after his wife's death, the foundation had been what saved him. Even if he'd found himself barely hanging on.

And during the dark days when he'd struggled with

guilt and his certainty had wavered, work had helped him once again find his way. He'd vowed nothing and no one would ever come between him and his charitable foundation ever again. Nor would he subject another woman to the kind of life that had clearly driven Noreen away. No matter how much he might long to.

Being with Ellie made him dangerously close to wanting something he couldn't and wouldn't have. Though he'd been completely up-front like always, and she'd agreed, he hadn't expected the emotions that accompanied the physical craving.

It was too dangerous. Yet he couldn't make himself stay away. It wasn't only the fact that until Aliana Martin was found Ellie's life was in danger, but the reality that his life had begun to feel dull and gray when she wasn't around.

He took several deep breaths before he felt composed enough to leave the bathroom. Checking his watch, he realized he'd spent quite a few minutes in there, lost in thought. After one last check in the mirror, satisfied he appeared composed and normal, he stepped out into the living room.

Looking around, he didn't see Ellie anywhere in the small apartment. His heart skipped a beat. Had Aliana somehow managed to get to her during the few minutes he'd been in the other room?

But wait. He'd heard no sign of a struggle. Ellie would have screamed or called for him. He checked out her bedroom again, went back to the living room and headed into the kitchen. There, he found a note propped up on the counter.

I went for a walk, the note read. *Needed to get some*

*air and clear my head. Please lock the door on the way
out. Hopefully, the bottom lock will be enough to keep
anyone from breaking in. I'll talk to you later. Ellie.*

Stunned, he read it again. What the hell? Earlier,
they'd discussed heading to Central Park together. Now
she'd gone out without him, leaving him alone in her
apartment. What if Aliana was watching her, waiting
for her? Ellie could be in danger and not even realize it.

Damn it. Heart pounding, he tried to figure out what
to do.

Though his first instinct was to go after her, he took
a minute to get a grip on his emotions. As he was trying to decide his plan of action, the front door burst
open. Ellie rushed into the room and stood facing him,
chest heaving.

"I'm glad I caught you before you left," she huffed,
as if she hadn't just run out on him. "I was on my way
out to walk when a brilliant thought occurred to me. I
have to share it with you and see what you think."

Bemused and not sure how he was supposed to react,
he went with the flow and nodded. "What is it?"

"I've figured out how we can grab Aliana," she said,
her dark eyes sparkling with excitement. "I want to set
a trap. She won't be able to resist it and we'll have her."

Even more cautious now, he crossed his arms. "A
trap? Using what for bait?"

"Me!" she replied, confirming his worst suspicion.

"But—"

She waved away his attempt to protest.

"Who better? If she wants me so badly, then let her
come to get me. This time, we'll be ready for her and we
can grab her."

Resisting the urge to groan out loud, he shook his head instead. "That's too dangerous. You can't seriously want to put yourself at risk like that."

He'd known her long enough to recognize the stubborn set of her chin.

"I don't know," she admitted. "This whole situation has really got me shook up. This isn't like me. I'm tired of jumping at every sound. I want to get her on my terms, not hers. You never know, maybe we can settle this once and for all."

"By letting her kill you?" The terror that rose up in his throat stunned him with its force. "Absolutely not."

"Liam, I'm not asking your permission," she said, her eyes narrowed. "I'm inviting you to help me. That's your choice, but either way, that's my plan. I'm going to do this with or without you."

She meant every word, he could tell. Though he'd only been reacquainted with Ellie a relatively short time, he knew her well enough to read the determination plain in her beautiful face.

Instead of arguing, he decided to appeal to her logic. "Say you are able to do this," he said. "If you manage to lure her into making her move, and outsmart her, managing to grab her without getting yourself hurt or killed, then what?"

"I'm not sure I follow," she replied. "What do you mean?"

"You can't arrest her since a) you're not a police officer and b) you don't have enough proof to bring up charges if you did. Say you get her and somehow subdue her. What's your plan after that?"

"I want to ask her to tell me the truth," she said.

"About all of it. I want to know why she disappeared like she did sixteen years ago. Why she broke her parents' and her best friend's heart." She took a deep breath before continuing. "And of course, I'd like her to tell me why, ever since I spotted her, she's been trying to kill me."

Though he wasn't sure whether to laugh or to cry, he waited a moment for her to hear her own words. The moment her expression changed, he realized she had.

"Damn," she muttered, dropping into one of her living room chairs. "It sounded better inside my head."

"I'm sure it did," he responded, his voice as dry as his throat. Relief made him slightly unsteady, though he knew better than to express this to her. Still, he had to know why she'd decided to bug out on him.

"Ellie, why'd you disappear earlier?" he asked.

Her gaze skittered away. "I wanted to go for a walk," she replied. "Get my thoughts together." She hesitated. "I just needed some time away from you."

Stung, he nodded. "You could have just asked me to leave."

When she raised her eyes to his, the conflict in her expression made him freeze.

"Liam, I like you a lot," she began. "But I think we've been spending too much time together, and it'd be best if—"

Ignoring a sharp stab of terror, he interrupted her. "Are you ending things with me?"

When she looked away, he had his answer.

"No need," he said, his tone as glib as he could manage. "We were only friends with benefits, Ellie. Nothing more. I completely understand if you don't want to continue with our arrangement. No harm, no foul."

Then, before she could see the pain all of this caused him, he strode to the door. "No need to see me out."

Not until he reached the sidewalk, walking fast and furious, did he allow himself to give in to the rush of emotion. He should have asked why, he realized. Though if he'd done so, she might have understood that his feelings had moved far past the friends with benefits stage. Way past. Already.

In fact, he felt as if his heart had been broken. After worrying about that possibility in the future, how could it have come to pass right now? They'd made no promises, no commitments, so how could he feel absolutely gutted? How?

He'd gone two blocks before he slowed his pace. Digging out his phone, he couldn't stop himself from checking for a text from her. But there was nothing. She'd really meant it.

Lost didn't even begin to describe how he felt.

Chapter 11

Ellie stared at the closed door, almost as if she thought he'd change his mind and open it. While she hadn't expected him to storm out, she guessed she couldn't blame him. After all, she'd taken off in a blind panic and left him alone in her apartment with no explanation. And then she'd told him she thought they might be seeing too much of each other. How else had she expected him to take it?

It had been the absolute right thing to do, but then why did it hurt so much? She'd only reconnected with Liam a few days ago. How had he come to mean so much to her so quickly?

Instead of giving in to the urge to crumple into a puddle of misery and give into weeping, she began pacing her small living room.

What had she done? And how on earth was she going to fix it?

In just a five short days, her life had become such a mess. She knew she'd been acting irrationally ever since her apartment had been broken into. In addition to struggling with her blossoming feelings for Liam, the realization that Aliana might have murdered someone in the past had hit hard. Because of that, she'd had no choice but to finally acknowledge that her childhood best friend actually *was* trying to kill her.

She covered her face with her hands, already missing Liam. He'd understood how difficult it had been for her to come to grips with realizing Aliana—someone she'd thought highly of for the past sixteen years—had never been who Ellie had thought she was. He'd helped her a lot with his presence, holding her and providing both comfort and a welcome distraction. He'd been a good friend—yes, a good friend with benefits, even though she hated that term. Not only was he extremely easy on the eyes, and the best kisser she'd ever known, but he'd seemed to genuinely care for her.

Liam Colton might just be the perfect man. And she'd sent him packing.

While trying to safeguard her heart, she felt as if she'd managed to break it instead. All because she'd been too afraid to face her own, burgeoning feelings for him.

Correction, she reminded herself. She had been afraid he'd do to her exactly what she'd done to him if he learned she'd begun to move way past the "keep things casual" relationship they'd agreed on.

Now what?

Torn, she ached to go after him. Or call him and beg him to come back. But how could she, without revealing how she really felt? Because if she exposed her secret heart, then when he left again, she'd feel even worse.

In the end, she did nothing. Though a walk might have helped, she no longer wanted to go without him.

Too restless to stay still, she continued to wear a path in her rug.

What had she done? Before, her existence might have been a bit sterile, focused on her work, but she'd been fine. She'd had her coworkers, friends and her parents. Sure, she might have fixated a little too much on an old cold case involving her childhood best friend, but she'd done so out of loyalty. Misplaced, clearly. But still.

Shaking her head, she tried to decide what to do now. Mostly, she wanted to go back to bed and crawl underneath the covers. Which wasn't like her at all and conversely, made her want to do the opposite.

Telling herself she wouldn't go after him, she waited a few more minutes to give Liam time to get far enough away. Then, packing a tote with a blanket and bottled water, she headed for the door, determined to take that walk anyway. Even if she did it alone. Times like these made her glad she didn't live close to work, because she knew she'd have ended up there if the lab had been within walking distance. Even on a Saturday.

Instead, she went to Central Park. Spreading her blanket on a sunny, grassy spot, surrounded by other New Yorkers, she sat down. With the sun on her face, she sipped her water and began some serious people watching.

Since it was a beautiful spring day, she had a lot to

choose from. A few people near her had brought their pets, and she enjoyed watching one tall, bearded man play Frisbee with an energetic black-and-white border collie.

People sunbathed, children played tag, and it all should have been enough to lift her out of her mood. But she couldn't help wishing Liam was here by her side. Several times she reached for her phone and almost texted him but stopped herself at the last minute. Intellectually, she knew they both needed space and time to reassess things.

In fact, the longer she thought, the more she realized she would no longer be satisfied with things remaining the way they were between her and Liam. She wanted more. Which she knew would all but guarantee scaring him off. And she'd have made herself vulnerable, only to end up in the exact same position she was now.

"Is this spot taken?" a pleasant, masculine voice asked.

She looked up to see a muscular man with dreads smiling down at her. "What spot?" she asked, glancing around and noticing several vacant places he could sit.

"This one right next to you," he said, a teasing lilt in his deep, rich voice.

"It's fine," she said, waving her hand dismissively. Wishing she'd brought a book, she grabbed her phone instead and began scrolling through social media.

Clearly undeterred, he spread his blanket a few feet away and stretched out. "Beautiful day, isn't it?" he asked.

Barely looking up, she nodded.

"I'm Jonah," he offered.

She couldn't even summon up a smile. Instead of volunteering her own name, she barely glanced at him before returning her attention to her screen.

"I'm just trying to be friendly," he said, his tone a bit more insistent.

"Sorry," she responded brusquely, eying him. "I'm just not in the mood."

Her phone chimed, indicating an incoming call. Eva. Relieved, she looked away from Jonah and answered. "Eva! What's up?"

"I wanted to see if you wanted to get together for dinner tonight. We're meeting at Mudville 9, that sports bar in Tribeca. I know how much you like their wings. Sean wants to meet up and discuss where we are on the Humphrey case."

Ellie's initial rush of pleasure faded. "Don't you people ever go out together and not discuss work?"

"Occasionally," Eva answered cheerfully. "But quite honestly, when we have an active case like this, it gives us an excuse."

"Is everyone else going?" By everyone else, Ellie specifically meant Liam, though she didn't want to ask.

"So far, yes. It'll be fun. What do you say?"

Trying to hedge, Ellie said the first thing that came to mind. "I'm not actually working on the Humphrey case, so I'd likely be a third wheel."

"Nonsense," Eva scoffed. "You know we all enjoy your company. Plus, it'll give you and Liam an excuse to spend more time together. Not that you need one, but still…"

Ellie swallowed. "About that," she began. "Liam and I just decided to take some time apart."

Judging from Eva's silence, Ellie had managed to shock her. When Eva finally spoke again, the enthusiasm in her voice had noticeably dimmed. "I'm sorry," she said. "I didn't know."

"It's okay," Ellie hastened to assure her. "But now you can see why I don't feel it would be a good idea for me to go tonight."

Eva swore. "If Liam wasn't my brother... All right, you're off the hook. You and I still need to get together soon. Maybe for brunch."

"Sounds good." Ending the call, Ellie looked up to see Jonah watching her, his expression now sympathetic. Clearly, he'd listened in on the conversation. How could he not? After all, he'd chosen to sit just a few feet away from her.

"Are you going through a breakup?" he asked, his expression hopeful.

Instead of answering, she pushed to her feet. "Nice to meet you, Jonah. I've got to run." She gathered up her things, ignoring his attempts to get her phone number or give her his.

As she walked off, she gave him a casual wave and a quick, dismissive smile. "Have a great rest of your weekend."

Once that adrenaline rush had faded, she slowed her pace. With all that had been going on lately, she found herself checking behind her constantly, to make sure she wasn't being followed.

Back at her apartment building, when she reached her unit and saw the door still closed and locked, she breathed a sigh of relief. Once inside, she slid the deadbolt into place and looked around. The same. Everything still in place, the apartment spotless, exactly like she'd left it.

She caught herself turning to tell Liam and then realized what she'd done. Which made her swear. All of this hurt more than it should have.

Piddling around the apartment, she went ahead and did meal prep for the next week. With the television on, she watched a couple of her favorite cooking shows even though she couldn't seem to concentrate.

There was nothing left to clean, so she sat down and got caught up on paying her bills. Then she went to the window and peered outside, hating that she was staying inside on such a beautiful afternoon.

As the hour inched closer to dinnertime, she could picture all the Coltons gathered together at Mudville 9. The rustic sports bar had great food. This time, Eva had chosen a place known for its excellent, eclectic menu. Ellie had enjoyed both the hamburgers and the chicken wings. Ellie considered herself a chicken wing connoisseur, and ate them as often as possible, the hotter the better.

Which meant she now craved chicken wings. Maybe she'd stop by Atomic Wings and grab some dinner. Or even better, order delivery.

Except now she wanted Mudville 9's wings. Craved them, actually. She toyed with the idea of simply showing up, greeting the Colton clan like nothing had happened and enjoying a nice meal. Who knows, maybe Liam hadn't gone.

This last thought made her grimace, wondering if she should add delusion to her list of her off behavior.

Naturally, Liam would go, and if she went, everyone would notice how off things were between them.

Liam would hate that. Heck, *she* would hate that. These people might be his family, but they were her coworkers. And friends.

Sitting in her formerly cozy apartment, she couldn't get comfortable. Every little sound made her jump, and she was afraid to walk in front of her windows, just in case Aliana might be out there with a high-powered rifle ready to take her down. She hated that she didn't feel safe in her own home.

Finally, she had to admit Liam had been right. She should have agreed to go with him and stay at his place. In addition to being better protected there, she'd get to enjoy the perks of his luxury apartment.

But she'd already turned him down. And worse, left him with the impression that she didn't want to see him anymore.

Ellie wished she had someone to talk to. A girlfriend, someone other than Eva, whom she could call and discuss these contradictory emotions. But most of the women she'd gone to college with had either moved away or were married and raising children. She'd lost touch with almost all of them and she'd never really minded since she'd chosen to focus on her career.

She and Eva had formed a friendship and occasionally went out for drinks, but she couldn't even begin to discuss her feelings for Liam with his own sister.

Her mother was also out. With her veiled comments and questions every time Ellie went home, wondering if she'd found anyone special yet, Ellie didn't want to start her mother down that path.

Sitting back on her couch, she closed her eyes. A slight sound from outside made her jump. Jittery, inside her own home. She had no idea how she'd sleep tonight. She thought about spending the night at her parents' place, but that would provoke questions she didn't want to answer.

She felt like such an idiot. Worse, she missed Liam.

Getting up, she paced, flinching as someone crashed into a garbage can outside. Ellie had always considered herself a strong, confident woman and now, she'd been reduced to this. Hiding out inside her own apartment, afraid of her own shadow.

Her idea of trapping Aliana began to sound reasonable again, even if Liam thought it wasn't.

Liam again. Never too far from her mind.

There had to be something she could do. She needed to fix this.

Eva made a beeline for Liam the instant he walked into the restaurant. "What did you do?" she hissed, her gaze shooting daggers at him. "I talked to Ellie and she told me you two decided to spend time apart. I just knew you were going to break Ellie's heart."

He shouldn't have been surprised, considering that his sister and Ellie were friends, but he couldn't believe Ellie would have lied about this. Still, the last thing he wanted to do was discuss their relationship with his baby sister.

"It's all good," he said, trying to keep his tone light. "I promise you, there are no broken hearts on either end."

Noticing him, Sean grinned and waved him over.

But when Liam tried to move past Eva, she stepped in front of him, effectively blocking his path.

"Oh, no, you don't," she told him, grabbing his arm. "I need you to tell me exactly what you did."

"Eva, stop." He shook his head. "This is none of your business."

Hearing that, she narrowed her eyes. "You're right," she finally admitted. She let go of him and stepped aside so he could pass.

Nodding to Sean, Liam dropped into one of the empty chairs. Eva sat down next to him, her expression still unsettled. If the others noticing her glaring at him, no one commented.

Once they were all seated at the table, Liam saw most of them already had their drinks in hand. Only he and Eva, clearly the last to arrive, were without. He'd just managed to catch the waiter's eye when Sean glanced around. "Where's Ellie?" he asked. "Eva, I though you invited her."

"I did," Eva replied. Liam caught her eye and gave a slight shake of his head, warning her not to say anything.

"But she declined," Eva continued, giving him the stink eye. "She said she and Liam are taking some time apart."

Hearing his sister say it out loud brought Liam a quick and surprising wave of pain.

"Damn it, Liam." Sean glared at him. Next to him, his fiancée, Orla, put a hand on his arm as if to caution him. "We talked about this. Ellie is not only a valuable member of our team, but she's our friend."

Liam clamped his jaw shut, glaring right back at his

brother. He looked around the table. Everyone was staring at him, his twin with amusement, Orla and Emily with curiosity, and Sean and Eva with outrage. "Fine," he muttered, then raised his voice. "Not that this is any of your concern, but I didn't dump Ellie. She dumped me. There. Are you satisfied? Now can we go back to our evening?"

The waiter appeared just then to take Eva's, then Liam's drink order. Instead of his usual beer, he ordered a double bourbon, straight up.

Due to the silence that had settled over the group, everyone heard his order. Liam dug out his phone, pretending to check emails. Anything would be better than seeing amusement or, heaven forbid, pity, on his family's faces.

The instant the waiter left, everyone started talking at once. Both relieved and perturbed, Liam continued to ignore them, now wishing he'd never come at all.

His drink arrived and Liam took a sip before raising his head to look around the table. Sean and Orla were engaged in a spirited discussion. Likewise, for Liam's twin brother and his fiancée. Only Eva continued to watch him, the earlier anger in her eyes now replaced with what looked suspiciously like pity.

"I'm sorry," she said, touching his arm. "I didn't know."

"It's no big deal," he replied, taking another sip of his bourbon. "We were only involved casually. It's not like we had a relationship or anything."

Despite his words, he suspected his sister saw right through him. He couldn't help but wonder what she thought, since he wasn't even sure how he himself felt.

The waiter appeared again to take their food orders. Since Liam hadn't even picked up his menu, he opened it and quickly scanned for anything that sounded even remotely interesting. Nothing did. Maybe he should just stick with the bourbon.

"Get a burger," Eva suggested, as if she knew. "You can always eat a burger."

He rolled his eyes, but when his turn came, he ordered the burger. And a second bourbon.

"Good choice," Eva said, nodding in approval. "You can't just drink on an empty stomach."

"I can, but I'd prefer not to," he corrected. "I honestly don't know why I'm so shook up about this. It wasn't like Ellie and I had a committed relationship or anything."

"Maybe not, but I could tell how much you liked being around her."

"I do. I did." He made no attempt to hide his misery. "And we had clear rules that we both agreed upon."

Sean stood and waved, grinning broadly. Both Eva and Liam turned to see who he greeted.

Ellie. Smiling and sauntering into the restaurant as if nothing had happened.

Liam's heart dropped to the sole of his boots. Quickly, he turned his attention away from the drop-dead gorgeous woman headed toward them and back to his bourbon.

Luckily, the waiter chose that moment to arrive with another.

"Ellie!" Grinning from ear to ear, Eva stood. "Here, you take my seat. I'll move to the other side of the table."

Liam could tell by the way Ellie briefly faltered that

sitting down next to him was the last thing she wanted to do. But with the entire group's eyes on her, she had no choice.

"Thanks, Eva." Smiling politely, Ellie took a seat. At first, Liam thought she intended to studiously ignore him. She greeted everyone, the tilt of her chin determined as she turned to give Liam a quick glance and a quiet hello.

When the waiter asked if he could take her drink order, she smiled. "I'll have an Allagash White beer and an order of classic wings, buffalo hot."

The waiter grinned. "You've got it," he said.

Now that the initial awkward silence had passed, conversations had started up again at their table. Aware of Eva trying not to conspicuously stare, he turned to Ellie. "What are you doing here?" he asked quietly.

Her smile dimmed, though she continued to hold his gaze. "Eva invited me." She swallowed, before raising her chin and continuing. "And I was hoping to talk to you."

He bit back his first instinctive response, aware it was far too snide. "Talk about what?" he asked instead, taking a deep drink of his bourbon. "I think you pretty much covered it all earlier. No worries." From somewhere, he summoned a smile. "It's all good."

"But it isn't," she replied, covering his hand with hers. "I owe you an apology."

"No apology necessary." Glib. He sounded so glib. "Actually, I completely understand." Sadly, he did. He'd given that *I think we're spending too much time together* speech more times than he could count.

Three servers arrived, bearing trays with all their

food. Somehow, they'd managed to get Ellie's wings out at the same time as everyone else's. Sean, Orla, Eva and Liam had gotten burgers, Cormac and Emily were sharing a large pizza. And Ellie had her wings and her beer.

Silence briefly fell as everyone dug in. Liam took a bite of his burger and chewed, trying not to watch Ellie eat her wings. She ate them with such gusto it fascinated him. After each one, she took a long drink of her beer.

"Want to try one?" she asked, gesturing at her plate. "They're pretty hot."

Realizing he still held his burger, he shook his head. "I'm good, thanks."

Mouth full, she wrinkled her pretty nose and nodded.

Trying to think of anything else to say, he took a bite of his burger, chewing deliberately. When he looked up, he realized everyone else at the table was openly staring. The moment he met each of their gazes, they looked away.

"Nice evening," Ellie said, drawing his attention back to her. His gut clenched as he watched, fascinated, while she licked hot sauce off her fingers. It shouldn't have been erotic, but all he could think about was that tongue on various parts of his body.

Damn.

"It is," he belatedly replied. "A nice evening, that is."

Stilted. Conversation between them had never been this awkward. Though he still wasn't quite sure why she'd decided to come to dinner, he realized he was actually glad she had.

"Listen," he said, leaning closer. "Do you think we could talk after all this is over?"

She raised one perfectly arched brow. "Have you given more thought to my plan to trap Aliana?"

Cormac caught that last bit from across the table. "You have a plan?" he asked, leaning forward. "I'd like to hear it."

Putting his burger down, Liam shook his head. "She wants to use herself as bait to draw Aliana out of hiding."

"And Liam's not a big fan of that idea," Ellie said sweetly.

"I can't blame him," Cormac replied. "That sounds dangerous. Especially since Aliana has made several attempts to kill you already. I think you should lie low and wait it out. She'll make a mistake and we'll get her then."

About to reach for another chicken wing, Ellie eyed him. "Did Liam tell you she broke into my apartment? She tore the place apart and stole my laptop and a file folder I'd been keeping full of information about her case."

"Yikes." Cormac looked at Liam. "Bro. Why don't you help her move over to your place?"

Now everyone else at the table had stopped their own conversations and were openly listening.

"I did," Liam said, as quietly as possible. Then, because he didn't want to rehash the rest of his and Ellie's conversation in front of his entire family, he pushed back his chair. "Excuse me," he said, glancing around the table at everyone except Ellie. "I need to go. Sean, let me know how much I owe and I'll Venmo you the money."

He strode toward the exit, not waiting on a reply.

"Wait up." Sean caught up with him outside. "What the hell was *that* all about?"

"Damned if I know. For as long as I live, I'll never understand women," Liam replied, shaking his head. "First, she tells me she thinks we're seeing too much of each other, and then she breezes in tonight like that conversation never happened."

"Maybe she regrets it?" Sean offered, his eyes twinkling, apparently amused at his younger brother's discomfort. "Did she say anything about wanting to talk to you later?"

Frustrated, Liam scowled. "Maybe. And I'm done talking about this. You have a good evening."

Sean opened his mouth to speak, but then something behind Liam caught his attention. "I will. And good luck," he muttered, grinning. "Hey, Ellie. Liam and I were just talking about you."

"I bet you were." She smiled back at Sean before turning to Liam. "Do you have a minute? I was hoping we could talk."

It took every ounce of resolve he possessed to not to walk away. "About what?" he asked. "I think you've already made yourself clear."

"In private," she said, glancing at Sean. Taking the hint, Sean beat a hasty retreat.

Once he'd gone, Ellie raised her chin and met Liam's gaze. "I got scared," she said, her voice quiet. "I'm the sort of person who thrives with a routine and well… nothing's been normal since all this started. Then when you suggested I come stay with you…"

She'd panicked, he thought, crossing his arms. Definitely relatable. But she'd also taken it out on him. No way was he letting her off easy. "What do you want, Ellie?"

"Two things," she replied. "I want to apologize. And second, I'd like to take you up on your offer to let me stay at your place."

Stunned, he stared. At that moment, she could have knocked him over with a feather. "What?" he managed.

"I thought about everything you said about Aliana escalating things. We see that a lot in CSI. If she does that, I won't feel safe in my apartment. Your place is definitely a lot safer."

Not sure what to say, he settled on nodding.

"And it'll be a bonus having you there to protect me if something happens."

Something warm bloomed in his chest at that.

"I only have one condition," she continued, her tone sweet. "I'll be there strictly as a friend. Nothing more, no benefits. Just friends."

Again, he managed to nod, hating the way she could twist up his insides without even trying. "When?" he asked.

"How about now?" she answered, surprising him again. "Let's go by my place so I can grab some things and then I can get settled in at yours. In the guest bedroom," she clarified.

He wasn't sure whether to laugh or to cry. "Sounds good."

Linking her arm in his, she smiled up at him. "And perhaps we can revisit my idea of trying to trap Aliana."

"Absolutely not."

"I kind of expected that." She patted his arm. "But maybe you should hear me out."

Glancing down at her, he thought she might just be the most beautiful woman he'd ever known. "How about we deal with one thing at a time? Let's go get your stuff and get you settled. We can discuss this another time."

With another smile, she nodded. "Sounds like a deal."

Blinking, he wondered how she couldn't notice the way his heart skipped a beat at the sight of that smile. "I was just about to call a cab," he told her. "Let's go to my place, grab my car and take it to yours, so you can pack whatever you need.

"Sounds great." She leaned into him for a second, bringing with her a trace of her scent.

Damn. He wondered how he'd survive with her in close proximity for a week or two. Had she really meant the no sex thing?

He guessed he'd find out soon enough

Chapter 12

To Ellie's surprise, gathering up a week's worth of clothing, jewelry and makeup with Liam waiting didn't feel even the slightest bit awkward. Instead, she had to tamp down her jumbled emotions. Just the idea of getting to use that rooftop garden brought her a sense of peace. Sharing space with Liam would also be... different, to say the least. And the fact that Aliana wouldn't be able to get to her while she stayed there was the icing on the cake.

Until then, she couldn't keep from constantly checking over her shoulder as she made several trips from her apartment to his vehicle parked in the street below.

Finally, she was done. Now that they had his car all loaded up, she got inside and buckled up. He did the same, glancing sideways at her. "Are you all good?" he asked.

Meeting his gaze, she nodded. "I think so. At least no one has shot at us this time."

He grimaced as he started the engine. "Yet. Let's not tempt fate."

Despite everything, this comment made her laugh. "Agreed."

As they made their way in the ever-present traffic, she noticed Liam continually checked his rearview mirror to make sure they weren't being followed. This not only made her feel even safer, but validated that her earlier fears were not mere paranoia.

Though she tried to relax, she couldn't. Not until they were safely inside his place. By the time he pulled into his parking garage, she let out her breath. "I hate this."

He glanced at her, his mouth curved in a teasing smile.

"Hate what? The parking garage?"

This coaxed a reluctant smile from her. "No," she answered. "Having to constantly check over my shoulder."

"I get that." He squeezed her shoulder. "Unfortunately, it's going to be that way until she is caught."

"I know." Though she didn't say it again, the idea of somehow trapping Aliana grew more and more appealing. At least that would finally make all this insanity stop.

Blinking, she shook her head. Right now, she needed to focus on what actually *was* under her control. Moving herself into her temporary lodgings.

It took two trips, but they managed to get all her clothing and toiletries inside. The guest bedroom was twice the size of Ellie's at home and boasted a huge walk-in closet.

She eyed the plush white and purple bedding, the queen size bed and matching nightstand and dresser. "It's really beautiful. Thank you for letting me use it."

This time, he didn't look away. Instead, he held her gaze, his own warm. "I'll enjoy having you here." He cleared his throat. "Anything to keep you safe."

Heart in her throat, she swallowed and looked away. "I really appreciate it," she replied. For the first time, she wondered how being in such close proximity to his sexy self would affect her decision to keep from jumping his bones.

Somehow, she managed.

Over the next couple of days, they fell into a comfortable routine, almost as if they'd always been roommates. They even worked out together. The act of watching Liam's muscular body glistening with sweat while he lifted weights was a more powerful aphrodisiac than Ellie could have ever imagined. If Liam thought the same thing about her, he never revealed it. To her mingled relief and disappointment, he maintained a hands-off approach, exactly as she'd asked. At least for her, this meant a constant sexual tension simmered underneath the surface. Her entire body lit on fire, blood humming, when he merely walked into the room, though she felt quite sure she kept this hidden from him.

At night was the worst. As she lay alone in that luxurious bed, aware he did the same in his own room down the hall, all she could think of was how badly she wanted him next to her. Twice, she'd actually gotten up in the middle of the night, burning with desire, intent on heading down the hall to his room. Both times, she'd managed to stop herself before making it to his room.

After all, she'd been the one to insist on these new rules, even if she did kind of regret it now.

With the ever-present need inside her, she couldn't help but wonder if he struggled as much as she, but if he did, he kept everything well concealed. Always friendly, he kept his distance without making her feel as if he was avoiding her.

She both hated it and loved it. More proof that she'd become a complete mess. Still, she enjoyed the patio area as much as she'd thought she would. She even found herself leaving work at normal quitting time, just so she could get up there, pour herself a glass of Pinot Noir and enjoy the sun setting over the city. Watching the lights come on as the sky darkened had become one of her favorite parts of her day.

Leaving her apartment to stay at Liam's, while hopefully confusing Aliana, in the end felt like a good thing. Ellie enjoyed having the run of the luxurious dwelling, which had begun to feel more and more familiar. Liam often came home late, which gave her the solitude she required after a long day at the lab interacting with people.

The first time he walked in the door at nine, he apologized profusely. She let him finish, and then reminded him she didn't need to be treated like a guest, and they'd both agreed to live their lives the same way they had before.

Staring at her, surprise and relief flickered across his handsome face. "Thank you," he said simply, before turning to make his way to his room to change.

Heart in her throat, she watched him go, her knees so weak she had to sit. Blindsided, she realized for the first time that she could actually imagine a life with this man. Even worse, she couldn't picture a life without him.

Eva showed up at the lab at lunchtime. She strolled into Ellie's office, wearing a pretty floral dress instead of her NYPD uniform. "It's my day off," she announced cheerfully. "And I thought I'd stop by and see if you wanted to go have lunch."

Glancing at the pile of reports on her desk, Ellie nodded. "I would love to. I really need to get out of here."

"I thought you might." Eva gave her a knowing grin. "Come on. There's a new sushi place that's not far from here. I've heard good things."

The idea of eating sushi, normally one of her favorites, made Ellie's stomach turn. She'd been feeling queasy all morning. At least enough time had passed that she knew it wasn't related to her having been poisoned. "I can't do sushi," she admitted. "Not today, at least. How about we grab something else?"

"Like what?"

"I can always eat a salad," Ellie said. "And the deli down the street makes a killer Reuben sandwich."

"Are you sure?" Eva regarded her dubiously. "You are the only other person I know who loves sushi as much as I do."

Briefly, Ellie considered telling her friend the truth—that she didn't want to venture too far from the lab in case Aliana might be lurking somewhere. In the end, she didn't, mainly because she didn't want Eva knowing how anxious she'd become. "I'm sure," she said instead. "I can't take too long a lunch break today anyway, so the closer the better."

"Fine." Eva sighed and capitulated. "Let's go. It's a beautiful day, so maybe we can take our sandwiches and eat in the park."

Though even considering this idea made Ellie break out into a cold sweat, she nodded. As she got up to go, a wave of fear hit her, so strong her knees buckled.

"Are you okay?" Eva peered at her. "You looked like you were about to pass out for a second."

Torn between determination to go and to remain in the relative safety of the lab, Ellie summoned up a smile. Damned if she'd let Aliana win. "I'm fine. I haven't been feeling too great today, but I'm sure a hot sandwich will go a long way toward helping with that."

Outside, the warm breeze ruffled her hair. "You're right," she told Eva. "It is a beautiful day. Maybe we can sit in the park and eat after all." She even had a particular bench in mind, as long as it wasn't occupied. It backed up to a stone wall and had a clear view of anyone coming or going. Even though her anxiety had ratcheted up her heart rate, she was determined to follow through with the plan.

At the deli, they got their sandwiches and drinks and after paying, turned to go. Another wave of dizziness hit Ellie, so strongly she had to grasp the back of a chair to orient herself.

"You know what?" she said, as Eva watched with a concerned expression. "How about we just eat here? I'm really not feeling up for a long walk."

"Of course." Dropping into an empty seat, Eva waited for Ellie to do the same. "Maybe you should take the rest of the day off. Go home and get some rest. I can see you safely to your apartment if you'd like."

The chair opposite Eva would have Ellie sitting with her back to the door, which wouldn't work. Instead, she went around the table and sat next to Eva. "I like being able to watch the door," she explained.

Eva raised an eyebrow. "So do I. You're starting to think like a cop."

"Maybe I am," Ellie replied. She took a sip of her drink and took her time opening her sandwich. As the scent of pastrami and sauerkraut hit her, her stomach roiled. "You know what? Maybe you're right. I do feel like I might be coming down with something. I'm thinking I should go home and rest."

"I'll walk you there," Eva offered.

"I appreciate that, but it's not necessary. I don't want to mess up your day off."

"Seriously." Eva rolled her eyes. "I don't mind. My only plan for today is to be outside and enjoy the fabulous spring weather."

Taking a tiny bite of her Reuben, Ellie managed to chew and swallow. "The thing is, I'm not actually staying at my place. Your brother has been kind enough to let me use his guest bedroom."

Eyes wide, Eva froze midchew. Slowly, she put her sandwich down on the wrapper and took a sip from her drink. "Say that again?" she asked.

"It's not a big deal," Ellie assured her. "After the break-in, I didn't feel safe, so Liam offered his place."

"Not. A. Big. Deal. If you believe that, then you don't really know my brother."

Ellie ignored the warm glow that coursed through her at Eva's words. Instead of answering, she took another bite of her lunch. Her stomach appeared to finally be settling down, and she was able to eat the rest of her meal without incident. "I think I'm feeling better," she announced. "Maybe I just needed to eat something."

Finishing up her own lunch, Eva eyed her. "Does that mean you're going back to work after all?"

"It does." Ellie checked her watch. "Which is probably a good thing, since I'm swamped. I'd better be getting back."

Eva stood. "All right. But you and I need to get together for drinks soon and talk. I have plans tonight, but soon. I definitely want to hear more about your current living situation."

"There's nothing to tell," Ellie replied. "But yes, I'd love to meet up after work for drinks. I'll text you."

"You do that."

Once she returned to the lab, Ellie got busy playing catch-up. Whatever stomach bug had plagued her earlier, appeared to have gone. When quitting time rolled around, she tidied her desk, eager to get back to Liam's apartment and that marvelous patio.

The next morning, Ellie woke up feeling slightly queasy. Remnants of whatever she'd had the day before? Instead of coffee, she grabbed a ginger ale to settle her stomach. Liam was running behind, so they barely had a chance to talk before it was time to head out the door.

Husting down the sidewalk side by side, Ellie couldn't help but steal glances at Liam. How he could manage to look so good first thing in the morning would always been one of life's better mysteries. Always on alert, trying to keep tabs on her surroundings, she was grateful for his presence, even when he appeared wrapped up in his own thoughts like this morning.

Though they walked to the same subway station together, they took different trains. Liam's came a few minutes before hers, so she always waved and watched him from the platform. As usual, he grinned and waved back before his train left.

Still smiling happily, she stood in the crowd waiting for hers to pull in. As usual, she continually searched faces, looking for Aliana and glancing behind her. As she heard the rumble of the approaching train, she got ready, bracing herself for the inevitable surge of people all eager to board.

Someone shoved her. Hard enough to push her forward, stumbling toward the edge of the platform and the train tracks below. A man grabbed her at the last moment, yanking her back from certain death and flinging her onto her behind.

Gasping for air, she tried to process what had just happened. The train arrived and the morning commuters surged forward, moving around her. She tried to find her rescuer, but couldn't, nor could she locate whoever had pushed her.

She got to her feet, realizing she'd miss her train if she didn't board now. Somehow, she got on. Grabbed a handrail and held on, despite the tremors that shook her body. In typical New Yorker fashion, no one noticed or if they did, they ignored her.

When she reached her stop, she got off, stumbling slightly. Feeling strangely detached, she kept going, amazed that her legs managed to move forward. All the way to the lab she kept her shoulders back, her chin up and stared straight ahead.

Only when she'd opened the door and stood inside

her lobby did she realize her slacks were torn and her knees bloody.

"Are you okay?" Mary, one of the techs, walked in and stopped, staring at her. "You look like you got run over by a bus."

"That bad?" Ellie attempted a wry smile, but as she turned to make her way toward the bathroom to see for herself, her legs buckled. Grabbing onto the edge of the reception desk just in time, she caught herself.

"Ellie? Should I call for help?"

"I'm fine." Waving Mary off, Ellie staggered into the bathroom. She barely made it inside and locked the door before she let the tears rip. Great, heaving sobs that made her clasp her hand over her mouth to keep from being heard.

Doubled over, clutching her stomach with her other hand, she let it all out. The trauma over what had almost just happened to her. The horror of being stalked, of having someone try to kill her not once, but four times. And the awful, unthinkable mess her once normal life had become.

"Ellie?" Mary tapped on the door. "Are you sure you're okay? Do you want me to call someone?"

"I'm fine," Ellie managed, though she knew she sounded anything but. The only person she wanted right now was Liam.

Hands still trembling, she dug out her phone.

"You did *what*?" The outrage in Sean's voice matched the anger in his eyes. He pushed to his feet, glaring.

"I didn't *do* anything," Liam replied, tamping his own temper down as he faced his older brother. "Ellie was having some problems with staying in her own apartment, so she's at my place. Temporarily," he added, almost as an afterthought.

Arms crossed, Sean regarded him with narrowed eyes. "That still sounds an awful lot like saying you two have moved in together."

"Not hardly," Liam scoffed. "For one thing, she's staying in my guest bedroom. For another, we've both agreed we're only friends. At least while she's there."

For whatever reason, this comment made Sean laugh. Not sure what to make of that, Liam simply waited.

"Must be rough," Sean finally managed, once he'd finished laughing. "But seriously, bruh. Do you expect me to believe that?"

"I don't really care what you believe," Liam replied. Before he could say anything else, his phone rang. About to let it go to voicemail, he glanced at it. When he saw Ellie's name on the screen, he held up a finger at Sean and went ahead and answered.

"Ellie," he began. And then she started sobbing, trying to talk while she cried. He could barely make out what she was trying to say. "Slow down," he urged. "Take a deep breath. I'm having trouble understanding you. What happened?"

It took a few seconds, but she finally caught her breath enough to be able to speak. "She pushed me onto the train tracks," she said. "Or tried to. A man grabbed me right before I went over. I was almost killed."

Liam swore. Through all of this insanity with Aliana, he'd worked hard to stay calm, cool and collected. From his time behind bars, he knew all too well how allowing emotions to take over increased vulnerability.

But this… He didn't know how he'd continue to live if that woman harmed a single hair on Ellie's head. A growl started low in his throat. Sean pushed to his feet at the sound, eying Liam.

"Enough is enough," Liam declared, fury simmering in his blood, mingling with stark, sheer terror. "Where are you?"

"At the lab," she managed. "Trying really hard to keep it together. I'm not doing so well."

"Don't move. I'll be there as soon as I can. I'm at the precinct and I'm on my way."

"Thank you." Her muffled voice made him think she'd started crying again, which ripped out his soul.

Jaw set, he slid his phone back into his pocket. "I've got to go," he told Sean. "Aliana tried to push Ellie in front of the train."

Sean simply nodded, his expression grim. To his credit, he didn't ask a single one of the questions no doubt swirling around in his police detective brain. "Go," he urged. And then, as Liam started for the door, Sean hollered after him. "Call me if you need any help."

The quickest way to get to the lab would be by taxi, if Liam could manage to flag one down. He lucked out, as one happened to be dropping someone off at the precinct. After hopping in, he gave the driver the lab's address and sat back. Jittery, he caught himself jiggling his leg, a bad habit he'd managed to kick back when he'd first gone to prison. Any sign of weakness there had indicated vulnerability, which could make one's life hell.

They pulled up in front of the lab in record time, mostly because traffic seemed to magically part in front of him. He tossed the cabbie the fare and a generous tip, muttering that he could keep the change, before rushing into the building.

The receptionist nodded when she saw them gave him a relieved smile and buzzed him back. He took off down the hall at a jog.

When he reached Ellie's office and knocked on her door, he waited, heart thumping in his chest.

"Come in," she said, her voice muffled.

He stepped inside and closed the door behind him, ready to take her into his arms and comfort her for as long as she needed.

Instead, she continued sitting behind her desk, making no move to meet him halfway. She glared at him instead. Her eyes were red and swollen, but free of tears.

"You seem…better," he said, jamming his hands into his pockets since he wasn't sure now what to do with them.

"Better?" Her bitter bark of laughter contained no humor. "I don't know about that. What I do know is this. I've had it. Enough is enough. I refuse to sit still and do nothing while this woman tries to kill me."

Drumming her fingers on her desk, she took a deep breath before continuing. "Clearly, Aliana is relentless. She's not going to stop. I'm still trying to process the fact that she almost got me killed by pushing me in front of the train this morning. I guess I should consider myself lucky she didn't stab me in the back."

Slowly, he nodded, briefly closing his eyes against the horror that image brought. When he opened them again, Ellie waited, glaring at him.

"I'm going on the offensive," she declared, her hard look daring him to contradict her. "Like I wanted to before. I'm going to set a trap so we can capture her. I'm fine with being the bait."

Chest tight, Liam swallowed. "If you're set on this plan, we need to call Sean, bring him in on this. The police should be the ones to set this all up. They have more experience in things like this."

"Maybe so," she acknowledged. "But there's only one person who can act as bait. Me. Since Aliana wants me dead so badly, it's got to be me."

A muscle worked in his jaw. Even the thought of Ellie getting hurt brought a swift, stabbing pain. "All right. Let's talk about some scenarios," he said, his voice clipped. "Because she's shot at you, attempted to poison you, broken into your apartment and now tried to push you in front of the train. What next? Stab you, like you mentioned?"

This made her wince. "Maybe so," she admitted, sagging back into her chair as if all the air had gone out from her. "I just wish I knew her motive. That would help."

"It would," he agreed. "And you're right, it is time to become proactive before she finally succeeds in killing you. But you know as well as I do that we've got to make a plan. You work in crime scene investigation. You know full well how awful some of these murderers can be."

Slowly, she nodded. "I do. Sure, we'll talk to Sean. And Eva. But I want you to know there's zero chance I'm going to let them talk me out of this. They have no idea what it's like to feel like this. I'm...prey."

The slight tremor in her voice made him ache to hold her. But because she didn't appear to want that kind of comfort right now, he merely nodded. If she simply needed him to listen, then that's what he'd do.

"I want my life back, Liam." She brushed a lock of hair away from her face. "While I appreciate you letting me stay at your place more than I can express, this is my city. I grew up here, I've never wanted to live anywhere else, and I absolutely despise the way Aliana is making me afraid to go anywhere or do anything. I went to lunch with Eva yesterday and every little sound had me jumping out of my skin."

"You did? That explains the three missed calls and the text ordering me to call her. I'm guessing you told her you were staying at my place."

Her gaze never leaving his face, she slowly nodded. "I made it clear I was staying in your guest bedroom. And I think I managed to keep the fact that I'm a nervous wreck hidden from her."

A nervous wreck? "I knew you were on edge," he said. "But you never let on that it was that bad."

"I'm telling you now. And today proved it's got to end. Now. I'm not waiting around anymore. She's going down."

He didn't like it, but he could see he had no choice. "All right. What's your plan?"

"I don't actually have one yet," she admitted. "But I will. Clearly, she's watching me. If I make myself available and the NYPD stations several undercover cops near me, they can grab her the second she makes a move."

"Can they?" He knew he didn't sound convinced. "What if they can't get to her in time? It doesn't take long for someone to stab you. You could be dead before they grab her."

"I'll wear body armor," she said, clearly improvising. "Every time I'm out on the street."

A begrudging approval made him nod. "That might work. Except your head would be unprotected. If she decided to take you out with a gun, she could shoot you in the head."

"We could argue and nitpick this all day," she pointed out, crossing her arms. "But I'm sick of feeling like a fugitive in my own city. I'm not used to this, being afraid of my own shadow. It has to end."

"I get that," he said. "But I can't help but worry you'll get hurt." Maybe even killed, though he didn't say that out loud.

She shrugged. "Damned if I do and damned if I don't."

Even thinking about what could happen made him want to grab her and spirit her away to somewhere private where Aliana could never find her. He tried to lighten the mood. "Are you that tired of staying at my place?"

This coaxed a reluctant smile from her. "That's not it at all and you know it."

"What about a vacation?" He eyed her, keeping his voice as casual as his posture. "Do you have any time you could take off, maybe go somewhere?"

"A vacation?" The frown came back. "With you?"

"Sure, why not? My treat. Anywhere you want to go."

"Wow." She whistled. "You must really hate the idea of me helping capture Aliana."

"I do," he admitted. "But that's not the only reason I

think getting out of town would be a good idea. You've been through a hell of a lot lately. You could use some time to recharge."

Still regarding him dubiously, she shook her head. "I don't know…"

"Think about it. Lying by a pool in the warm sun somewhere, with an umbrella drink in your hand. Gourmet meals, white sand beaches and nothing to worry about except making sure you don't wake up with a hangover."

"You should work for a travel company," she told him. "And while that admittedly does sound heavenly, I'm not the kind of person who runs away from their problems."

Begrudgingly, he had to give her props for that. Still, he'd tried.

"I might take you up on that offer, *after* all this is over," she said. "I'm thinking Turks and Caicos."

"You got it," he replied, laughing a little. "Just hit me up with some dates and I'll book the tickets."

"I'll hold you to that." Gaze serious, she sighed. "I should only be a few more minutes before I'm ready to go."

Watching her, with her silky curtain of dark hair falling down over her face, he couldn't help thinking she was the most beautiful woman he'd ever met. "Take your time," he said, not telling her he could sit and watch her for hours.

Chapter 13

Most of what Ellie had left on her desk would qualify as busy work. She went ahead and did it anyway, partly because she like things nice and tidy when she returned to work in the morning, and partly because she was once again nervous about going outside. She absolutely despised feeling that way. Yet another reason to get Aliana into police custody.

Liam patiently stayed until she was ready to go home, his large presence reassuring. Ellie appreciated that more than she could express. These days, she felt like she walked a thin tightrope between normalcy and something out of a thriller movie. She could even imagine the headlines—*Woman Who Vanished Sixteen Years Ago Returns to Kill Former Best Friend*.

The thought sent a shiver up her spine. Once again,

she felt queasy, no doubt due to her skyrocketing anxiety. Maybe a vacation wouldn't be a bad idea after all.

Finally, she'd done all she could do. With her desk organized, everything ready for her to start again the next morning, she took a deep breath. Wiping her hands on the front of her slacks, she stood up.

"Are you ready?" Liam asked, glancing up from the magazine he'd been leafing through while he waited.

Though it wasn't yet five, she nodded, placing a hand on her stomach. "I haven't been able to concentrate much on work today. All this stress is giving me a stomachache."

He slipped his arm around her shoulders and gently tugged her close. "I can imagine. Come on, let's get you home. I foresee a glass of wine on the patio in your future."

With a flash of heat, she realized she wanted more than that. So much more. Leaning into him, inhaling his masculine scent, she figured she'd better use the ride home to talk herself out of jumping his bones.

Instead, as she sat next to him in the car and watched him navigate traffic, she found herself in a state of heightened sensual awareness. Eying his long-fingered, capable hands on the steering wheel, she sighed. Even his bare, muscular arms with their fine dusting of hair sent a quiver of awareness through her.

Dang it. She forced her gaze away from him, trying to concentrate on the noisy traffic outside. Finally, they pulled into his parking garage. The instant he'd parked, she unhooked her seat belt and opened her door. She'd never been so relieved to get out of a car in her entire life.

Together, they walked to the elevator. Once they'd stepped inside and the doors closed, Liam glanced at her. "Are you all right?" he asked. "You seem a little quiet. Is your stomach still bothering you?"

She shook her head. "I'm okay. Just trying to figure something out."

Luckily, he didn't ask her for details. She'd have had a heck of a time trying to explain her inner war over what she wanted to do with him and why she knew she shouldn't.

Inside the apartment, she headed straight to her room and closed the door behind her. The ache of wanting him had only intensified, and she needed to take it down a notch.

Or did she? Slowly, she shook her head. Here she was, staying in a fabulous apartment with the sexiest man she'd ever met, and she'd been deliberately keeping herself shut off from him. No wonder she now felt starving.

Decision made, she turned on her heel and marched back into the living room. Liam still stood where she'd left him, having dropped his keys on the end table. He looked up at her approach, the dazed expression on his face catching at her heart.

"I want you," she said, speaking the truth before she lost her nerve. "I really, really want you."

He made a sound; part passion and part something else, she wasn't sure what. Crossing the space between them, he pulled her to him and slanted his lips over hers. This! She kissed him back in kind, hungry and lost and needing this more than she'd ever needed anything.

Tongue to tongue, on fire, they managed to strip off

their clothes while still locked together. He backed her against the wall and took her standing up, slipping deep inside of her with one fluid thrust.

She met him push for push, her body pulsing, alive for what felt like the first time in forever.

Only when he pulled out of her with a tortured groan, did she realize he hadn't used a condom.

"I need a minute," he rasped. With his back to her, he snatched his jeans up off the floor and fumbled in the pocket. When he located one, he struggled with getting the wrapper off.

"Let me," she offered softly, taking the packet out of his hand. Easing the condom over his hard and swollen body was one of the most sensual things she'd ever experienced.

And when he entered her again, even with that slight barrier between their bodies, she felt that same deep connection. He filled her, both physically and mentally, in a way no one else ever had.

The first time, rough and wild and mindless, was nothing but raw, unfettered passion. Later, when she woke up beside him in his bed, they made love again, taking it slow and exploring each other's bodies. She wondered how she'd ever lived without him and the clarity of that thought brought a stab of pain. Because she knew, when all this was over, she'd have to learn to live her life alone again. Liam had made it clear he wasn't looking for a relationship. And she'd gladly done the same, because at that time she wasn't. She simply hadn't realized how this man would manage to work his way deep inside her heart.

Since she knew she couldn't share her feelings with

him, she bit back words of endearment, though they echoed silently in her head. He made her feel as if they were meant to be together. No other man had ever been able to touch her the way Liam did, both physically and inside her heart.

How ironic it was that Aliana had indirectly been responsible for bringing Liam back into Ellie's life. Especially since back in the day, Aliana had made it clear she despised him. Her scathing remarks and snarky comments had bothered sixteen-year-old Ellie, but not enough to make her give him up. She'd been way too into him to do that.

They'd been polar opposites back in high school. Liam had been the quintessential bad boy, while wholesome, innocent Ellie had been more like the squeakyclean academic. Yet somehow, they'd clicked. For two entire years, Liam had treated Ellie with respectful tenderness while he'd unleashed a wild side she hadn't even realized she possessed.

She loved him then, worried over him and his stubborn insistence on running with a bad crowd. At first, the trouble he'd gotten into had been minor. When Ellie's mother had caught wind of it, she'd stopped short of forbidding her daughter to see him. Instead, she'd sat Ellie down for a heart-to-heart, warned her to be careful and left it at that.

In the end, Liam had gotten into the kind of trouble that had taken him away from her. A few months after graduation, when Ellie was reviewing college offers, Liam had gotten caught with an expensive stolen car. Since he'd turned eighteen a few days before, he'd been arrested, convicted and sent off to prison. When Ellie had tried to go see him, he'd ended things, telling her she'd be better off without him.

Brokenhearted, Ellie had moved on with her life. Time had done as it always did and healed her wounds. She couldn't explain why Liam had been the first person she'd thought to call when she'd seen Aliana after so many years, or why she'd still had his number saved in her phone.

Fate, maybe. No matter the reason, she was glad she'd called him. Even after so long, they still had that same spark between them.

With these thoughts swirling inside, she fell asleep in his bed, with his arms wrapped around her.

A few hours later, she'd awakened. Glancing at him while he slept, she felt her heart expand. She felt at home with him, as if in his arms was exactly where she belonged. In addition to the undeniable heat between them, a kind of comfortable familiarity had slowly blossomed inside of her that until now, she'd tried not to think about, never mind question.

Scary as hell.

But it sure felt…right.

She could easily imagine spending the rest of her life like this, with him by her side. Which was all kinds of wrong, especially since he'd made it abundantly clear that he didn't want anything even remotely permanent. And, until this very moment, neither had she.

Now that she knew she loved him, everything had changed, at least for her. Unsettled, raw, with her heart exposed.

Aching, her eyes filled with tears. She took one more look at his handsome face, features relaxed in slum-

her, and sighed. Then she slid out from underneath the
sheets and slipped away from him, to spend the rest of
the night in her own bed. As if by doing so, she could
at least retain some small piece of her own heart.

Liam woke to an empty bed. Sometime after he'd
fallen asleep, Ellie had gone back to her own room.
Her insistence on not spending the entire night with
him hurt him far more than it should have. Of course,
she had no idea how he felt about her. And he intended
to make sure it stayed that way. He suspected if she
learned the truth, she'd completely shut him out. Especially since they'd agreed on the parameters of their
relationship early on.

A sharp rapping from the other room had him sitting up. What the…?

That kind of insistent knock on his front door could
only be one person. Sean. Liam climbed out of bed,
dragged his hand through his hair, and padded toward
the door. Stifling a yawn, he checked through the peep-
hole.

Yep. Sean. With his fist raised to knock again. And
he hadn't sent his usual text.

Liam opened the door and stepped back. "Have you
lost your mind? It's six thirty in the morning."

"Best time to catch you at home," a feminine voice
drawled as Eva stepped around the corner. Cormac,
looking half-asleep, trailed behind her.

Aware he was about to be ambushed, Liam motioned
them in. "Come on, then. But for God's sake, be quiet.
Ellie's still asleep."

They followed him into the kitchen where blessedly,

they stayed quiet long enough for him to turn the coffee machine on, insert a pod and stick a cup underneath. He kept his back to them, struggling to wake up while his coffee finished brewing. Inhaling the scent, he grabbed the mug and took a tentative sip before remembering his manners. Turning slowly, he eyed his siblings. "Would any of you like me to make you a cup?"

In unison, Sean and Eva held up their to-go cups. "We're good, thanks."

Cormac yawned, covering his mouth with his hand. "Do you have any espresso? I need two or three shots to help me wake up."

Liam shook his head. "Sorry, man. Black coffee is about as strong as it gets around here."

"Fine. I'll take a cup. A large one." Cormac leaned against the wall and closed his eyes, as if he intended to doze standing up. Sadly, Liam could relate.

Once the coffee had finished brewing and Liam had handed the mug to Cormac, he turned to face the others.

"Okay." Liam took another drink of his own coffee. "Now tell me why you're all here."

"I asked them to come," Ellie said, strolling into the kitchen. With her tousled hair, long T-shirt and shorts that showed off her shapely legs, she looked sexy as hell.

Liam's mouth went dry. He caught himself staring before forcing his attention back to his coffee. "Why?" he asked. "Have there been any new developments in Humphrey's case?"

"Not that I know of," Ellie answered, strolling over to make her own cup of coffee. She turned to face them while it brewed. "Liam, I wanted to ask Sean, Cormac and Eva here to discuss my plan to trap Aliana."

Her plan. Damn it. When had she even had time to call anyone?

He managed to suppress his groan, but something must have shown on his face because Sean eyed him. "I take it you're not a fan of this idea?" Sean asked.

"He's not," Ellie replied before Liam could answer. "That's why I texted you all last night. I knew Liam wouldn't like it. But it's not his decision to make."

Eyes still half-closed, Cormac snorted. "She's right, you know."

"I'm aware," Liam said immediately, resisting the urge to glare at his twin. Instead, he sighed. "Why don't we all go into the living room and discuss this?"

They all trooped past him, drinks in hand. Ellie went last, glancing sideways at him and giving him an encouraging and somehow sexy smile. Liam froze, his pulse thundering in his ears.

Damn. The realization hit him like a lightning bolt. He was in love with Ellie Mathers.

Somehow, he managed to compose himself enough to follow the others. He dropped into his favorite chair, struggling to push his swirling emotions out of his mind. He'd have to figure this out later. Right now, he needed to slow his racing heartbeat, take a deep breath and calm himself down before anyone noticed.

Luckily, everyone watched Ellie as she waited for them to get settled. Once everyone had taken a seat, she started talking. "I know I've brought up the idea of trying to set a trap for Aliana multiple times over the last few weeks, but until she nearly succeeded in killing me by pushing me in front of the train, I wasn't really ready."

"But you are now?" Eva asked, clearly intrigued.

"Yes, I am now," Ellie replied. "And that's why I asked you all here. I need your help. Right now, I don't have much of a concrete plan, other than to make myself available for her to attack me."

Immediately, Sean shook his head. "I don't think that's a good idea. Aliana might have been inept and unsuccessful so far with her attempts to take you out, but there's a truth to that old saying *if at first you don't succeed, try and try again.*"

"I don't know," Eva chimed in, sitting on the edge of her chair. "If we made sure she had enough police protection—undercover of course—this might work. Aliana would make her move, and we could take her down."

"Unless she used a gun," Liam interjected. "She could take Ellie out from a distance, without us getting a chance to even get close to her."

"Good point," Sean acknowledged, glancing from Liam to Ellie. "What about body armor?"

"That's what I suggested," Ellie said. "But then Liam pointed out she could still get me in the head."

"Except she appears to be a lousy shot," Eva mused. "At least from what you've told me. Ellie, I get you wanting to be done with this, but maybe you should just wait and let the police do their job."

Ellie started shaking her head before Eva even finished speaking. "I'm done waiting. My life is in shambles, and I'm a mess. This isn't me, and I don't like it. I'll take my chances and hope that we can get her. Because this has to stop."

"I agree." Sean stood. "But we can't go about this

without a solid, workable plan. And I'll have to call in some favors, because I can't realistically use department resources for an off-the-book operation like this."

"Off-the-book?" Ellie asked. "What do you mean? We'd be stopping someone who has repeatedly attempted to kill me."

"Allegedly," Sean pointed out. "You know how this works. Aliana hasn't been charged with any crime."

"Yet." Ellie raised her chin. "But once she tries to get at me in front of witnesses, it'll all be over for her."

"This might just work." Excitement colored Eva's voice. "As long as we hammer out the details."

Feeling outnumbered, Liam glanced at his older brother. Sean shrugged.

Cormac, who'd remained silent through all of this, grimaced. "Damned if you do, and damned if you don't," he muttered.

This made Ellie chuckle. "I said that exact same thing to Liam yesterday," she said. "And that summarizes my situation exactly."

"What do you hope to gain?" Sean asked, directing the question at Ellie.

She stared at him, her expression perplexed. "I thought I made that clear. I want my life back. I'm tired of her trying to kill me. I want to know why. Plus, I'd really like some answers about what happened to her when she disappeared sixteen years ago."

"Me too," Eva chimed in. "Ellie's right. This needs to end. Come on, guys. Let's get serious here. Help us figure out what we're going to do."

"Let me talk to my buddy who works in SWAT,"

Sean said. "He's got a lot more experience at this type of thing. If anyone can come up with a plan, it's him."

Grateful to his brother for buying a little time, Liam exhaled. Maybe he could still talk Ellie out of this.

Ellie considered. "How long will that take? I don't want to drag this out too much longer."

"I'll call him right now," Sean offered, digging out his phone. He scrolled through his contacts and chose one. With his phone to his ear, he waited, and then left a message asking his friend to call him.

"He's probably asleep," Cormac drawled. "Like I was, before you two dragged me out of bed to come over here."

"I forgot about the time," Sean admitted. "I'll make sure to apologize when I talk to him."

Ellie made a face, clearly frustrated. "It doesn't seem like it should be this difficult to come up with a plan. I just need to make myself available, you three stay in the background and watch, and grab her when she comes for me."

"It's never that simple," Sean started to explain. "There are so many things that could go wrong with that scenario. You could get killed, or seriously hurt, and she'd still get away."

Eva nodded. "Sorry, Ell. But I agree. You don't want to put your life in danger. I don't want to lose you."

Relieved, Liam took a deep breath. He looked up and caught Cormac staring at him with a knowing expression, as if he knew Liam's thoughts. "I need more coffee," he said out loud, draining his cup. "I didn't get much sleep last night."

"Me neither," Ellie yawned. Her comment made Eva snicker.

"What?" Ellie asked, apparently oblivious. "What's so funny?"

Eva went over and whispered in her ear. Ellie blinked twice. "You need to get your mind out of the gutter," she said primly.

For whatever reason, this struck Liam as hilarious. Once he stared laughing, Cormac joined in. A moment later, so did Sean and Eva. Finally, Ellie shook her head and smiled too. "Focus, people. I can't believe we can have two police officers and a private investigator and we can't come up with a simple plan to capture Aliana."

She had a point. Even if she'd left him—and herself—out of this list.

"The problem is this," Liam felt compelled to interject, especially since she hadn't asked for his opinion. "Aliana is completely unpredictable. There's no way to even guess what she'll try next."

"I agree," Sean said. "Do you think she is watching you?"

"I don't know," Ellie answered. "Maybe some of the time."

"Obviously, she must be," Cormac pointed out. "How else does she keep turning up where you happen to be?"

Staring at Sean with a stricken expression, Ellie swallowed.

Liam recognized the worry and fear she tried so hard to conceal and ached to take her in his arms and comfort her. Since he couldn't— not with his entire family around—he cleared his throat. "Except not here," he said. "So far, Aliana doesn't appear to have any idea

Ellie has been staying here. And we hope to keep it that way."

Expression relieved, Ellie nodded. "That's right."

"What about the train station?" Cormac asked. "How'd she know where you'd be getting on?"

Ellie considered. "I'm not sure about that. While this isn't too far from my normal route, I'm guessing she just saw me and decided to take the opportunity."

Gaze narrowed, Cormac looked from Liam to Ellie. "Have either of you felt even the slightest suspicion you were being followed?"

"No," Liam and Ellie answered in unison.

"Even when someone shot at your car?"

This time, Liam shrugged. "I did feel like someone might be following us right before then. But we weren't anywhere near here. And after, I made sure we weren't followed. I'm certain Aliana has no idea that Ellie is staying here."

"Does she even know you two are together?" Cormac asked. "I mean now. I'm aware you three were all friends back in high school."

"Would she even recognize you?" Ellie eyed Liam. "You definitely look different than you did back then."

This made him laugh. "I certainly hope so. But to answer your question, Cormac, I don't know. Since she shot at my car, I have to think she does."

"Or she may just know some man is helping me," Ellie added.

Cormac nodded.

"Why would that matter?" Ellie asked. "Even if she recognized Liam, I don't think she has any idea where he lives."

"That's good," Eva said. "I feel better knowing you're safe."

"Relatively," Ellie corrected. "At least when I'm here. But after her trying to push me in front of the train, I feel truly hunted." She glanced at Sean. "I filed a police report. But since no one got a good look at her, I can't even prove it was Aliana."

Sean nodded. "You know, this could be completely random."

Ellie and Eva both made rude noises. Even Liam found himself shaking his head in disbelief. "You know better than that," Liam said.

Sean nodded. "I do. But I had to throw out that possibility. Let me make some phone calls, talk to a few people and I'll get back with you with a plan."

"When?" Ellie wanted to know.

"Hopefully before Monday," Sean replied. "I know that's not as soon as you want, but it's the weekend. I need time to round up these guys."

With a sigh, Ellie nodded. "If I don't hear back from you, I'll follow up with you on Sunday afternoon."

"Sounds good." Sean checked his watch. "I need to run. Eva, Cormac, are you coming with me?"

After his siblings finally left, Liam closed the door behind them, engaged the dead bolt, and sighed. "I sure wish you would have given me a heads-up," he told Ellie. "Even if you had to wake me up to do it."

Her gaze locked on his, she slowly nodded. "You're right. I'm sorry if we ambushed you. I should have told you they were coming over."

Heart in his throat, he couldn't look away. "Ellie, there's something I need to discuss with you."

Before he could continue, her phone rang. "Just one sec," she said, glancing at the screen. "It's the lab. Since we're technically closed on the weekend, this must be important."

He watched as she answered the phone, saw the way her eyes went wide. Still clutching it, she took a staggering step toward him. "Thank you," she managed to grind out, before ending the call. Fumbling with the phone, she nearly dropped it before managing to shove it into her back pocket.

Sensing she might be about to fall, he rushed over, reached out and pulled her into his arms. Trembling, she clung to him, making tiny sounds of anguish.

"What happened?" he asked, smoothing her hair back from her face, aching with love for her.

"One of the other investigators was stabbed," she got out. "Sarah Peterson. Some of us go in and work on the weekends, trying to catch up. Sarah was leaving to go grab something to eat and someone rushed up and stabbed her."

"Where? Is there video footage?" he asked.

"Outside, from the sound of it. So I doubt there's anything on video."

"Did they catch the guy?"

Ellie shook her head. "That's just it. Eyewitnesses who saw it said that the attacker was a woman."

He froze. "Aliana?"

"Yes." Ellie exhaled. "It had to be her. This is all my fault."

"But why would she stab someone else?" he asked. "That makes no sense."

Slowly, Ellie pulled enough out of his arms to look

him in the eye. "Because the woman she stabbed looks a lot like me. Similar build, hair and style. If Aliana only got a quick glance at Sarah, she could easily have mistaken her for me. Which, clearly she did."

"How about Sarah? How is she? Is she...?" he asked.

"They've rushed her into emergency surgery at Langone. I need to go there." Stepping away, she straightened her shoulders. "I have to go change. Will you drive me?"

"Of course. I should change too."

On the drive to the hospital, he called Sean, putting the phone on speaker. Once he'd relayed what had happened, Ellie chimed in. "Now it's even more imperative that we capture her," she said, her voice shaky.

"I agree." Sean's measured tone contained an undercurrent of anger. "And by her attacking someone and injuring them, with an eyewitness or two, the NYPD is now actively looking for her."

"Which means what?" Ellie asked. "That they'll be willing to help me implement my plan?"

Sean went silent for a moment. Liam could picture his brother's expression while he tried to formulate the right words.

"Ellie, how about we give the department a chance to capture her first," Sean finally said. "One of our own was stabbed, and nothing pisses us off more than that. We'll find her, I promise."

Turning into the hospital parking garage, Liam glanced at Ellie. She'd raised her chin, that stubborn quirk he'd begun to recognize.

"We're at the hospital. We'll have to call you back,"

Liam said, disconnecting the call. He expected Ellie to protest, but she simply stared straight ahead.

Once he'd parked, he got out and hurried over to her side to open the door. But when he did, she made no move to exit his vehicle.

"Are you okay?" he asked, holding out his hand for her to take.

After allowing him to assist her up, she shrugged. "Not really. If Sarah dies, I'll never forgive myself."

"This is not your fault," he began.

"Stop." She held up her hand. "If I'd been more pro-active and set a trap the way I wanted to, none of this would have happened." Starting toward the elevator, she didn't look back.

Which saved Liam from pointing out to her the truth. Ellie could have been the one Aliana stabbed. He felt a jolt of terror at the thought.

"You're right," he called after her, relieved when she turned and waited for him to catch up. "This has to end. Aliana must be stopped."

"Yes, she does. Right now."

He touched her arm. "First, let's make sure Sarah is all right. Sean needs time to contact his guys, though I think this might change things. Either way, we'll get with Sean, Eva and Cormac and work out a plan. We can't try to do this on our own."

He could see a gut-wrenching mix of pain and anger warring in her expression. In that moment, if there had been anything he could do to help her, he'd have done it. No matter what. Even if it meant putting his own life at risk.

"They'll understand the urgency," he continued. "Let's give them one more shot. Please."

"We'll see," she finally said.

Inside the ER, Ellie greeted several other coworkers who were all sitting together. One by one, they stood up and hugged her, their faces somber. "She's in surgery," someone said. "In critical condition. That's all they'll tell us."

Just then, Sean walked in. He wore street clothes like usual, but a quick flash of his badge had the triage nurse picking up her phone and making a call. A moment later, two uniformed NYPD officers emerged.

Liam hurried over, joining his brother just as the two policemen reached him. "Hey, Liam," one of the officers greeted him. He glanced over at Ellie and her coworkers, still gathered together and offering each other comfort.

"Any word on the suspect?" Sean asked.

"Not yet," the officer replied, his expression grim. "But every beat cop on the street is actively looking. This is an attack on one of our own."

"Agreed," Sean said. "We need to bring this person in."

"Person?" The description had Liam frowning. "I understand the attacker was a woman."

Now Sean and both the officers turned to stare. Liam didn't blink. He just crossed his arms and waited.

"According to an eyewitness, yes," the uniform responded. "How do you know that?"

Instead of responding, Liam just glanced at Ellie, making sure his brother followed his gaze.

"Liam," Sean warned. "Why don't you go sit back down?"

Liam ignored him. "And I assume you have a detailed physical description?"

This time, the officer glanced at Sean instead of responding. "If there's nothing else…"

"Sure, go ahead back," Sean said, his smile forced. He waited until the two officers had disappeared before turning back to Liam.

"What's your point, Liam?" he snapped. "I promise you, we are searching for her. And we'll find her."

Keeping his gaze locked on his brother, Liam slowly nodded. "You better hope you do. And quickly. Before Ellie goes looking for her and gets herself hurt."

Now that he'd said his piece, Liam turned away and headed back to Ellie. He didn't look back to see if Sean came with him or not.

Chapter 14

Watching Liam confer with his brother and two of NYPD's uniformed finest, Ellie felt numb. When she'd first gotten the call and learned what had happened to Sarah, she'd thought the guilt would cripple her. This was all her fault. And also wasn't. Sometime between hugging her coworkers and seeing their own anguish, she'd ruthlessly shoved away all emotions. It was bad enough that Aliana wanted to kill her. But now she'd hurt someone else, and that Ellie could not abide.

Aliana was going down.

She knew Liam wanted her to wait. Sean, Eva and Cormac too. For now, she would, but only because she didn't have a concrete plan. She didn't want to mess this up. Aliana not only had to be stopped, but she needed to face justice for what she'd done. Ellie could only hope Sarah survived.

Tomorrow, she thought. She'd do something tomorrow. Even if she had to wing it. With or without anyone else's help. Eying Liam, she felt certain he'd back her up. He might not like it, but he'd be there for her. That knowledge warmed her cold, cold heart. She'd fix this. Stop Aliana. No matter what it took.

Around her, the forensic lab crew talked in hushed voices. No one bothered Ellie. She guessed they understood she was dealing with this her own way.

A wave of dizziness passed over her. She swallowed hard and bent over until it passed, wondering if maybe she really had caught some sort of virus. Hopefully not, because she didn't have time to be sick. Unless... No. She refused to even consider the possibility of pregnancy. Not right now.

When she looked up again, the two uniformed officers had turned and were headed back inside the ER. Had the NYPD posted a guard? Ellie sat up straighter. This might mean that they thought Aliana would try again. If so, Ellie wanted to be ready. A mental picture of taking the other woman down at the knees made Ellie smile grimly. She normally didn't consider herself a violent person, but Aliana had pushed her to the absolute limit. The next time Aliana came after her, Ellie planned to be ready. She wasn't sure how exactly, but she planned to defend herself.

Liam came over, Sean walking a few paces behind him. The small group of her coworkers fell silent as they approached.

"There's no word yet," Sean told the group. "We've asked the surgeon to keep us all updated."

"What's the status on the search for her attacker?"

Ellie asked. No one in the tight-knit group of her co-workers knew Ellie had been the intended target. Ellie wasn't sure how she'd ever live with the weight of that guilt.

"The NYPD has taken witness statements," Sean replied carefully. "And we've put out an APB. Sarah Peterson is one of our own. We don't take such attacks lightly."

"Good." Ellie sat back down. Normally, her gruffness might have earned her a few concerned looks from her group, but everyone else was on edge and worried too.

Liam took the empty chair next to her. He took her hand. Startled, she glanced at him, but didn't pull away. Of anyone in this room, he was likely the only person who understood the tempest raging inside her.

After answering a few more questions from the others, Sean got a phone call and walked away to take it. The group talked among themselves in low voices. Gripping Liam's hand, Ellie made no attempt to participate in the conversation.

Liam leaned in close. "Are you okay?"

Still staring straight ahead, she clenched her jaw. "I want to run out into the street right now and scream," she admitted, keeping her voice low. "If she wants me so bad, let her come get me."

"I get it. But please don't," he replied, squeezing her hand once more. "We'll get this figured out."

Since several of her coworkers were now eying her, she didn't respond.

A moment later, a man wearing surgical scrubs came

through the double doors. Immediately, everyone went silent, some twisting their hands together anxiously.

"I'm Dr. Randall," he announced, briefly making eye contact with everyone. "Your friend is out of surgery. We repaired a tear to her small intestine and she's in recovery right now. She's in stable condition. We'll be keeping a close watch on her for the next twenty-four hours, but we expect her to be okay. I'll tell the nurses to let you know if anything changes, but my suggestion right now is to go home and get some rest."

Once the doctor left, most of the others stood and murmured their goodbyes. Still seated, Ellie watched them go.

Now that she knew Sarah would be all right, exhaustion swamped her. She said her goodbyes to various members of her team, recognizing and relating to their dazed expressions. One by one, they trooped out, until only she and Liam remained sitting in the waiting area.

If she closed her eyes, she thought she might just be able to go to sleep sitting upright.

"Let me take you home," Liam murmured, his breath hot against her ear. "We can sit out on the patio and see if we can come up with a plan."

Though she figured the last was mostly to appease her, she appreciated the effort. Struggling to get to her feet, she allowed him to tug her up since her hand was still in his. "Thank you," she said, stifling a yawn. "That actually sounds heavenly."

As they walked to the parking garage, she noticed an unusually high police presence. "Are they here to watch over Sarah?" she wondered out loud.

"Maybe," Liam answered. "I'm sure they want to

make certain the attacker doesn't come back to finish the job. Especially since it's doubtful Aliana realizes it wasn't you she stabbed."

This stopped Ellie in her tracks. "I didn't think of that. If she believes it's me lying in that hospital bed, she might just do exactly that."

They'd reached Liam's car and he pressed the key fob to unlock the doors.

Still chewing on that thought, she got in. "This would be the perfect time to go after her," she said, her growing excitement revitalizing her flagging energy. Though he glanced at her, he didn't speak until he'd fastened his seat belt and started the engine.

"Maybe so," he replied, putting the car in Reverse and backing out. "But she's likely holed up somewhere, waiting to see how much damage she inflicted. She's managed to stay under the radar for sixteen years. I don't think she'd be foolish enough to go to the hospital and try to finish the job."

Ellie started to argue but then thought better of it. "You might be right. But then again, she seems to have grown more and more determined to wipe me off the face of the earth."

"Fifty-fifty. It could go either way." Before pulling out of the parking garage, he reached over and squeezed her shoulder. "But you need to rest. I saw how tired you were back there. At least give it a day."

Aware he was probably right, she nodded. "I will."

"Perfect. Might be a good night for pizza and wine."

If she could stay awake that long.

Eva called as they were stopped in traffic. "I just

heard about Sarah," she said. "I'm glad the damage wasn't worse. You know how bad stab wounds can be."

"If the person wielding the knife knows how to do it," Ellie replied. "Luckily, Aliana doesn't appear to be too skilled."

"You're that sure it was her?" Eva asked.

"I am. The witness's descriptions match. And like I told you guys this morning, I'm done sitting around and letting her wreak havoc on my life." Next to her, Liam made a sound, no doubt to remind her of her promise. "Tonight, I'm going to rest up," she told Eva, earning an approving nod from Liam. "Liam promised me pizza and wine. Then tomorrow, I'm going hunting."

"Not without a plan," Eva protested immediately. "Sean is talking to some of his friends and seeing what he can work up."

Right now, Ellie couldn't have cared less about any of that. This needed to end. She was done waiting. Of course, she said none of that. "Good," she replied, earning a skeptical sound from Eva, who must have detected something in her tone.

"Promise me you won't go out there looking for her on your own. At least wait and hear what Sean comes up with," Eva pleaded. "I don't want you to end up like Sarah."

Since Ellie didn't want to make a promise she had no intention of keeping, she said nothing.

Luckily, Eva kept going and didn't appear to notice. "I'll call you later, okay?"

"Sure." And Ellie ended the call. Again, a wave of exhaustion swamped her. Stifling a yawn, she tried to watch traffic but instead found herself nodding off.

The next thing she knew, Liam was gently waking her. Somehow, they'd arrived and parked and he'd turned off the engine, with her completely oblivious.

"We're here," he said. "You looked so out of it that I considered letting you sleep, but I'd feel a lot safer inside the apartment."

Blinking, she nodded. "I don't know what's wrong with me," she muttered, pushing herself out of the car. "I've never been this tired for no reason."

Liam took her arm. "You've been under a lot of stress. Or maybe you've caught a bug. Weren't you feeling kind of crummy the other day?"

"I was. I thought about that while in the hospital waiting room too. That must be it." Inside the elevator, she allowed herself to lean into him. Even as muddled as she felt, his large muscular body gave her strength.

Once inside his apartment, she headed straight for the couch since her legs felt as if they'd turned to jelly.

"Would you like some wine?" Liam asked. "I've got a great new red I've been wanting to try."

"You go ahead," she said. "I'm still not feeling great, so I think I'll have water instead."

He brought her a bottle of sparkling water. "I'll take this out to the patio for you," he said, his gaze warm. He waited until she'd gotten settled before returning with the open bottle of wine and a single glass.

Watching as he eased himself onto one of the lounge chairs, she took a sip of her water and sighed. "This is exactly what I needed."

"I can tell." He leaned over and took her hand. "We're going to get her, Ellie. All of the NYPD is looking for her. She won't be able to hide."

Closing her eyes once more, Ellie nodded. The urge to sleep tugged at her, slowly pulling her under. For whatever reason, she went with it.

When she woke again, Liam had gone inside. The smell of bacon made her raise her head and sniff, momentarily disoriented.

She grabbed her water, drank a few swallows and pushed to her feet. Not as foggy, she thought, shaking her head. Another scent, maybe toast, drifted out through the open patio door, making her mouth water. Breakfast for dinner? Her stomach growled.

Inside, she saw Liam in the kitchen, moving with that efficient sort of grace that she always found so sexy in such a large man.

"Hey," he said when he saw her. "I made some BLT's. It's been awhile since we ate and I thought you might be hungry."

No nausea. "That sounds just about perfect," she said, taking a seat on one of the barstools at his kitchen island. She sipped her water while he finished making their food, relieved that she felt almost normal once more. Maybe whatever bug she'd caught had finally lost its grip on her.

It turned out she was ravenous. Devouring her sandwich, she looked up to find Liam grinning at her.

"Maybe you just needed to eat," he said.

"Maybe so." Then, giving into impulse, she leaned over and kissed him. He tasted like bacon and sin. More energized than she'd felt all day, she straddled him on the barstool and kissed him again. She felt his arousal pressing against her, electrifying her.

Frantic for more, she slid her hands up under his

shirt, making him groan. "Not here," he managed, lifting her off him. "Bedroom."

Poor man could barely walk, but they somehow made it, shedding clothing as they went. He grabbed a condom from his bedside table and managed to get it on. Ellie's every sense felt heightened, each touch and kiss sending shudders of delight rocketing through her body.

On the bed, she once again climbed on top. For whatever reason, she needed to feel in control. Fierce, wild, she took him inside of her and rode him until sparks of pleasure ignited into a full-blown flame. She cried out, allowing the orgasm to overtake her. A moment later, he joined her, his body pulsing in time to hers.

After, he held her like he always did. She liked that about him, how he always held her close. Snuggling into him, she relaxed, her gaze drifting closed.

This time, instead of trying to lightly doze until she could get up and go to her own room, she curled up in Liam's arms and feel into a deep, dreamless sleep.

After making love, Liam held her, just as he always did, and breathed in the sweetly spicy vanilla scent of her hair. Her chest rose and fell in even breaths. She appeared to be soundly asleep, lush mouth slightly parted and making the cutest little snores.

She'd been truly, deeply exhausted.

In all the time he'd known Ellie, he had never seen her like this. He'd come to admire not only her intelligence, but her tenacity and determination. Even when she drove him out of his mind with worry, she'd always seemed to be in motion, like a lithe tigress. She'd wormed her way into his psyche, haunted his dreams and even his waking hours. In addition to being the sexiest woman he'd ever known, he couldn't even begin to imagine his life without her.

He loved Ellie Mathers. More and more with each passing day. And holding her close, her lithe body curled into his, he knew he'd have to tell her how he felt.

He could only hope making this admission wouldn't have her running away.

For now, she was his. At least until she woke and crept back to her own bed, the way she always did.

Watching her sleep, his chest tight, he wondered if he should have had her checked out at the hospital. Though he knew the stress of everything could have gotten to her, knowing Ellie, he doubted it.

Especially since she'd announced her plans to shut Aliana down if the police didn't capture her first.

Making a muffled sound, she rolled over, still soundly asleep. Just as he debated whether to gather her to him again, his phone pinged. Moving quietly, he reached for it on the nightstand and checked the screen. A text from Sean. Turn on your television. In addition to putting out an APB on Aliana, we've got media coverage. By noon tomorrow, every New Yorker will have seen her face and be on the lookout for her.

Not wanting to wake Ellie, Liam slipped from the bed, closing the door behind him, and went into the den. Then, still worried the noise would disturb her, he grabbed his half-empty wineglass and went outside onto the patio. There, he grabbed a remote and opened the outside TV cabinet. Once the television rose from its stand, he turned it on.

Sure enough, a reporter had been stationed outside

the hospital and was talking excitedly about the stabbing earlier in the day. Then a grainy photo of a younger Aliana appeared on the screen, along with an artist sketch of what they believed she'd look like today.

Despite his attempts not to bother her, Ellie came staggering outside, carrying her water. She eyed him with sleep-filled eyes. She wore her T-shirt, but nothing else.

"That's her," she mumbled, staring at the screen. "The police artist is good. They managed to capture exactly what she looks like."

His heart squeezed as he took in her tousled hair and legs that seemed to go on forever. "Good. Hopefully, that means they'll be easily able to locate her."

Dropping into the same chair she'd occupied earlier, Ellie took a large drink of her water, wrinkling her nose slightly as the bubbles tickled her. "I hope so. But she's a sly one. And all of this is only going to make her more desperate and determined to get to me."

Curious, he eyed her. "Even though she's now been exposed? I figured the reason she wanted to take you out was to keep your from revealing her existence."

"That's kind of what I thought too," Ellie admitted, yawning again and covering her mouth with her free hand. "But even if it was, I suspect she's going to blame me for all of this. I don't think she'll rest until she gets to me."

Alarmed, he tore his gaze away from her and took a sip of his wine. "Well, at least she doesn't know where to find you. You're safe for now."

"For now," she agreed. "But all of that is going to change tomorrow."

He decided to let that one go. As exhausted as she seemed to be, he figured once she actually went to bed, she'd sleep late in the morning. That's what Sundays were great for. Lazy mornings, coffee and bagels. With a jolt, he realized he wanted to share mornings—and more—with her for the rest of his life.

Dusk had settled over the city and lights were coming on. The never-ending stream of traffic continued far below. He'd lived in this apartment for several years now, but not until Ellie had come to stay had it felt like home.

Glancing at her, he smiled, aching to tell her how he felt. He knew he would, as soon as Aliana was safely behind bars.

Yawning again, she caught him watching her and grimaced. "I'm sorry, but I think I'm going back to bed. I know it's early, but I can't seem to shake this tiredness. Hopefully some extra sleep and I'll feel more like myself in the morning."

He jumped to his feet and helped her up, pulling her up close for a tender kiss. "Sleep well," he murmured.

Her smile momentarily chased the sleepiness from her eyes. "I imagine I will," she said dryly. With a quick wave, she disappeared back inside. "I hope I can count on your help tomorrow."

Not sure how to respond, he settled on the truth. "I'll think about it."

"Then that'll have to be good enough," she responded, turning and drifting back inside, leaving him alone.

The news had gone on to another story, so he turned the TV off. Sipping his wine, he realized in his desire to keep Ellie safe, he would be ignoring what she wanted. Instead, he had to figure out a way to help her. Because until Aliana was caught, neither of them could have any kind of normal life. Which he wanted more than anything.

Since it wasn't too late, he grabbed his phone and called Sean. His brother picked up on the second ring.

"Are you calling about the news story?" Sean asked.

"Not really. Though Ellie said the police sketch artist did a great job picture what Aliana looks like today." Liam cleared his throat. "I'm actually calling to see if you had a chance to talk to your SWAT buddies about a plan."

"You've got to be kidding me. We've got every uniform in the city looking for her. She can't hide. Why would we allow Ellie to put herself in danger when we're so close?"

Grimacing, Liam took a deep breath. "Ellie isn't the kind of woman you *allow* to do anything. She's an intelligent, rational adult."

"You know what I meant," Sean groused. "I get that she wants this over with—and it will be, if she gives it a day or two. And while she works in our crime scene lab, she's an investigator, not a peace officer. A civilian. Just like you are."

"Cut the BS. I take it this means you're not going to offer your assistance."

Silence. When Sean spoke again, he sounded incredulous. "You're serious?"

"I am. Ellie has already informed me that come hell or high water, she's going out looking for Aliana herself tomorrow."

Sean cursed. "Then I hope and pray the NYPD captures her tonight. That woman is dangerous. I don't want Ellie to end up in the hospital like Sarah."

"I don't either," Liam answered quietly. "Which is why I thought we could count on you for help."

"We?"

"I'm going with her," Liam responded. "I'll do what I can to protect her, but I won't stand in her way. She deserves to have closure."

"Closure," Sean scoffed. "I despise that word. I don't see how that would have anything to do with this situation."

"Let me explain it to you then. Ellie has looked for answers into Aliana's disappearance for sixteen years! They were best friends. Ellie never gave up on trying to figure out what happened to her, not even once."

Liam took a deep breath, working on keeping his voice down. "Then, in a freak coincidence," he continued, "Ellie happens to see her long-vanished, so-called friend in the subway. From that moment on, Aliana has made numerous attempts to kill her. If something like that doesn't need closure, I don't know what does."

"Point taken," Sean replied. "But is there any way you can get Ellie to hold off, just for a few days? I'm confident the NYPD can get her."

"I can try," Liam said. "But she's let me know she's done waiting around. I'm ninety-nine percent sure she's planning on trying to locate Aliana tomorrow."

Sean cursed. "Isn't there anything you can do?"

"Not really. I promised her I'd help." With a sigh, Liam polished off the last of his wine and debated pouring another glass. "My suggestion to you is to get busy.

Capture Aliana before tomorrow if you really want to keep Ellie safe."

After ending the call, Liam tried to settle down, relax and enjoy the view. Instead, he found himself picturing all the ways things could go wrong if Ellie insisted on putting herself out there in hopes of drawing out Aliana.

He couldn't imagine a world without Ellie in it.

Shaking his head at himself, Liam got up and went inside. All he wanted to do was climb under the covers with Ellie and wrap her up tight in his arms. But since she'd never actually invited him into her bed, he didn't. Clearly, she needed her sleep. Hopefully, whatever bug had gotten into her system would be gone by morning.

Instead, he settled into the living room and tried to read the newest psychological thriller by one of his favorite authors. Though he usually found this type of story engrossing, instead he found himself constantly checking the clock, counting down until it would be a reasonable hour to go to bed. Part of him hoped Ellie would make her way back to his room, though the other part of him simply wanted her to get her rest. Since she preferred to sleep in her own room, and sleep was what she needed, he felt selfish for his own desire to hold her through the night.

But now, he felt…lonely. Sitting outside, on a perfect evening, on his beautiful patio, alone. Aching for the woman who slept inside, oblivious to his feelings.

He'd need to change that. Soon. He poured himself another glass of wine and tried to relax.

Around eight, he went inside and made himself some cheese and crackers and ate that along with an apple. He'd waited as long as he could in the hopes that Ellie might wake up hungry despite the earlier BLTs and wander out of her room. But she didn't.

He read some more, made very little progress, and finally gave up and turned on the television. Keeping the volume low, he watched some old sitcom reruns, until boredom made him get up and pace.

Resisting the urge to check on Ellie in her room, instead he stepped back outside onto the patio, hoping the night air and city sounds might help soothe his restlessness. Instead of sitting, he walked to the railing and stood, taking in the sight and sounds of the vibrant city below.

Until now, his life had been good. Thanks to the money Noreen had left him, he'd been able to indulge his passion working to help troubled teens. He'd kept himself busy, believing work could be enough, until it wasn't.

He'd found someone he wanted to share his life with. He wanted to wake up beside her, kiss over coffee and bagels, walk to the train together, and reconnect at the end of the workday. When something went bad, Ellie was the first person he wanted to share with. And when things were good, he only wanted to celebrate with her. All of life's little moments, the successes and tears and frustrations and joy, belonged to Ellie.

Just like his heart.

Finishing off the last of his wine, he went back inside, locking up as he went and turning off the lights. He forced himself to go directly to his own room, not wanting to take a chance of waking Ellie.

As he entered his bedroom, he flicked on the light and then froze. There, in his bed, sound asleep, lay Ellie.

Quickly, he turned the light off. Chest aching, cautiously joyful and humble all at once, he quietly got ready in the dark. Then, careful not to wake her, he slipped into bed next to her. With Ellie by his side, he couldn't help but feel as if everything would be all right.

Chapter 15

When Ellie opened her eyes the next morning, for the space of a few heartbeats, she had absolutely no idea where she was. Then, as she adjusted to the brightness of the sunlight, she realized she was still in Liam's bed. And the bedside clock said it was close to nine o'clock. She hadn't slept this late since college.

Despite this, she didn't feel any compulsion to hurry. Sitting up, she stretched and swung her legs over the side of the bed. When she caught sight of her reflection in the dresser mirror, she wasn't sure whether to grimace or grin. With her tousled hair and swollen lips, the woman staring back at her had clearly been thoroughly made love to the night before.

More than once, actually. Her smile widened. She had a clear recollection of waking up Liam with her mouth in the middle of the night.

She slipped out of Liam's room and headed down the hall to the bathroom she used. After washing up and brushing her teeth, she decided to grab a cup of coffee before she showered.

Walking in that direction, she wondered why the place seemed so quiet. No sign of Liam, though maybe he'd taken his coffee out to the patio. Which was exactly what she wanted to do, before she showered and got ready to start the day.

Anticipation normally made her jittery, but for whatever reason, today she felt confident and focused. Aliana had finally gone too far. Not only was the entire NYPD looking for her, but today Ellie Mathers was done being the victim. To coin an old and admittedly corny phrase, the hunted would now become the hunter.

Her coffee finished brewing. She fixed it up, took a sip and headed out to the terrace to find Liam.

Except he wasn't there. Frowning, she looked around. This wasn't like him at all. When he went out, he usually left her a note. Thinking maybe she'd missed it, she went back inside.

Nothing in the kitchen. Same with the living room and his bedroom. She even checked his bathroom, just in case. An ominous chill of foreboding snaked up her spine. Had something happened? Something so awful that he'd had to rush out of the apartment with no time to leave her a note?

The thought made her gasp. Had…had Sarah died?

Setting her coffee down, she hurried to find her phone. Surely, someone would have texted or called her if that were the case.

Grabbing her cell up off the nightstand, she checked the screen. Nothing. No missed texts or calls.

Then where was Liam? Scrolling to his contact info, she called him. It went straight to voicemail.

Weird. Just in case, she went ahead and left a message. Then, because why the hell not, she sent a text. Liam, can you call me?

Staring at her phone, she waited. Nothing. No little dots to indicate he was in the process of texting her back.

Likely she was just overreacting. He'd probably gotten tired of waiting for her to wake up and headed out to get the bagels he liked to share on Sunday morning. The thought made her smile. Though she hadn't been there long, she and Liam already had started a routine. One that she loved.

Her stomach growled. She needed more coffee. Hopefully, Liam would be back soon with food. Then she'd jump in the shower. After that, the two of them could head out and see if they could find Aliana. Not much of a plan, but since no one else seemed inclined to help her, she was winging it. At least she knew she could count on Liam.

Locating her coffee cup, she raised it to her mouth. The scent made her gag. What the…? She loved the smell of coffee, along with the taste. Not to mention the welcome effect of the caffeine.

She shook her head and tried again. And found herself sprinting for the bathroom so she could puke up the entire contents of her stomach. Which luckily wasn't much at the moment.

Apparently, whatever bug she'd caught was still

hanging on. When she felt sure she was done, she washed her face, rinsed her mouth out with mouthwash and tried to think. Things had been so crazy, she hadn't even noticed that she'd missed her period.

She froze, her heartbeat stuttering in her chest.

Could she possibly be pregnant?

Thinking back, she tried to remember. Until all this craziness with Aliana had started, she'd always had her period like clockwork. Reminding herself that stress could cause one's body to be off, she tried not to panic. She could only deal with one thing at a time.

Today would be devoted to catching Aliana. She'd figure out the rest after that.

Once she decided that, calmness settled over her. Checking her phone again and wondering why she hadn't heard back from Liam, she decided she might as well go ahead and take a shower while she waited. That way, she'd be all freshened up by the time Liam returned.

Twenty minutes later, she'd finished blow-drying her hair and Liam still hadn't returned. Nor had he returned her text or call. Slightly worried, she called Sean. That call also went to voicemail. Feeling slightly foolish, she went ahead and left a message, asking Sean to call her.

Feeling a bit like an overreacting parent on prom night, she tried Eva next. Her friend answered on the second ring.

"Ellie! What's up?"

"You sound cheerful," Ellie said. "And wide awake."

"I am. I'm about to start my shift but my partner is out again today, so they're pairing me up with someone else. It's bound to be a good day!"

Despite everything, this comment made Ellie laugh. "Well, I won't keep you. I'm just wondering if you've heard from Liam. He wasn't here when I woke up and he's not answering his phone or responding to texts. I tried Sean but got his voicemail."

"That's weird." In the background, someone called Eva's name. "Listen, it's Sunday. He's probably doing something with Sean and Cormac. I'm sure he'll turn up. If I hear from him, I'll tell him to call you. I've got to go." And she ended the call.

When Ellie's stomach growled again, she decided to go ahead and make herself something to eat. She scrambled some eggs and ate them with a glass of orange juice standing up. Once she'd finished, she rinsed her plate and waited to see if the food would stay down. She couldn't be pregnant, she just couldn't. This wasn't in her plans, not even a little bit.

Her cell rang, jarring her out of the thoughts. Liam. Finally. "Hey there," she answered, hoping her racing heart and anxiety didn't transfer to her voice.

"Sorry I didn't leave you a note," he said. "I went out to get our bagels and on the way there, I think I spotted Aliana. I called Sean and he's here too."

"Where?" she asked. "I want to come."

"Not yet," he responded. "Sean brought backup and I don't want to spook her. This could be it, Ellie. We're really close to capturing her."

Without her. She wasn't sure whether to be relieved or angry. While she'd kind of wanted to have a part in taking Aliana down, what mattered in the end was getting her off the streets. Ellie could always go see her in jail.

Still, she tried another tack. "Are you in between here and the deli?" she asked. He usually got their bagels at Liam's favorite deli, a block west.

"No, I ended up seeing her and going the opposite way," Liam replied. "I didn't get a chance to pick up my order. You can go grab it, if you're hungry. There shouldn't be any risk, since I know Aliana isn't anywhere near there."

Tamping down a sliver of regret, she sighed. "I'll run out and get it. Stay safe, Liam. And call me if you need me, okay? If she goes into hiding, she might come out if she sees me." Part of her couldn't help but hope he'd tell her to join them.

Of course, he did not. "Stay safe," she repeated.

"Will do," Liam replied. "I hope we get her, Ellie. Then this could all be over and we could resume normal lives."

After ending the call, Ellie debated simply going out and trying to find them. Instead, she decided she'd simply wait her turn. If Liam and Sean weren't successful, then she'd have to try. She'd rather have Liam at her side than try to face Aliana alone.

Decision made, she got dressed, grabbed her purse and sent Liam a quick text to let him know she'd left. Then she headed out the door to pick up their bagels. No sense in letting a perfectly good Sunday morning go completely to waste. Hopefully, by the time Liam returned to enjoy them with her, they could celebrate the news that Aliana had been taken into police custody.

Outside, the sun was shining and there was a light breeze. As she joined the crowds of people walking, the sidewalk energy felt different. Sunday funday, she thought, smiling slightly to herself. During the work week, everyone seemed fixated on the need to get where they were going. Today, more of them were actually enjoying the journey.

Spring in New York could be a wonderful thing.

She reached the deli and stepped inside, noting the smaller line at this time of the day. Patiently waiting her turn, she greeted Hector, the owner, and his wife, Samara, by name. Smiling, they bagged up the order Liam had placed. She thanked them and paid, stepping back out into the sunshine. Despite her good mood, she made sure to check her surroundings before beginning her walk back to Liam's building.

Scanning the faces of the crowd, she stepped out into the middle of them after making sure Aliana wasn't among them. Even though Liam and Sean had been certain they were on the other woman's tail several blocks away, Ellie figured she couldn't be too careful. Aliana wouldn't be taking her by surprise ever again.

Still, Ellie's mood remained light. Swinging the bag with the bagels, humming to herself, she couldn't think of anywhere else she'd rather be. Soon, maybe, she'd be able to enjoy the city with Liam without always looking over her shoulder. Liam…

With a smile on her face, she rounded the corner.

Someone came out of nowhere, head low, and barreled into her, knocking her to the ground and sending her bagels flying.

Too startled to be afraid, Ellie scrambled to get up, still thinking this had to be some sort of accident. But when the person—wearing a hoody despite the warm day—rushed her again, she realized her nemesis had found her.

"Aliana," she cried out, pivoting so she had her back to the brick building. "Stop. Why are you doing this?"

Instead of answering, Aliana raised her hand, the metal knife blade glinting in the sun. She came at Ellie again, her face hidden by her hood.

Ellie stepped sideways. Rather than panic, a grim determination settled over her. This would end now. Acting instinctively, she brought her knee up and kicked, catching Aliana right in the midsection.

Aliana went down. But somehow, she kept her grip on her weapon.

Unarmed, Ellie swung the only thing she had. Her purse.

She caught Aliana squarely in the face, knocking down the hoody. Ellie used the forward motion to kick again, this time aiming for Ariana's chest. But instead Aliana grabbed Ellie's leg and yanked her down.

She hit the ground hard, momentarily knocking the breath from her. Snarling, Aliana leaped for her, arm raised.

The knife! Ellie barely managed to roll sideways. Even so, the blade caught her in the arm. Adrenaline pumping, Ellie barely felt it. Must have been a scratch.

Pushing up, she head-bumped Ariana, catching the other woman right under the chin. That hurt worse, and Aliana went down. Ellie took immediate advantage and jumped on top of her, pinning her arms as best she could.

But Aliana still had the knife. Expression murder-

ous, she fought back, slamming her shoulder into Ellie's injured arm.

Ellie pushed the pain away and fought back. A rush
of adrenaline fueled her strength. "I'm not going to
die today," she declared, shoving Aliana down hard.
And again.

"Ellie!" Liam's voice, from a distance. But she couldn't
let herself be distracted, not now. Not if she wanted to
live.

"Bitch," Aliana spat, struggling to get up. Ellie
slammed her again. Ariana's head hit concrete. Hard.
Her grip on Ellie loosened, though she didn't completely
let go.

From a distance, through her haze of pain and rage,
Ellie heard a familiar voice. Liam, shouting to his
brother, and then calling her name.

Her momentary loss in concentration nearly hurt her.
Aliana attempted to roll sideways and brought her knee
up to knock Ellie off her.

With a strength born of desperation, Ellie was able
to push back, slamming Aliana into the concrete again.
When she went limp, Ellie continued to hold her there,
not wanting to take even the slightest chance of Aliana
getting the upper hand.

Spotting Ellie fighting with a slender person wearing a hoodie, Liam thought his heart would stop. Aliana. Somehow, she'd evaded him and Sean and gotten
to Ellie.

Shouting to his brother, Liam ran. Even from this
distance, he saw the glint of metal in her hand as she
raised her arm. A knife. She'd almost killed one of El-

lie's coworkers. And now she meant to finish the job with Ellie.

Crossing the next intersection without waiting, he was almost hit by a cab. The driver blared his horn, screaming at him out the open window. With Sean hot on his heels, Liam kept going. He had to get to Ellie before Aliana hurt her.

Unbelievably, most of the people on the crowded sidewalk paid absolutely no mind to the two women grappling with each other. But then someone must have noticed the knife, because one woman started screaming.

By the time Liam reached them, Ellie had knocked Aliana unconscious, but she didn't relax her grip.

Liam crouched down beside her. "You can let her go, Ellie. She's out."

Eyes blank, Ellie met his gaze, but he doubted she saw him. She blinked and her breath hitched. He recognized the moment when she collected herself enough to realize what had happened.

By then Sean had reached them. He nodded at Sean and together they helped Ellie get up. The instant Liam saw the blood running down her arm, his throat went dry.

"You're hurt," he managed, resisting the urge to sweep her up into his arms and try to carry her. "We need to get you to the hospital."

"Wait." Expression intense, Ellie watched as Sean crouched down, checked Ariana's pulse, and then called for an ambulance for the still unconscious woman.

"Is she alive?" Ellie asked, taking a faltering step and almost falling. If not for Liam, she would have fallen.

"Ellie needs an ambulance too," Liam told his brother, right before Ellie went limp in his arms. Heart pounding, Liam held her close. He couldn't help but flash back to the night he'd found his former wife, still trapped in the wreckage of her car crash. He'd tried to save her and failed. For years, he'd blamed himself, especially since they'd been arguing right before she drove off.

With a flash of illumination, he realized this guilt over his failure to save her, along with the horrible, gut-wrenching pain, had been why he'd run from any kind of true relationship. He'd never wanted to feel that way again.

Now, holding Ellie, the woman he knew he loved more deeply than he ever had any other, he remembered. While he understood, he wouldn't trade one single second he and Ellie had shared. And he damned sure wasn't going to lose her.

No matter what.

The next few minutes passed both excruciatingly slowly and in a blur. Liam held on to Ellie's unconscious body, more terrified than he'd ever been as he watched the pulse beating in her throat. "Come on," he muttered, an invocation and a prayer. He could hear the ambulance getting closer, sirens wailing and lights flashing as it weaved through traffic. Finally, it reached them and parked. EMTs jumped out and rushed over to Aliana, still on the concrete.

Liam called out to them, still managing to hold Ellie upright, her blood soaking his shirt. They turned, took quick stock of the situation and gently took her from

Liam. He watched as they eased Ellie onto the stretcher they'd brought for Aliana.

At that moment, Liam could barely remain standing. He couldn't lose Ellie. Not when they'd finally found each other.

A police car pulled up and Sean hustled him inside. "I called for backup," he told Liam. "I've got a couple of units meeting us at the hospital. Aliana's not going to get away this time."

Liam nodded. "I'm more concerned about Ellie. Aliana stabbed her."

"I know." Sean patted his arm. "I'm sure she's going to be fine. From what I could see, Ellie's wound looked superficial."

"I hope you're right." Watching as the uniformed police officer navigated traffic, Liam suppressed the urge to ask him to go faster somehow, as if they could magically move vehicles out of his way. Peering up ahead, he tried to find the ambulance, but he'd lost sight of it. A good thing, right? Because that meant they'd get Ellie to the ER faster.

Finally, they reached the hospital. As soon as the patrol car coasted to a stop, Liam jumped out and hit the entrance running. Behind him, Sean urged him to slow down, a command Liam ignored.

At the front desk, Liam tried to catch the busy triage nurse's attention, but it wasn't until Sean flashed his badge that she hurried over. Sean was directed toward where Aliana had been taken, the nurse buzzing him through. Liam went with him, planning to find out where they were treating Ellie.

Sean stopped to speak with a nurse about the two

women who'd been brought in. "They're both being worked on right now," she said. "I'd suggest you two go back to the waiting room. Someone will be out to speak with you later."

Again, Sean flashed his badge. "One of them is under arrest. The other is an NYPD employee."

Her harried expression softened at that. She pointed to one door at the opposite end of the hall. "One woman is in there. The other is in the room three doors up, on the opposite side."

"Which is which?" Liam asked, trying to keep his voice level.

"I don't know, but you can't go in either room yet," the nurse replied. "Station a police guard outside the door if you need to, but let the doctors do their work."

With that, she hurried away.

"Stay with me," Sean ordered. "We can at least take a look in and see what's going on."

First, they checked on Aliana, despite Liam's wishes. They'd barely opened the door and poked their heads in when someone in the group of medical personnel around the bed turned and ushered them out.

"Wait outside," one of the medical staff said, closing the door firmly before they could protest.

Sean and Liam exchanged a glance. "You go," Sean said. "Check on Ellie. I'm going to wait here until I can get a few officers in place."

Liam didn't need to be told twice. He found Ellie's room easily, relieved to see she was alone and appeared to be sleeping peacefully. He dropped into the chair next to the bed and gently took her hand into his.

Watching her sleep, he felt like he could breathe

again. Just being there with her, knowing she'd be okay, filled his heart to bursting. Love. So much love.

Ellie stirred, which made him lean forward.

"Where is she?" These were Ellie's first words once she'd opened her eyes.

Still holding her hand, Liam didn't bother to ask who she meant. "Somewhere here in the ER," he replied. "Sean is with her to make sure she doesn't get away."

"Is she conscious?"

"I don't know." He squeezed her fingers. "I haven't left your side to check on her."

"Let's go find out." She pulled her hand from his. The determined lift of her chin told him she wouldn't be dissuaded. As she struggled to swing her legs over the side of the bed, she seemed to notice her IV for the first time. Once she took stock of that, she glanced at her other arm, which had been well bandaged.

"What's all this?" she asked. Before he could answer, her eyes widened. "Aliana stabbed me."

"Yes. And you lost consciousness." Emotion made his voice raw, so he cleared his throat before continuing. "But the doctor thinks you're going to be just fine. The knife didn't hit any major arteries, just muscle. They cleaned the stab wound, stitched you up, and got a bandage on."

Slowly, she nodded. "Then take me to where she is. I have some questions I want to ask her."

Just then Sean came in. "Oh, you're awake," he said. "Good."

Ellie nodded. "Why aren't you with Aliana? What if she escapes?"

"She won't. I cuffed her to the bed until she can be

transported. I've got some guys on the way to handle transport to the jail."

"What's wrong with her?" Ellie asked.

Sean eyed her. "Looks like she has a concussion. She has a pretty big bump on the back of her head."

"Is she awake?"

Sean glanced at Liam, who shrugged. "She is. And she's damned lucky you didn't kill her. But I'm not letting you in there to finish the job."

For a second, Ellie recoiled, appearing stunned. "I just want to ask her some questions," she said. "Geez, Sean."

Finally, Sean cracked a smile. "Just kidding. But I wouldn't blame you, you know. Yeah, you have every right to try and get answers from her." He motioned toward the door. "Come on. I'll take you to her."

This time when Ellie struggled to get out of the bed, Liam helped her. When she realized she was only wearing one of those hospital gowns that opened in the back over her underwear, she froze. "Where are my clothes?"

Grimacing, Liam pointed to a plastic bag on one of the chairs. "Your jeans, socks and sneakers are in there. They had to cut your shirt off you, so that gown is it for now."

"Would you mind texting Eva and asking her to bring one of her T-shirts up here?" Ellie asked. "I just need something to wear on the way home."

"Already done," Liam replied. "It was actually her idea. I had to give her status updates while you were out, and she's the one who realized you'd need a shirt."

Sean's phone pinged. He glanced at the screen and texted a reply. After sliding his cell back into his pocket, he smiled at Ellie. "Eva just got here. She'll be up in a minute. Just hang tight and you should be all set."

He'd barely finished speaking when Eva breezed into the room. "Ellie!" she exclaimed, rushing to the bed for a careful hug. "I'm so glad you're okay."

"Me too." Ellie eyed Eva's oversized tote. "Did you bring a shirt?"

"I did." Turning to glare at her brothers, Eva motioned them to leave the room. "Give us a sec so Ellie can get dressed please."

The instant Liam stepped back, Eva drew the curtain around the bed, giving her and Ellie some privacy.

"Come on." Sean motioned for Liam to follow him out to the hallway. Once there, Sean glanced back at the hospital room. "Aliana is restrained. She's been read her rights and we've already spoken to the district attorney, even though it's Sunday. Charges will be filed."

"Good."

"Yeah. As you know, we normally would go straight to court, but since it's not open until Monday, Aliana is aware her next stop will be a holding cell." Again, Sean glanced back at the room and kept his voice low. "I should warn you, even restrained, she is very combative. For whatever reason, she really seems to have it in for Ellie."

Liam shook his head. "That much was already obvious. What none of us know is why."

Just then Eva pulled the curtain open and she and Ellie emerged. Despite the dose of pain meds Ellie had been given, she appeared alert and steady.

"I'm ready," she said. "Time to find out why my former best friend has been trying to kill me."

As they walked down the hallway, Sean relayed to Ellie what he'd already told Liam.

Ellie shrugged. "As long as she can't physically hurt me, I don't care what insults she wants to hurl my way. I just want an explanation. After all this, she owes me that."

At the end of the hallway, they reached a room with a uniformed officer standing watch outside.

"She's in here," Sean said, stepping aside so Ellie could enter. Since there was zero chance Liam intended to let Ellie be alone with that awful woman, he went in with her.

At that moment, Aliana appeared to be asleep. With her eyes closed and her dark, curly hair spread out around her pillow, she didn't look at all threatening.

But then, as Ellie approached the bed, Aliana's eyes snapped open. She pinned Ellie with a glare, her gaze full of malice. "You," she spat. "You ruined everything."

Ellie froze. Liam knew there were a hundred things she wanted to ask. He stepped up next to her and placed a hand lightly on her shoulder to offer support.

"How?" Ellie asked, getting right to the point. "How did I ruin everything?"

Instead of answering, Aliana turned her face away, ignoring her.

"You know what?" Ellie continued, moving a tiny bit closer. "After you disappeared when we were sixteen, I never stopped looking for you. I never gave up. I watched your parents fall apart with grief. Even when they finally, reluctantly, accepted the inevitable and thought you were dead, I refused to believe. I got into law enforcement because of you."

Ellie took a deep breath, her voice shaky. "Aliana, we were best friends. In all the years that have gone by, I've never stopped looking for you. I couldn't believe it when I saw you in the subway. And then you tried to kill me. Not once, but multiple times. Don't you think you at least owe me an explanation?"

Slowly, Aliana swung her head back around. "I wanted to stay dead," she replied, her voice dripping with venom. "You should have left well enough alone."

"Because you killed John Dobby." Eva strode into the room. "We know that's the guy you left with."

Aliana didn't even flinch. Instead, she transferred her now dead-eyed gaze to Eva. "John deserved to die. He promised me the moon and then, right after we left, he changed his mind. We argued, he pulled a gun. I took it away from him and shot him with it."

"Then you ran the car into the river," Eva finished for her. "Trying to hide all evidence of your crime."

"Not a crime," Aliana retorted. "Self-defense."

"Then why try to cover it up?" Sean moved forward, arms crossed, in what Liam always thought of as his police detective stance. "Most people who've done nothing wrong don't run and hide."

"I wanted my freedom." Aliana glanced at him, before swinging her gaze back to Ellie. "A new life, a new everything.

Ellie shook her head, her expression sad. "We were sixteen. Just two more years until we graduated and turned eighteen. You could have waited, just like the rest of us. Either you don't know or worse, don't care, what kind of pain your disappearance caused your family. And me—hell, everyone who cared about you."

Liam had never loved her more. Even now, facing the woman who'd tried to kill her, Ellie still managed to think of others with her huge heart.

A nurse poked her head in the room. "Ellie Mathers? The doctor is looking for you. I think we need to get you back to your room."

"Is he ready to discharge me?" Without waiting for the nurse to answer, Ellie grabbed Liam's arm. "Come on. Let's go get this over with so I can go home."

Behind her, Liam noticed the way Eva and Sean exchanged a look. "We'll meet up with you later," Sean said, waving them away. "Eva and I have a bit of work to do here."

As they followed the nurse down the hallway, Ellie clutched Liam's arm. "Are you okay?" he asked, concerned.

"A bit nauseated, but otherwise yes."

Back at her room, the nurse asked them to wait, promising a doctor would be with them shorty. Ellie took a seat on the edge of the hospital bed while Liam remained standing.

"I can't wait to go home," she announced, smiling up at him.

Staring down into her beautiful dark eyes, he decided to take a chance. Swallowing, he ignored his suddenly racing heartbeat, and reached for her hand. "About that," he said. "I'm wondering if you might want to make it more permanent."

Before she could answer, the doctor entered the room. He glanced from Ellie to Liam, beaming. "I have some news," he said. "We ran a lot of tests when you came in. They were mostly all normal, except one."

Liam froze. "Is she going to be all right?" he asked, his fingers still entwined with hers.

Still smiling, the doctor hesitated. "Ellie, do I have your permission to share your test results with him?"

Slowly, Ellie nodded. "Yes of course."

Now the doctor glanced at Liam. "To answer your question then, if by all right, you mean pregnant, then yes. She is." He handed Ellie a sheaf of paper. "You should go see your ob-gyn right away."

Stunned, Liam and Ellie stared at each other. The doctor patted Liam's shoulder as he walked toward the door. Once there, he turned. "Oh, I've already signed your discharge papers. You two are free to go home and start preparing for your baby."

As soon as the doctor left, Ellie shook her head. "That explains my exhaustion and nausea. Still, it's awfully presumptuous of him to assume anything. How does he know if we even want this baby? Or," she swallowed. "That you're even the father?"

Liam met her gaze. He didn't even have to ask if he was, because he knew the truth deep inside. He found himself blinking back tears. "I don't know how you feel, but I want our child more than anything. Ellie, I was about to ask you to marry me."

"What?" She searched his face. "Marriage is an awfully big step. I thought you wanted to talk about us moving in together."

"I love you, Ellie. I want to wake up every morning with you next to me. I want to come home to you at the end of every day. And now this. A baby. Unexpected, sure. But I think we both have enough love between us to spread it three ways."

By the time he'd finished talking, she was crying. "You couldn't have said it any better, Liam. Now let's go home and figure this out together."

Home. As long as she was there with him, he knew anyplace would feel like home.

And, he thought with a private smile, Cormac's child would have a cousin. The timing couldn't be more perfect.

Monday morning, Ellie called in to work and took a personal day off. She and Liam went ring shopping in the diamond district. She found the perfect ring at the second place they stopped at. Not too big, nor too small, just a single solitary diamond mounted on a simple platinum band. For Liam, he chose a matching men's ring. When the jeweler stated the price, Ellie almost gasped, but Liam simply kissed her and then handed over his credit card.

Since her ring fit perfectly, Liam slipped it on her finger and kissed her again while the jeweler grinned at them. "Now it's official," Liam told her.

Kissing him back, she laughed. The joy in that sound had them both grinning at each other like fools.

Liam had asked everyone to meet them at Trattoria Trecolori, Ellie's favorite Italian restaurant, for dinner Monday. He made reservations for the whole crew and their plus ones. Sean immediately assumed it was to celebrate finally closing the Aliana Martin case. Liam let him think that, even though he felt about to burst with the need to share the good news. They'd decided not to mention Ellie's pregnancy, not until she made it past the first trimester, but their engagement would be more than enough joy to spread around.

Now that she knew the reason for her fatigue and nausea, Ellie allowed herself to revel in both their love and her pregnancy. More beautiful than ever, she positively glowed. Liam had hired a company to move her belongings into his place—now their place—which would happen this coming weekend.

Tonight though, they'd be letting both families in on their news. After they met up with his family for dinner, Ellie and Liam were heading over to her parents' place to tell them as well. Though he knew her mother, Liam would be meeting her father for the first time since he'd been a teenager, as well as announcing their engagement. Despite knowing a lot had changed since then, he couldn't help but worry.

"Don't be nervous," Ellie teased, giving him a long, lingering kiss. "My mother has been after me to get married for as long as I can remember. And she's a big fan of yours. She'll be thrilled." Placing one hand on her still flat belly, she sighed. "Even more so when we can finally tell her she's going to be a grandmother."

She looked so beautiful in her little black dress, he wanted to sweep her into the bedroom right then and show her once more how much he loved her. But because if he did that, they'd be late, he simply smiled at her and said one word. "Later."

Since she knew exactly what he meant, this made her laugh. "Come on, fiancé of mine. We've got some major news to share."

When they walked into the restaurant, arm in arm,

everyone else had already been seated. Sean and Orla both looked up as Liam and Ellie approached, grinning. Cormac and Emily sat next to Eva.

Liam pulled out a chair for Ellie and helped her get settled before he took a seat. Sean had taken the head of the table and Liam ended up at the foot, which would be perfect since he wanted to make his big announcement.

Since everyone already had their drinks, the waiter came to take Ellie and Liam's. She ordered a ginger ale and Liam got his usual Italian beer.

Heart racing, Liam could barely contain himself. He waited until everyone had given their food orders, before standing up and tapping on his water glass. "Everyone, Ellie and I have an announcement we want to make."

Before he could say another word, Eva let out a loud *whoop.* "I knew it," she said. "Congratulations, you two."

"Can you at least let the man tell us himself?" Sean asked, fighting a smile.

"Thank you," Liam replied, with a mock glare at his sister. He went around to Ellie's chair, took her hand and pulled her to her feet. As she stood, he put his arm around her before they both turned to face his family. "As you all apparently guessed, Ellie and I are engaged."

Now the entire table erupted. Sean came over and patted Liam on the back, before sweeping Ellie up in a hug. Orla was right behind him. Cormac and Emily were next, and then Eva, who hugged them both. "I'm getting another sister," she said, wiping away a tear. "Orla and Emily and now you! It's enough to make a girl cry."

"Don't cry, celebrate!" Eva said, lifting her glass of ginger ale. "We should all have a toast."

So they did. They toasted each other, celebrating their close family, and most important of all, finding true love.

* * * * *

Don't miss the next exciting story from
The Coltons of New York series:
Colton's Undercover Seduction *by Beth Cornelison*
Available from Harlequin Romantic Suspense!

#2227 COLTON'S UNDERCOVER SEDUCTION
The Coltons of New York • by Beth Cornelison

To investigate the Westmore family, rookie cop Eva Colton goes undercover as ladies' man detective Carmine DiRico's wife on a marriage-retreat cruise. As the "marriage" starts feeling alarmingly real, Eva becomes the lone witness to a shipboard murder and the target of a killer determined to silence her...permanently.

#2228 SAVED BY THE TEXAS COWBOY
by Karen Whiddon

When Marissa Noll's former high school sweetheart and now-injured rodeo star Jared Miller returns to Anniversary, Texas, and needs her help with physical therapy, she vows to be professional. After all, she's moved on with her life. But when she starts receiving threats, the coincidental timing makes her wonder if Jared might have something to do with it.

#2229 THE BOUNTY HUNTER'S BABY SEARCH
Sierra's Web • by Tara Taylor Quinn

Haley Carmichael discovers her recently deceased sister had a baby—a baby who's currently missing—and she knows her ex-husband, Paul Wright, is the only one who can help. Reuniting with his ex is the last thing the expert bounty hunter wants, but he isn't willing to risk a child's life, either—and a second chance might help both of them put past demons to rest.

#2230 HUNTED ON THE BAY
by Amber Leigh Williams

Desiree Gardet will change her address, her name, her hair—anything—to leave her past behind, but when fate brings her to sweet and sexy barkeep William Leighton and the small town he calls home, she longs for somewhere to belong more than ever before. Unfortunately, her past has a way of catching up with her no matter what she does, only this time Desiree finds that she isn't alone in the crosshairs.

YOU CAN FIND MORE INFORMATION ON UPCOMING HARLEQUIN TITLES,
FREE EXCERPTS AND MORE AT HARLEQUIN.COM.

HRSCNM0323

HARLEQUIN
PLUS

Try the best multimedia subscription service for romance readers like you!

Read, Watch and Play.

Experience the easiest way to get the romance content you crave.

Start your **FREE TRIAL** at
www.harlequinplus.com/freetrial.